The Change

The Change

Deanne Smith

Love & Prayers,
Deanne Smith
2015

THE CHANGE

Published by Deanne Smith

409 Hemlock Avenue

Glendive, MT 59330, USA

Copyright © 2014 by Deanne Smith

Cover Photograph Copyright ©
<ahref='http://www.123rf.com/profile_soloway'>soloway/123RFStock Photo</a>

Author photograph by Darla Torgerson

ISBN 978-1-502-41402-1

A Note from the Author

When I began writing this novel, I primarily wanted to tell of a series of tragic insanity cases that occurred in the tiny Montana town in which I was raised. Between 1914 and 1919, fourteen men had their menopausal wives arrested and sent to the Montana State Hospital, or as it was called back then, the Insane Asylum. Court transcripts and records reveal these women were arrested, tried, found to be insane and indigent, and sentenced to the "asylum." Most of the trials lasted less than one day. Their husbands, physicians, neighbors, sons, and others testified against them. The women's voices, however, were silent. I feel it is time they were heard.

I wish those women would have had advocates like the main characters in this book; however, they did not. Please know that my vision for this book does not include placing blame on anyone, for I believe ignorance about menopause and the lack of women's rights at the time are at fault. As you read this book, please keep in mind that although it is rooted in truth, it is a story of fiction.

As I researched this time period and wrote the book, I was overcome with gratitude for the many doctors, state officials, lawmakers, and women who, over time, have changed the perceptions people have of menopause. It is no longer regarded as a cause of insanity, as it was in the early twentieth century. It is no longer a taboo subject, something to be endured but not discussed. For that, I am thankful.

I also am thankful for the rights women now have. Before I wrote this story, I seldom thought about the fact that I am free to be whatever I want and that I own property and have the means to live independently. Now, I often think of the many women – and men, too – who suffered and fought for these rights, and I will never again take them for granted.

Most of all, my wish is that you enjoy the story, most of which was created in my mind. Any similarities to actual people, places, or events are coincidence since only the deep root of the story is true.

Deanne

For the fourteen women who inspired this book.

And for women everywhere who feel they have no choice but to silently suffer.

PROLOGUE

April 25, 1920
Bergen

The smell of fresh mown hay and horse permeated the barn where the five men gathered. A pinkish orange glow illuminated the large doorway, throwing shadows onto the heavy wood walls.

"She just ain't actin' right lately, I tell you. I just don't know what a guy's supposed to do. It just don't make no sense to me."

"Now, Bob, don't go getting all riled up about such a simple matter. We've all been where you are at one time or another. Haven't we, gentlemen?" Judge Edward Valsted paused and continued when the other men nodded their agreement. "Isn't that why you asked us to come out here?" The judge's eyes followed the disheveled man pacing in front of him.

"Well, I guess I did ask you all to come out here all right, Judge, but I'm tellin' you, she's crazy and I just don't know what to do any more. I tried everything I could think of to get her back to her old self, but it ain't no good. Ain't no use tryin' nothing else with her." Bob Terrell stopped pacing, took a healthy swig out of the mug he clutched, belched, and smacked his lips.

"We'll talk this out this morning, and you'll feel a whole lot better about everything after we're done. Okay?" Bob grunted his assent, so the portly, well-dressed judge continued, "We're here to offer a solution to your problem, if you're willing to hear us out and then keep your mouth shut about it afterward. What do you say?"

"Well, I'm guessin' that I need your help; otherwise, I don't know what to do, really. I know'd from a long while back that you all lost your wives somehow, but I don't know any specifics." Bob stopped pacing and swayed on his feet, waving his mug at the other four men.

Doctor Henry Belzer heaved himself up from the wooden chair he sat in, smoothed his vest, cleared his throat, and said, "Well, then, perhaps it's time we were upfront with you so you know what happened to our wives and then you can make up your mind about Clara. I'll start with my Mary." Doctor Belzer paced heavily. "You knew her, Bob. She was the sweetest-tempered woman a man could ask for. A wonderful cook, housekeeper, hostess, and mother. For twenty-three years she served me well."

"Yep, I remember her real good, Doc, a real sweet thing."

"Thanks, Bob, but hear me out now. A few years ago, I started noticing changes in her like she became ill-tempered, crying without any reason, and arguing with me about something almost every day. One time she even threw a plate of food on the floor in a fit of rage."

"Well, I'll be. That sounds just like my Clara, it does," Bob interrupted, swaying and sloshing his drink.

2

"Yes. Lucretia was the same way," Judge Valsted said.

"My wife, too. Even worse if ya ask me. Meaner than hell, she was," Frank Larson spoke for the first time.

"What was wrong with 'em, Doc?" Bob asked, his eyes widening.

The doctor sat back down and replied, "I had no idea what was happening to Mary, but this ill temper lasted for about a year until finally I had enough and went to the judge here and we figured it out together."

"What'd you all figure out? What's the matter with my wife? And what can be done 'bout it?" Bob slurred his words and waved his mug in front of the doctor.

"Now, just calm yourself down a little. We're getting to that," Doctor Belzer said, raising his hand as if to protect himself.

"Well, you're a doctor, ain't ya? What's ailin' my Clara? Is it something that can be fixed?"

"No, I'm sorry, but it's nothing that can be fixed, Bob, not physically anyway. Now, what we're going to tell you about happened to all of us here. Our wives had almost the exact same symptoms, and they were almost all of the same age when it happened - about fifty years, give or take." Doctor Belzer cleared his throat and spit on the floor. "Joshua here should go next. Joshua, why don't you go ahead and tell Bob your story."

Joshua Miller had been sitting in a shadowed corner listening to the other men, but now he rose to his feet, glared at the doctor, and said, "Hell no, I won't. You told me we was comin' out here to see about a problem Bob was having. You never said that Clara was the problem. I'm just a simple farmer trying to make a livin' for my family, and I won't be a part of this, no how." Thin-lipped, Joshua slammed his cup on to the shelf next to him, sloshing dark amber liquid on the dirt floor. He stalked out of the barn, mounted his horse, and galloped out of the yard.

CHAPTER 1

Our little brown and white border collie mix, Champ, carried on terribly in the yard, barking and yapping, indicating something was amiss in his world. I turned from the stew on the woodstove, poked my head out the door of the small shack I shared with my husband Bob, and saw the back of Joshua Miller as he galloped down our lane. The dog ran from the house to the barn to the lane, trying to alert someone to the trouble he felt in the air. That is when I noticed a horse tethered to the fence and two vehicles parked near the barn.

"Champ!" I yelled from the doorway. "Come here!" The dog slinked toward me, occasionally looking back and giving another short "woof."

I was always cognizant of the different tones the dog made, since that was his primary job around the place, and he certainly did it well. Reaching down, I scratched him behind his ears all the while looking down the lane where Joshua had gone.

He certainly looked angry. Who was in the barn with Bob? Bob's remaining in the barn except for meals and bed was completely normal; his having company out there was not.

A sense of curiosity mixed with fear of what was going on in that barn washed over me, so I shushed the dog, told him to stay, and moved on silent feet from the shack to the side of the open doorway to the barn. The hot late morning breeze blew on my brow, underarms, and between my breasts, drying the sweat that gathered there due in equal parts to concern for my husband and fear of getting caught eavesdropping, something I never had cause to do before. Now, though, Bob might need my help, so I pressed my body against the building, feeling its sun-warmed splintery wood through my thin cotton dress. I silently arranged myself so I could hear what the men inside were saying.

"...have to be careful about what we all share with old Miller from now on, I think, but just so you know, Bob, his story is the same as all of ours. Here's what happened with Joshua." Not recognizing the deep voice, I stayed as still as possible, straining to hear what the man was saying. "One night I was having a few drinks in the Shade Tree with the good doctor here, and Joshua was pretty drunk and spouting off about his wife, Rebecca's, crazy behavior. Right, Doc?"

"Yes, that's right, Judge." I instantly recognized our county's doctor, Doctor Belzer, as the speaker. My mind raced. It could only be Judge Valsted who was being addressed since he was the only judge around these parts, but what in the world was he doing in our barn, and with Doctor Belzer, too? What was going on in there?

The judge's deep voice continued, "So I told him that if he was interested, something could be done about her, but that he would have to be willing to follow my advice to the letter."

"What's the advice ya gave him?" Bob's voice came to me. He sounded agitated.

"I'll get to that in a minute," the judge said. "Anyway, he was eager to listen to my plan and agreed to follow through with all the steps necessary. So that is what he did. He did the same thing with Rebecca that we did with all our crazy wives. Right, guys?"

"Yes, the same exact thing," Doctor Belzer said. "Only now, it seems that Joshua might be having second thoughts about what he did. Hmm...I don't like that at all."

"Me either, not one bit," the judge said. "But anyway, enough about him. Let's get down to the business at hand."

"And what's that, Judge?" Bob asked. I heard a long sigh and scuffling of boots on straw-covered dirt. I tensed.

"I'm getting to it, Bob. Just be patient."

"Humph! I'm not known to be a patient man and you all know it," Bob said. I heard the other men chuckle before Bob's loud obnoxious laugh drowned them out. He had been drinking this morning. My heart skipped a beat.

Doctor Belzer said, "Okay, let's move on for the sake of Bob here and so that we can all get home before lunch. I said my piece already, so let's hear from you, Frank," At Frank Larson's name, the only Frank I knew, I could not help but pull my head back as one would pull away from a coiled rattlesnake, quickly and silently.

I recognized this terrible man's loud, raspy voice. "Well, now, it's about time you heard my story, Bob. You know, Sarah wasn't anythin' like ole Doc's wife. Why, if I didn't straighten her out with the back of my hand near every day, nothin' at all would've got done. She was the laziest, dumbest woman I ever did lay eyes on. Stupid thing had to be taught everything

7

under the sun, by God." He loudly slurped something and continued.

"Anyhow, she was usually pretty good, not cryin' much or nothing when I was teachin' her things…you know, with the back of my hand or my belt or whatever. Not crying but maybe whimperin' every now and again. She always had the sense, though, to duck or cringe away, even though she was so stupid."

"Well, Clara's not stupid, no siree. She's just a smart-mouthed one, she is." I sucked in a quick breath and stopped the urge to step into the barn and confront Bob. I needed to continue eavesdropping so I could find out why they were talking about me.

"Then, all the bad started about two years ago," Frank continued. "All of a sudden, ole Sarah started talkin' back to me. Why, she'd become right mean-spirited, I say." Rivulets of perspiration ran down my body, sticking my dress to me.

"One day I come in from cuttin' firewood to get some grub, and there she stood with her fists on her hips yappin' about how I was early to lunch and there wasn't no food ready and that it was my fault because I never was any good at huntin' and couldn't rustle her up no meat to cook…only roots and such and a rabbit every now and then."

"Good Lord, Frank. Just the facts and make it quick," the judge's deep voice sounded tight.

But Frank continued on, "Why, she was fit to be tied that day. I pulled my belt off right then, expectin' her to turn away or crouch down or duck like she usually did, but nope, instead, she just stood there and took it without even flinching. Spookiest thing I ever did see, I'm telling you." Heat coursed through me and my jaw clenched at the casual mention of the abuse.

"Okay, okay, Frank. Let's move this along," Doctor Belzer said.

"And that's not the end of it neither…she just kept on like that for months. Yellin' at me about nothing at all and taking her punishment all silent and still. The only times she cried out was when she thought I wasn't in hearing distance. Then, I'd hear her yowlin' like a treed lion, I'm telling you. So loud it'd wake the dead. And about nothin' at all, I can tell you that."

"Yep. That's just how Clara's been actin' lately," Bob said. I tensed. What was he talking about? I barely breathed.

"Lucretia, too, at the end," the judge said.

"Stupid woman," Frank continued as though he had not heard the other men, "she was old enough not to be carrying on so, even in private…fifty some odd years old. Hmph! Pitiful, how she went from bein' my Sarah to bein' this crazy loon that I didn't even recognize no more."

"Frank, that's enough –" Doctor Belzer interrupted.

Frank kept right on talking. "So anyhow, Bob, this behavior went on for about a year, and then I got wind of what some other guys had done when this sickness struck their women, and I decided to do somethin' about it. I went to ole Judge here and had her sent away to Whispering Pines. You know, that place where people who's sick in the head go? Yep, took less than one week to get that all taken care of."

My mind raced. I must have heard wrong. What were these men talking about? Slowly, this despicable man's words came to me once again: Sarah, crazy, Whispering Pines, other wives, sickness. A whimper arose in my mouth, so I quickly shushed myself, clamping my hand over my mouth. I could barely hear Frank Larson's voice over the roaring in my ears, so I held my breath.

"Now, I don't have no worries. Started plumb over with a new one. You know her, Laura, nicest thing you'd ever see. Barely ever makes a peep at all." Finally, he wound down, and I heard him slurp again and then belch loudly, probably to indicate that he had finished his story.

I was having trouble making sense of what I was hearing. Was I just dreaming all of this, like those nightmares full of red rage and hate that I had been having lately? Would I wake up soon, drenched in perspiration yet again and have all of this be some awful dream? Somewhere deep inside me, though, I knew this was real, just as real as the spring sun hot upon my cheek. The shuffling of boots came to me, and I startled as one of the men cleared his throat.

Even though I knew I should leave, I could not will my feet to move. I needed to hear more, in case they disclosed any other information that might help these poor women. Bob's voice broke through and I concentrated on it rather than on the thoughts that were humming in my brain. I was hopeful and confident that Bob would put these men in their place, kick them off the property as he must have kicked Joshua Miller off earlier, and then report them to the authorities. Upon hearing the loud slurring of Bob's drunken voice, though, I realized that he was probably not in any condition to help at all.

Bob said, "Well, those are some interestin' stories, I tell ya. I never really knew what all happened to your wives. Did you send 'em all to that Whisper Pines?"

"Whisper-*ing* Pines," the judge corrected him. "And yes, all of our wives as well as Joshua Miller's wife and as far as I know there have been ten others in the past four or four and a half years."

"Ten others? Why, tha's…well…tha's how many?"

"A total of fourteen and if I may speak bluntly here, Clara would be the fifteenth," the judge calmly replied.

"Fourteen? Are ya all crazy? Somebody's bound to find out about this and get all of you in trouble, don't ya see? I can't be no part of this here," Bob said.

My knees suddenly went weak, and I struggled to keep my shaking hand over my mouth to keep from crying out. Was I to be sent to this place, too? The judge said I would be the fifteenth. This just could not be possible. What in the world had I done to make them think I am crazy and need to be locked away? My mind whirled, and although I wanted desperately to run, I kept my wits about me.

"We have absolutely nothing to be afraid of, Bob. You see, people around here trust us, and we use Doctor Belzer here as a witness to corroborate what the husbands say about the women. It's a foolproof plan, and nobody in this area has caught on in the past four years, so why would they now?"

"I dunno, I guess you're right, Judge. And my Clara's been actin' so strange lately that I don't think nobody would question my actions anyhow. So what goes on to bring this all about?"

A dark tunnel surrounded me, and bright spots of light came at me from all sides. The sharp tang of fear mixed in my nose with the scent of the sweat that poured down my face and torso. I was in danger and had to get away from the barn before the men found me and before the darkness engulfing my mind was complete.

As from a faraway place, the judge's voice came to me. "Well, first of all, you need to think this over, and when you're ready, come on in to the sheriff's office and get a complaint issued against Clara. Then, the sheriff will write up an arrest warrant and come out here and get her. He will bring her back to town and put her in jail. The next day, in the afternoon, you need to come to town for the trial. It'll just be a formality, really. Clara won't even be there." I bit down on my hand to keep from crying out.

"It's better if the woman just stays in her cell during these 'cuz she wouldn't have nothin' worthwhile to say anyway," Frank Larson said. My eyes bulged.

"Yes, well, the trials never take longer than a half hour, so you will not have to be gone from the farm for too long that day," the judge continued. "Charles Littman, the lawyer who travels with me and handles these things, will ask you to tell me about Clara's actions and about her financial means, essentially that she does not own any property and that she is dangerous to herself or to other folks."

"Dangerous? I don't think Clara's dangerous to nobody. Who said that anyhow?"

"Nobody said that she actually is dangerous, Bob," Doctor Belzer answered. "The judge here was just explaining that you need to say that she is if you want Clara sent to Whispering Pines so you don't have to put up with this insanity of hers anymore."

"Oh, I get it now. Ya know, that sounds easy enough. I'm thinkin' I just might do that."

CHAPTER 2

Of their own volition, my bare feet turned away from the barn door and somehow my trembling, weak legs carried me silently back to the shack. Champ, his tail dragging in the dirt and his head down, came off the porch to greet me. I did not have the energy to even acknowledge the poor thing. Instead, I just plodded along into the shack. Once I reached the bed I had shared for twenty-four years with my husband, I collapsed, spent and exhausted. Darkness encroached as the words I had heard came at me with the force of a train. That is when my instincts took over. I sprang to my feet. Spots of light still played at the edges of my vision, so I just stood at the edge of the bed. A ball of heat took up residence in my head, bouncing from one side to the other. I raised one hand to my temple and rubbed the spots of light away. What do I do now?

As though slogging through dense fog, I felt my way into the other room of the shack and over to the basin filled with murky water I had used earlier to wash the vegetables for the stew. Suddenly, the fog lifted and my thoughts became crisp as a winter day on the prairie. I splashed some of the dirty water on my face and stood dripping next to the basin. The ball of heat in my head retreated some.

I inched my way to the doorway and peeked toward the barn. The vehicles and horse were still there. My guts tensed. What if they come and get me right now and haul me off to jail? No, they can't do that. They need to do it all official-like, with the sheriff and a warrant. I had a little time to think this through. What should I do, though? The desire to run was strong, but if I did, the men might figure out that I knew what they had done and then I would be in real danger. Taking a deep breath helped to slow my thoughts, so I took another. There was nothing I could do right now except wait for them to leave. With any luck, Bob would go with them.

Suddenly, and for no reason that made sense, the thought of the stew entered my mind, and always priding myself on my ability to cook a good hearty meal, I went to the stove which had gone cold. The stew was a mess, vegetables mushy and meat burned to the bottom of the Dutch oven. With tears welling in my eyes, I took up the big wooden spoon, shakily stirred the mess, and tasted it. Not bad, not my best work, but the best I could do today.

A slight giggle suddenly escaped, and knowing that hysteria approached, I clamped down hard to keep it at bay. If I can just keep myself together for a little while longer, maybe I can think this through and come up with a solution, just a little while longer. I sneaked another look outside. The horse and vehicles were still there.

I always did my best thinking when my hands were busy and I definitely needed to think straight, so I took out the rags and soap powder used to clean house and set to my work, allowing my mind to run freely.

Because of what I had just heard Bob say about my behavior, my thoughts drifted to the past few months. He told those men I was acting strangely, and in a way, he was right. Rage often built up in me and bubbled out after a few days, manifesting itself in actions that surprised even me. About a month ago, Bob had been gone to town for three days leaving me to tend to all of the chores and to worry about the various things that might have happened to him. When he returned, I verbally attacked him, calling him names and accusing him of all sorts of improprieties. Why had I done that? It was as though I was provoking the physical attack that naturally followed. The rage I expressed evaporated almost immediately; the bruises took a few days.

Another day I awakened with a terrible headache, and nothing seemed to go right. I was clumsy, dropping a whole bowl of soup onto the newly swept floor and tripping twice over that stupid loose floorboard that Bob never seemed to find the time to fix. By suppertime the anger overtook me, and I ended up yelling terrible things at my husband, that he was lazy and did not care enough about me to fix up the floor, that I never should have married him and moved out to this God-forsaken country in the first place. I knew I had crossed the line with that one, but that day Bob actually said that he agreed with me on that point, saying that I should have stayed in Wisconsin where my mother could have taken care of me forever. His sarcasm accompanied me as I rushed out of the house, walking until my tears were spent before returning and climbing into bed with Bob who was sleeping soundly.

I quickly looked outside again. The men were still in the barn, so I fairly sprinted out to the pump and filled the basin with clean water. As I walked back to the house with it, my mind continued on its earlier path.

There were several similar incidences that I was ashamed of, but after most of them I apologized and asked Bob to forgive me, which he said he did a couple of times but not lately. My outbursts had become more frequent. Subsequently, he had been gone to town more and more often, staying away for days, which only fueled my anger toward him for leaving me alone with no one but Champ to talk to. But really, who could blame him when my moods were so unpredictable? He never knew which Clara would await him when he came in the house, the lunatic or the kindly wife he married…did I just think 'lunatic'? My goodness, that's just what got those other women sent to that place they were talking about, Whispering Pines. I need to find out more about that place. It's a nice sounding name, for sure, but one of the men said that is where crazy people are sent, so the name must be a deception. At any rate, I certainly do not want to be "sent" there.

I busied myself, sprinkling powder on the wooden counters in the kitchen area, then scrubbing and rinsing them with water from the basin. My mind went to these women. What was the judge's wife's name again? She and the judge lived in the larger town of Glendive, twenty-five miles west of our place, so I only saw her once. It was in the market, but I could still picture the petite, dark-haired woman with creamy smooth skin, not a freckle or wrinkle on her face or hands to be seen. Probably never had the sun beat on her. Servants, no doubt, did her work for her, which left her with nothing much to do except take care of that hair and skin. A tinge of jealousy crept in until it dawned on me that the woman now resided in a place called Whispering Pines because she had lost her mind. Lucretia, that's the name. I smiled at the prettiness of it and the way it sounded in my mind. I tried it aloud, "Lucretia." It almost sounded like a sigh, but add the last name, Valsted...Lucretia Valsted, and it sounded suddenly evil, like the sound of a snake poised to strike. Maybe I'm crazy after all. Who thinks these things anyway? Occasionally over the past two years or so, I had that same thought...who thinks these kinds of things anyway? Or, why do I feel like that sometimes? And the forgetfulness and clumsiness. So unlike me.

I moved on to the table, powdering, scrubbing, and rinsing the hard surface worn smooth by elbows, hands, plates, and the life of my family. Henry Belzer's wife I knew quite well, not well enough to call her a friend, but more an acquaintance. She often helped her husband in his duties as our small town doctor, even helping care for my own children when they were sick. Mary Belzer was admired as a kind, helpful woman. When she disappeared in late December about four years ago, the rumors were that she had gone back to Illinois to care for her dying mother. She simply never returned, and no one questioned it. People on the prairie were just too busy trying to live to notice things like that and if they did notice, they were too cognizant of other people's privacy to mention it.

Now, I knew Mary was not in Illinois, and the sheer gravity of her situation overwhelmed me. I also knew that I knew too much and these men were a dangerous lot who were not to be trifled with. Now, Bob had thrown in with them.

Putting my rag down, I finally allowed the tears to flow, and my knees buckled under me. Thankfully, a chair was nearby. I plunked into it. Sobs racked my tense body.

Once the episode subsided and I was able to stand, I went to refill the wash basin and splashed some tepid water on my face, relieving some of the physical discomfort but not the mental anguish. Quickly, I finished cleaning the table, and after peeking outside yet again, I moved on to dusting the few pieces of furniture in the house, my mind moving now on to more practical things like what I should do about my situation.

My options were few. Basically, I could stay and confront Bob about what I overheard in the barn. Doing so in a cool-headed, rational manner would be paramount, though, and I was far too emotional for that. It was just that type of irrational behavior that made him think I was crazy enough to send away. If I did that, I would be gone within two days, for sure. Another option was just to stay and act like my old self from now on which is what Bob wanted anyway; I did too, if truth be known. But things were too far out of hand for that. If I tripped up even once more, which I was sure to do since I really had no control over my actions when those feelings overtook me, Bob would send me away. Away, away, that is all I could think of.

The dusting complete and the men still in the barn, I put away the cleaning supplies, took up the straw broom, and began working on the old wood floor. As my hands and body moved in a rhythm with the broom, I tried to fetter out some acceptable solution. Suddenly, it came to me. My best friend in all the world, Annie Hazelton, would know what I should do. I would go to her for advice. The only problem was that she lived five miles away in the little town of Bergen. Too far to walk on these old feet. The horses were Bob's and only Bob's according to the laws of our state, and if I took one and rode it to town without his knowing, I could be arrested. Then, I would be in a worse position. Even though it would be an exceedingly difficult trip, I would have to walk.

That decision made, I sighed and felt the weight lift from my body and my spirit. Just then, Champ gave a 'woof,' and I heard men's voices and laughter. I quickly moved to hide behind the door. What if they came to the house? Dark fear threatened me again, so I took a deep breath. I stayed completely still until the sounds of the vehicle engines and the clomping of hooves faded. I briefly wondered why I had not heard the engines when they drove up. I must have been too busy to notice. Only then did I dare look outside. Was Bob still in the barn? My eyes flew from the barn to the corral and saw that Bob's favorite old horse, the bay, was missing. Bob was gone. Flooded with relief and even a bit of giddiness, I breathed the fresh sagey air of the prairie.

The desire to leave and get to Annie's was intense, but my sense of duty and compassion for the animals was stronger, so with Champ scampering along beside me, I did the quick version of my chores, taking care of the horses and chickens. Back at the house, I made sure Champ had plenty of water in his bowl and then took the entire Dutch oven filled with stew to the porch and placed it beside the door. Champ ambled over, sniffed the pot, looked up at me in gratitude, and let out a high whine as he bent his head to eat.

I went inside and quickly packed a few pieces of clothing, my beloved Bible, the silver grooming set my Mama had given me, and the professional photographs of Bob and me on our wedding day, a hopeful, wide-eyed countenance showing in each of the two photographs. Taking a moment to study them, I also noticed the sobriety on our faces, perhaps a precognition of the hardships and heartaches that lay ahead of us. I carefully placed the photographs face down between two dresses and closed the lid on the small valise.

Before I left, maybe for good, I had one important place to visit. Walking toward the large cottonwood tree on the hill behind the house, my mind went to our children. The sweet scent of infants came to me on the breeze, and the warmth of a tiny hand around my forefinger as I nursed made my heart fill to nearly bursting. I heard the three boys' tinkling laughter as they played outside. I felt their thin arms around my neck and their small, warm bodies as I held them through various scraped knees, bumblebee bites, and thunderstorms of the prairie. But, as their voices grew deep and their arms grew sinewy with muscle, they became more distant from me, emulating Bob and following him everywhere, learning from him how to be a man. One at a time, they moved from the prairies of Eastern Montana to various parts of the country, married, and made their own lives, taking with them the knowledge and love of ranching; the sweet sounds of their rising in the morning, their soft breathing in the night, and their perpetual hunger and motions in between; and most of all, a part of their mother's heart.

21

I knelt under the huge tree, tucked my long skirt under my knees, and brushed fallen leaves from the small plot where my fourth child lay so far under the packed dirt with the prairie grass growing over her.

"Well, my little Julia, I must bid you farewell now. Mommy must go away for a while and try to get all this mess straightened out somehow. I know you're watching over us all, little angel, and that you know what has happened to Daddy and Mommy." A sob caught in my thick throat and tears dampened the front of my shirt, sticking the cotton to my chest. "Oh, how I miss you, my baby darling." I swiped the tears from my face and blew a kiss skyward. "I love you, Julia." As I rose, my knees cracking, I remembered my baby girl and the two short years she was with us.

I could still feel the hot pain of the birth and then the joyous filling of my heart at the first tiny "mew" emitted from this long-awaited daughter's little lungs. But, those tiny mews never grew into normal loud cryings. The lungs were faulty, come to find out, and Julia did not grow robust from my milk, remaining smaller and weaker than her brothers had been. Although she walked at about one year, she never wanted to run and play outside as she grew older, wishing instead to remain inside where she sat silently watching me work. When Julia could talk a little, her voice was raspy and soft, and she spoke few words as the effort seemed too much for the little one to bear.

Annie begged me to bring Julia to Chicago where she lived for what she called proper doctoring, but Bob constantly shushed my worries. A girl was just weaker than boys, that was all. He also convinced me there was no money to take her all the way to Chicago.

For the rest of my life, I would regret allowing Bob to convince me of these things. Hot resentment built in my chest as I revisited the times I sat rocking Julia as she gasped, her body working too hard just to make her little chest rise and fall. Bob was not the one who made plasters of various plants and medicines and placed them on our daughter's chest and prayed that this one would be the one that would cure whatever it was that ailed our precious baby. Taking Julia to Doctor Belzer in Bergen when she got really bad was my job as well. Bob thought it was all nonsense until after that one worst night when he awakened to find me rocking gently and holding Julia's little two-year-old body which struggled no more. She was blue, cold, stiff, and finally at peace.

The days and nights after that were a blur, the swaddling of the tiny body in her favorite afghan, the building of the small wooden box, the digging under the cottonwood tree, the plunk of the soil as it covered my most wondrous gift and with it, my happiness. Yet somehow I lived on, full of grief and self-pity for the first year or two. Life was divided now, the 'with Julia' and the 'without Julia.' Before and after. For Bob, this time after Julia passed found him slipping slowly from a loving, hardworking husband and father into an angry, lazy drunk who often forgot his family even existed, drowning his sorrow in the taverns in town. He and I knew not how to heal each other which caused problems, for sure, and our family was never the same, deteriorating even more after the boys left.

Julia would be eighteen years old now, had she lived, and my heart hurt at the thought of all the two of us have missed. On this day of leaving, though, I was relieved that Julia was not here. This was not a day that my dearest child needed to be a part of, that was for sure.

As my thoughts fell once again on leaving, Annie came to mind. My childhood friend moved to Bergen about five years ago when her husband Walter passed away, and it was joyous to have her nearby again. She was not next door, as she had been for the first eighteen years of our lives, but she was nearby and that was all that mattered to me. I desperately wanted to get her advice and feel her soothing embrace. This feeling was the only thing that could possibly pull me from my baby's grave.

I walked to the house, and once inside I composed myself, donned my sunbonnet, and put on my only pair of shoes. Taking up my valise, I strode out the door, forcing myself not to look around our home, fearing I would lose the courage to leave.

CHAPTER 3

Champ walked a ways with me before turning
back, which he always did whenever I went to town. I
wobbled a little and wondered if I would ever see him
again, but I swallowed around the lump in my throat
and carried on. I trudged up the steep rise called
Beaver Hill, so named because most things in these
parts were named after the sharp-toothed nuisance of
an animal. Beaver Creek, Beaver Ridge, Beaver
Hollow, Beaver County, the list went on.

Spring had always been my favorite time of the
year, but since this doggone drought started some four
or five years ago, it was no longer so beautiful out here.
In fact, it was downright ugly. The ground had dried to
an awful grayish color, and sagebrush, also gray, was
about the only thing that could live in it. Before the
drought, the animals had been able to get their feed in
the way of fresh grass and bugs and such, and water
was abundant and clean in the small streams and
coulees found all over the land that they traversed
during the day. These days, though, people had to buy
feed for their livestock year round, hoping they could
afford it. Many could not, and had sold out and
headed back to wherever they came from or headed
onward to try their fortune out West.

Bob and I were doing all right; however, I had
no idea how. Finances were Bob's thing, not mine. I
had been told enough times that it "weren't none of my
business" to know not to ask questions. I figured we

25

might just make it if the drought did not last much longer, but none of that mattered after what I heard this morning. There simply was no "Bob and me." My heart thudded, and knowing panic and tears would slow my journey, I forced my thoughts toward what had brought me to this place.

In my mind I saw my father with his twinkling blue eyes, tall thin build, and shock of reddish-blond hair which never did recede or turn gray before he passed away some twenty-five years ago, the year before I married Bob. In fact, it was Father's passing that really brought me here. Back when I was in my teenage years, living in Green Bay, Wisconsin, next door to Annie, I had numerous beaus, including two who proposed marriage. I was too fussy, though, and perhaps thought too highly of myself, so I rejected the proposals and soon developed the reputation of being headstrong and spoiled. Thus, the attention of young men and the marriage proposals soon dried up, and it looked as if I would live out my days in the house in which I grew up, being cared for by the servants.

Annie, on the other hand, did the acceptable thing and got married at age eighteen to an adorable man named Walter who was from Chicago. They moved to that large city right after their marriage which disappointed me terribly. For some odd reason, I figured Annie and I would live our lives forever next door to each other.

I was twenty-six years old and an "old maid" when Father died, and it came to light that he had many more debts than income and had lived far beyond his means for the last years of his life. Our family was suddenly poor, and the creditors wanted to be paid immediately since they knew Mama had no way of earning income. The stately house and land were sold, the servants let go, and my dear Mama and I moved into a small home in the not-so-affluent section of Green Bay.

Although our addresses changed, the kinship between Annie and I did not. Many of our friends shunned Mama and me, but not Annie. She and I wrote weekly letters, and I came to cherish her news of parties, festivals, concerts, and political functions. Soon after her arrival in Chicago, she began a crusade to get the right to vote for women. She was a Suffragette, and as was her nature, completely engulfed herself in her cause. Her dear husband Walter stood by her side, encouraging her to do whatever it was that she wanted to do. I longed for a man in my life who would treat me as Walter did Annie.

After we moved from the affluent section of town, my mother and I needed an income, so regretfully I began searching the newspaper for employment. I figured I could be some kind of domestic help, having watched my family's servants for years. That was when I saw the advertisements for brides. I poured over them and answered a couple, one of which was from a man named Robert Terrell. Bob and I corresponded for a little over two months, during which time I worked as a maid, and not a very good one at that. Bob came to Green Bay only once and although he was a bit rough around the edges, he also presented himself as hard-working, generous, and kind, so when he wrote and asked for my hand in marriage a few weeks after his visit, I readily accepted even though it would mean moving to Eastern Montana where Bob had recently homesteaded. Mama was devastated, not wanting the daughter she treasured most to move so far away.

I tried to reassure her by explaining that I would be able to send her money and that I would be happy and raise a family with a man that I would grow to love in time.

Mama did not live long after I left, probably died from a broken heart over the loss of her husband, her home, and her daughter. Thankfully, my sisters who had married young and moved to the East Coast, somehow were able to send her some money they squirreled away from their wealthy husbands because I never was able to send Mama the promised money. Bob controlled all of our finances, and he was more frugal than generous, especially with me.

Self-pity began sprouting again, so I tried to think positively about this morning. Perhaps there is a simple explanation for what I overheard. Perhaps I didn't hear the men correctly, and Bob has no plans to send me away. Perhaps I have nothing to fear and will be home before dark.

However, after an hour of walking and the temperature rising, my entire body felt every bit of its fifty years. And with the pain came the ugly truth. Bob fully intends to send me away, and I can't let that happen. I heard what I heard and it wasn't a figment of my imagination. Plus, Bob can't just change his mind and not send me away because he knows far too much about those other men's lives now. They will not allow him to back down. They need him to do what they did so that they are all in cahoots on it together, so that not one of them can tell the authorities about the others.

28

Although my feet, unaccustomed to the shoes I rarely wore, sent sharp pains up my legs, I managed to keep moving them. Bugs buzzing in the knee-high grasses beside the road periodically drowned out the ringing in my ears. As I passed the occasional cottonwood or juniper, flustered blackbirds and wrens took flight, making their perches tremble, the air rustle, and my mind still for a moment.

Certainly, Annie would be able to think clearly about this and give me some good solid advice. Between Annie and me, we could solve almost any problem, or at the very least, help the troubled one feel better. A woman needs her best friend to help her through these types of things. Annie would help me, I just knew it.

By the time I arrived at the outskirts of Bergen, my feet had swelled and blistered and my arms ached under the weight of the valise, but my heart was lighter.

When the country road intersected the main street, I turned to the right and paused to gather my thoughts. The little town was growing rapidly. It now boasted a brand new church on the corner where I stood. The bright white paint shone in the sun and I smiled. More churches meant more families and fewer single men and the women who profited from their loneliness. Someday, maybe there would be more churches here than saloons. Shaking my head at my silliness, I walked down the street toward the main part of town.

"Why, Clara Terrell, is that you?" A shrill voice interrupted my reverie, and I turned so quickly my valise caught in my skirt and I had to drop it to the ground and untangle myself. The very large

Mrs. Carlson, whose husband owned the only bank in town, crossed the street with one arm in the air, waving and drawing other people's stares. My cheeks flamed at the attention.

"Yes, Mrs. Carlson, it's me. How are you doing these days?" Quickly, I realized my mistake. I had forgotten that that question almost always elicited an hour's worth of babble from the woman.

"Oh, so sweet of you to ask, dear Clara. Why, I have had to go to Doctor Belzer I don't know how many times in the last month or two. It started out as a small pain in the side of my head right behind my right ear here and then..." I nodded occasionally and made a sound of compassion every once in a while so as not to be rude, yet I was only listening with half an ear.

Nervous and trapped, I looked down the street at the numerous buildings that had sprung up in the last couple of years. People could get almost anything they needed here, so the town bustled with activity. I turned toward a ruckus coming from Patty's Saloon just two buildings down from where we stood. Horses were tied to the hitching post in front of the saloon. Many horses. Bob's horse. That meant he was inside. My heart lurched at the thought of being so close to my husband. Blood pounded in my temples and I shivered in the heat. The desire to run was overwhelming.

"...going somewhere, Clara? Why do you have a valise with you?" Mrs. Carlson broke into my thoughts.

Shaken, I replied, "Uh, I guess I was thinking about going down to see Robby and Lillian and the little ones." I could not look her in the eye.

"Oh my, how delightful! Where are they now? Still in South Dakota?"

"Yes, they're near Rapid City. Robby ranches down --"

"Wonderful! And how are the children? What are their ages now? I'll bet they are just the most beautiful children in the whole world, well other than my Mae and Ralphie…" And Mrs. Carlson was chattering again. The fear of Bob coming out of the saloon and seeing me got stronger by the minute, so knowing it was rude but not caring all that much, I interrupted.

"Um, Mrs. Carlson, I'm very sorry, but I do need to do some errands before embarking on my trip, so if you'll excuse me. I really must go now." And without even glancing at her, I picked up my valise and walked off, my feet and legs screaming at me for the movement.

Thankfully, the other people I met were either strangers or merely acquaintances who required only a passing nod and "Good day" as I was in a hurry to get down to The Marquis, a hotel and restaurant where I could get a bite to eat so that I would not put undue bother on Annie. I also would be out of sight of my husband if he were to wander out of the saloon.

The hotel was the largest building in town. Its false front had once been bright yellow but had faded to a color that could only be described as dull. Large windows flanked the door leading to the restaurant and allowed sunlight to stream into the eatery.

As always when I entered the hotel, I was struck by the brightness and cleanliness of the place, so unlike its exterior. And the onslaught of smells was heavenly, especially today as I was extremely hungry after my long walk. Beatrice Mulhaney and her husband Samuel were doing a booming business today. I took a seat at one of the only empty tables, set my valise next to my feet, and removed my bonnet. I glanced around, hoping no one would recognize me. I really hoped to get Annie's help before anyone else noticed me and my valise. Too many tongues might wag, and the wrong ears, namely Bob and those cronies from the barn, might get wind of the fact that I was leaving and start to wonder.

"Why, Clara Terrell!" It's been forever and a day since I seen the likes of you! How have you been?" The booming voice of Bea Mulhaney brought me startling back to the present. So much for privacy. Everyone in the place seemed to stop mid-bite to look over at the whirlwind proprietor and me. I sank down a little.

"Why, I'm just fine, Bea." My voice was quiet and shaky. I looked up at Bea, and as always, noticed how strikingly beautiful the woman was, despite the smear of flour that ran from her temple to her nose. A gingham dress the exact color of the crocuses I saw that morning pulled tightly across her ample bosom, gathered with a wide sash at her tiny waist, and flowed elegantly around her white leather boots. With her flawless, olive-shaded skin and snapping blue eyes, the woman was stunning. I hoped Bea would not examine me as closely and notice my swollen eyelids, red cheeks, and shaky hands.

Too tightly strung even to sit down, Bea thankfully did not appear to notice my plight. She took my order and rushed to the kitchen to help take huge plates of food out to the patrons. I watched and marveled at her energy. Oh, to be young and exuberant again.

"Here you go, Mrs. Terrell. A mighty helping of our special meat loaf for you to feast on!" Bea said as she returned with my food, her raven black hair shimmering in the sunlight.

"Thank you, Bea. It looks mighty good."

"You just holler for me if you need anything else at all." Bea disappeared in a whirl to the kitchen again.

My mouth watered at the smell of the meat loaf. After a quick prayer to the Lord, I put a small bite into my mouth. I chewed and chewed, unable to swallow. Mortified, I tried again and again, but the lump in my throat would not subside enough to allow me to eat. Finally, I gave up and reached into the tiny purse containing what little money I had been able to squirrel away over the years.

Suddenly, Bea was sitting across from me. "Was the food okay, Mrs. Terrell?" The young woman asked hopefully. I averted my eyes. "It looks to me as though you haven't eaten a bite and you're pale as a sheet."

"No, Bea, the food is fine. I'm just not feeling as hungry as I thought I was when I came in."

"Well then, what's the trouble? Are you in town to see the doc? 'Cuz if you are, you just missed him. He went out to the old Krauss place to help doctor on one of their horses that's having trouble."

"No, I'm not here to see Doctor Be-belzer," I stumbled over the man's name, knowing now what kind of man he really was. "I'm just in town to visit with Annie Hazelton. I haven't seen her for quite a while and thought I'd stop in for a chat."

I noticed a slight change in Bea's demeanor, a tightness around the woman's eyes and a small pursing of her lips. I had never really cared what others thought about Annie; I loved my friend, and her radical political views just went along with the rest of the package. However, many people in town did not care for Annie with her strong opinions, her immense wealth, and her sense of style. Bea's disapproval did not surprise me; however, a feeling of unease came upon me and I wished I had not spoken the truth to her.

Bea rose from her chair, the visit obviously over, and said, "Well, have a nice day, Mrs. Terrell. And don't bother with your money. There's no charge for food you don't eat!" Bea huffed and stomped away.

My cheeks turned pink as I rose with creaking knees. I left thirty-five cents for the food, grabbed my valise, and strode out the door. Sweat beaded on my forehead and a small rivulet dribbled down my chest.

CHAPTER 4

It was a short walk to Annie's house, but I was exhausted. Finally, I made it to the immense two-story brick house that, according to Annie, was done in a neoclassical style which she had grown to love while she and Walter lived in Chicago. I paused only a moment before raising the brass knocker on the beautiful door. It took a full minute or two for my friend to open the door, but then, there she was. Relief flooded me, and pent-up tears shot from my eyes. Annie stepped onto the porch and pulled me into her ample arms, smelling of vanilla as she always did.

"What in the world is this all about?" Annie asked as she gently urged me into the massive entry of the home and, taking the valise, placed it by the front door.

"What brings you here, sweetie?"

"W-well, it's a long story. But what I'm hoping for is a friend right now and some advice, too, I guess." I blotted the tears with my handkerchief and felt better with Annie's comforting arm around me.

She led me into the bright parlor. The room was huge, almost the size of my entire house, but it was beautiful, too, with papered walls, polished wainscoting, and a massive fireplace. Annie guided me to an embroidered, cushioned settee and sat next to me. The late afternoon sun shined in on us.

"Now, you tell me all about your troubles, Clara. This is so unlike you to be so upset. What is it?"

And so I set about telling my story, tentatively at first. Saying it aloud made it all so unbelievable. But as I progressed, anger and concern came to Annie's face, and I knew I had come to the right place and that my friend would help all she could. But what could she really do to help?

Annie listened intently, nodding at times, but when I said the words "Whispering Pines," her blue eyes widened and her breath made a "shh" sound as it sucked between her teeth. She ran a pudgy hand over her unruly blond hair that was gathered into a thick bun.

"Whispering Pines! Isn't that where they send crazy people, people who have committed horrible crimes and such? Isn't that a lunatic place?"

I nodded. "I believe it is. I remember the men saying that it is, in fact. But they said their wives are actually crazy. And that's what the judge said they are, too. I'm so scared, I just don't know what to do. What if they send me there, too?" The words tumbled out of my mouth, and I was surprised how much calmer and more controlled I felt as they did. The fog in my mind lifted and the lump in my throat disappeared.

"Is that why you brought your valise with you today? Are you leaving Bob?" I felt my hair bob as I nodded. "Good!" she exclaimed as she leapt to her feet and began pacing gracefully despite her large size.

"I have to leave him, I think. But, that's what I hoped you would help me with. I'm not sure what to do or where to go. I'm so confused and all of this is so sudden and so ter..." Suddenly, my neck was hot and wet with tears I had not felt slide down my cheeks. Annie leaned over me, engulfing me in vanilla and softness as I continued, "I just have no idea what to do, and I don't know what's happening to me. One minute I feel as if everything is just fine and then the next a cloud comes over me and I can't breathe, can't even function. And then there's the red feeling of hot anger that comes upon me every now and again. I'm scared, Annie. Maybe I really am going crazy." My voice faded off as I fought for control of my emotions.

"There, there," Annie said, patting my clenched hands. "I'm not sure what you should do, either, but I do know this...you have no choice but to leave that son-of-a-bitch. Oh, sorry, I know you don't like my swearing." Her chubby fingers covered her lips for a second. Somehow, her self-chastisement helped me feel better. This was my Annie, strong, confident, and ready for a fight.

"Oh, Clara, what will we do about this?" She was up and pacing again. "We need to think clearly right now, really clearly. This is actually very dangerous information you have."

"But what can we do? I can't even think straight right now, I'm so scared. I just feel trapped and..." My voice was tinny. I took a shaky breath.

"You just stop your worrying and allow me to think this through." Annie continued pacing and wringing her hands. "For Heaven's sake, where are my manners? You must be terribly parched after your journey," she said as she rang for the housekeeper. "And I haven't even offered you anything yet."

Martha, the housekeeper, was there within seconds. Annie asked her to bring us refreshments and then continued talking the problem through, whether to herself or to me, I could not be sure.

37

"Now, let's see. One thing we must do right away is go to the authorities for help."

"But, Annie, we can't go to the authorities because it's the authorities who were in the barn. They're the ones who've sent their wives away!" I did not even recognize the high, tight voice coming from me. I just might be losing my mind after all. Wouldn't that be ironic? I would be carted off to that dreadful place in the end anyway, and all because of these nerves shattering my mind into a thousand puzzle pieces. I had to keep a cooler head.

"I see….Well, even those bast-, oops! Even those men have bosses. We just need to find out who is above these yahoos and go over their heads for help. Now, though, who can help us do that? Who can we trust? Oh! I know! There's a man named Connor Sullivan who might be able to help us. He's just the nicest young man you'll ever meet." Martha quietly entered, placed a refreshment tray on the table, and left as silently as she had appeared. "Oh good, I'm parched myself now!" Annie said as she poured iced tea into glasses, placed plum scones on dessert plates, and placed them on a table next to me. She continued, "Now, where was I? Why, I can't remember what the heck I was just saying." Annie laughed heartily and sat down. Her eyes closed as she took a large bite of scone. "Mmm – now that is some mighty good scone, I tell you. Don't you think so, Clara?"

I took a dainty bite and found that I had relaxed enough to actually swallow some of the food, washing it down with the sweet tea. "Oh, it is truly delightful. Thank you."

"But now what was I saying before Martha brought these distracting scones in?"

I smiled at my friend's delight in food and in her forgetfulness. "You were talking about a young man who might be able to help me."

"Oh, yes! Connor Sullivan." Annie was pacing again, the scone devoured. "He's pretty new here in town. I already had him do some legal work for me and got to know him a little from that. He's a very good lawyer and such a nice man. Comes from somewhere out East. New York or someplace like that. He told me he wanted a more rustic life, so he came out here and set up shop as a lawyer. Ha! He'll do well here, just you wait and see."

"I've heard talk of a new lawyer in town, actually. I just never heard his name or where he's from, I guess."

"He will give that terrible Charles Littman who traipses around sniffing after the judge some competition, that's for sure. I never did like that Littman fella, you know. Just like you said, he's in cahoots with Judge Valsted and that's enough to make me distrust him. But now with Mr. Sullivan here, our little town will be far better off. Oh, here I am babbling on about nothing and it's only you who matters right now. Clara, I'm just so sorry that this is happening to you." Annie crouched in front of me as well as her large body would allow and took my face in her hands. Her fingers were like pieces of icy silk. A sigh escaped my lips and my fingers unclenched and lay still in my lap.

I was completely willing to let this Sullivan fellow help, if he could, and I told Annie so. My eyes, though, were getting heavy and my head was aching. Luckily, Annie was perceptive enough to notice.

"Well, we know what our first step will be. Tomorrow morning we will go see Mr. Sullivan. Now though, you need to go lie down for a while. Upstairs you go!" She helped me to my feet and led me up the wide staircase, each step covered with a lovely rose colored carpet patterned with gold swirls. At the bedroom door, I turned to Annie, wishing to thank her for all of her help, but she would hear none of it.

"What are old friends for, anyway, if not to help one another? Why, think of all the times you've given me advice and helped calm me down. You are a dear, dear friend, and I want to help you…and all of those other women, too. Now, off to bed with you. I'll have Martha bring your valise up here and once supper is served, I'll come to get you."

My feet were lead as I walked to the white iron four-poster bed where I sat and removed my shoes, sighing as I freed my blistered feet. I still cannot recall settling into the soft mattress as I fell immediately into the deep darkness of uninterrupted sleep, for a while that is.

CHAPTER 5

Seemingly from far away, angry voices came to me and I slowly came to the surface of awareness, struggling to comprehend where I was and why I was in a strange bed. Then, I remembered and became fully awake.

"You can NOT go up there, Bob Terrell, you dirty rotten son-of-a-bitch! This is my house and you will not trespass in it!" Annie's voice was loud and desperate.

"Get out of my way, you dumb woman, or I'll...so help me, I'll...well, I don't know what, but it won't be good for you!" My mind screamed in panic at the sound of Bob's drunken voice. How did he find me? How in the world could he have known where I was? Then, there was a loud thump and a shriek from Annie that brought me upright and running for the door. Bob's boots clumped on each of the carpeted stairs, and knowing I could not get past him to help Annie, I scrambled to the other side of the room, hoping he would not find me.

"Clara, where's ya at, dolly? You come out now and see old Bob here. You need to come on home with me so we can talk this through." I cringed at the sickening syrupy voice of my husband. I cowered in the corner, and before I realized I was trapped, Bob appeared in the doorway and strode quickly to me, his speed belying his drunken state. The rage, though, was clearly marked on his face. I knew as soon as I saw

41

him that he had no intention at all of "talking this through." His rough hands grabbed my arm, pulling me out the door. Squirming and pushing at him, I tried to get loose, but his grip was too strong for me. As he dragged me down the stairs, my long hair pulled loose and caught in his hands. I yelped at the pain and the humiliation of having my husband abuse me so in front of my friend.

It all happened so quickly. I got a glimpse of Annie rising from the floor at the bottom of the stairs and then of Martha rushing into the entryway. I screamed and reached desperately for them, but Bob manhandled me out of the house, threw me onto his horse, and jumped up behind me. Annie and Martha were in the open doorway, and I could see their mouths moving, screaming words I could not hear over the roaring in my ears, a waterfall of sound so intense that I was deaf to all else. Bob gripped me tightly around my middle with one arm, and with the other, wheeled the horse to a gallop and headed home.

My mind was in a whirlwind and I could not think straight. I knew what would happen once we arrived at home but was trapped and helpless to stop it. Frightened beyond belief, I fought against the darkness threatening my consciousness. I focused on staying awake. After a while, my hearing returned and the words I heard solidified my fears. "You'll see, you dumb bitch, I'll always be the boss of you. You don't have no rights at all, no siree, you stupid...."

Somehow, I was able to block out his voice and I used the time to assess my rather slim options. I had no choice now but to be at home with him. Thankfully, there was no way he knew the real reason I was at

Annie's. I might as well listen and agree as he ranted and raved in his drunkenness, and then with any luck at all he would fall asleep quickly, allowing me time to think the next step through.

I heard Champ's barks as we came down the lane to our farm and I stirred slightly. Bob's grip around my waist tightened and made breathing difficult. The rancid smell of days' old sweat and whiskey made my throat burn with acidic bile. Finally, he stopped near the door of the shack and threw me off the horse, roughly shouting for me to get into the house. Then, he steered the animal to the barn where he began caring for him. I was relieved to see that he had the clarity of mind to at least do that small kindness for the faithful horse. Maybe he was coming out of his rage and would treat me with that same kindness.

Once inside, I paced and waited for Bob, dreading the confrontation. Before long I heard his heavy footsteps on the porch and he lurched into the room. My hope for kind treatment was smothered under a heavy cloak of fear when I stared into his face, once so handsome and smiling but now a mottled purple with red-rimmed fiery eyes.

"Just what in hell were you thinkin' going into town and shamin' me by goin' to that worthless pig's house? Huh? Just what? Answer me now, you stupid bitch!"

Words stuck in my throat and I backed away. "I-I was just going for a visit is all, Bob. Now calm down."

"Calm down, ya say? You really are stupid! Calm down!" Bob's voice was high-pitched in an attempt to imitate me. "You don't think I'm dumb enough to believe that bullshit about just visitin' do you? Ha! I know better than that, I'm telling you! You ain't got no right to go anywhere without my say-so, ole lady, and you need to get that straight in your head right now!" Bob's fist came down sharply on the table and almost overturned the lantern that sat in the middle of it. I backed another step away. I was almost at the door to our bedroom.

Bob continued his ranting, swaying on his feet and punctuating his words by pumping his fists in the air. "How do you think it felt for me when ole Ben Wilson come into the saloon there and told me that he'd just overheard you tellin' Bea that you was headed to that man-hatin' worthless pig Annie's place? Why, no God-fearing respectful woman goes to her house! You hear me? No, siree, no wife of mine's gonna shame me that way! Didn't you ever hear that Annie was one of them there Suffgettes, wife? That there's the truth; that dumb bitch is nothing but trouble, and you'll have nothing to do with her. Never! Just for a visit, my ass! You all is cookin' something up against us men is what I think you're doing! Ain't that right, woman? Answer me, dammit!"

"Wh-why no, Bob. I just wanted to go to town is all and thought a visit to Annie's would be an all right thing to do while I was there." My words stumbled out. Lying to Bob was uncharacteristic, but I hoped to calm his rage. It came to me in a sudden rush that my husband had always felt threatened by Annie. Our lifelong friendship created a bond that, although different from the one I had with Bob, was equally strong. At times, even stronger. I remembered having

44

these thoughts before, right after Annie moved to Bergen to be closer to me. Bob knew of our friendship and did not feel threatened much by it until she moved here, complete with her independence, her outspoken nature, and her wealth. I think he feared she would see him for what he was and convince me to leave him. She did not, though, much to her credit, saying very few negative things about Bob. But now, something or someone was poisoning Bob's mind against women, it seemed to me, and the threat he perceived Annie to be was coming out in force.

Bob came raging toward me, his unblinking eyes bulging and his lips curled in a sneer not unlike an angry wolf, and my ears roared as he advanced on me. I stumbled backward into the bedroom, putting my arms in front of my face just in time to partially ward off a backhand blow. I yelped which fueled his anger so that he grabbed both my wrists in his left hand, pulled them to the side, and rained blows with his right fist into my face and alongside my head. I screamed at the pain and terror that filled me. Suddenly, he pushed me backward. My head hit the footboard of the bed on the way to the floor. White spots danced in the darkness. I pulled my knees as far up to my chest as I could and covered my head with my arms. Then, I was aware of Bob's boots pounding into my back and legs. I cried out for him to stop and finally, blessedly, a heavy velvety cloak surrounded me, and I snuggled against its thickness and felt no more of the battery.

I came to as if from the bottom of an empty well, up and toward a small square of light. For a second I rejoiced. I was dead and would see my Julia and blessed Jesus at any moment, but then the

45

excruciating pain came, and I knew that was not the case. By inches, I moved to a sitting position, trying not to moan. At one point I almost retreated again to the blackness, but self-preservation created a determination to stay awake.

Finally, I rose to my knees and looked around, assuring myself that Bob was there, passed out cold on the top of our quilted bed. His feet, still enclosed in those boots that he used to kick me nearly to death, hung off the end of the bed. I got to my feet and staggered out of the bedroom and to the washbasin which I took out to the pump and filled with clean water. Champ followed closely, his high whine mirroring my despair. The coppery taste of blood made me nauseous, so I drank from the ladle at the well. Somehow I stumbled back to the house and told Champ to stay on the porch.

Once inside, I tenderly and slowly washed myself as best I could. My reflection in the mirror showed blood caked around my mouth and splotched on the front of my blouse. Dark red marks formed like continents on the parts of me that I could see. Once I finished, as quietly as possible, I stepped back to the bedroom and changed into a dress I had not taken to town. I attempted to put my hair up, but pain prevented me from raising my arms. For some strange reason, this all was quite important, as if company would arrive at any moment, and I wanted to appear put together for them.

Bob snored from the bed, snorting every now and then. My pulse pounded throughout my body as I stood a ways from him and stared at his form. How and why was this happening? My husband had never been a brutal man, just a frustrated one. For sure he had struck me several times before, but he always gained control of himself quickly and left the house before he beat me too badly. This time, though, something overtook him. It was as if he was an animal with no control of itself.

Aching from head to toe, I stepped like a whisper into the other room where I paced back and forth trying to work the knots out of my muscles, all the while trying to think of a solution to this problem. My knees weakened, causing me to fall into a ladder-backed chair, and I put my battered head into my hands, weeping loudly. Defeated, I no longer cared if Bob heard me and woke up and came to finish what he had started. My head weighed too much to hold up, so I let it fall on my arms crossed on the table. I tilted it to the right side since my left eye was swollen nearly shut. Just the movement in my neck made me wince. Weariness overtook me and my right eye closed; however, sleep eluded me and my mind took over, too strong to give up the fight.

For some reason I still cannot fathom, I was able to think rationally and not give in to my emotions. I had to move forward if I was to survive. Clearly, my life here with Bob was over. Although he had never beaten me this badly, I had endured his violence too often over the years, especially the past couple of years after I had begun to act "strangely." Both Bob and I had always blamed the liquor for his outbursts. This time, though, there was no excuse. He had brought this on, and I knew he intended to see it through, even if he had to kill me, which would be even easier for him to accomplish than having me committed to that awful asylum. I was dispensable. I shuddered at the dawning of this new reality.

I really had nowhere to go except back to Annie's, although I doubted my ability to make a second trip to town in my battered state, and I figured Bob would just come and get me again. Next time, I probably would not survive. Hope, though, is a powerful drug. I thought that perhaps Annie was right and Mr. Sullivan would help me somehow. Fear and desperation are also good catalysts. They took over and I stumbled to my feet, almost overturning the chair as I did so. Righting the chair, I stood, not daring to breathe, like a mouse caught in the glare of a cat on the prowl. What if Bob came to at the sound? As quietly as possible, I crept to the door. Once on the porch, I took a deep, ragged, painful breath of the cool night air which made me feel a little sturdier.

Naturally, Champ followed me as I trudged down the lane for the second time that day. I groaned as I stooped to pet his head and told him how good he was but that he needed to go home. The dog whimpered as though he felt my despair and understood he might never see me again. Always obedient, though, he started walking back home, turning his head back to me every now and then, just to be sure I had not changed my mind. I groaned in pain as I straightened my back. My bare feet struck out toward Bergen an exhausting five miles away. At least that heavy valise and those dreaded shoes were already at Annie's this time, so I traveled unencumbered except for the pain that threatened to overwhelm both my body and my heart. But I walked on through the darkness, thankful for a little bit of light from the moon to show the way.

About a mile down the road, I saw the lights of a vehicle coming toward me. Who would be out here so late, I wondered? Very few people in these parts drove vehicles. The vision of the two parked near our barn, Judge Valsted's and Doctor Belzer's, swam through my mind. Quickly moving behind the cover of a bush of fragrant sage lest I be seen, I held my breath.

"Look out! There's a goddamned huge rock in the road right there!" The voice was female, loud, and familiar. It was Annie. Relief nearly made me faint.

I stumbled noisily out from my hiding place, tripping over a small bush. I dropped to my knees, hands splayed out in front of me. The car was only a little ways past me, so I raised my hundred-pound drooping head to shout to them, "Annie. H-help me. Over here. Please." My voice, however, was barely over a whisper, but by some miracle Annie heard me.

"Shh! I just heard something!" Annie said. Suddenly, the brake lights illuminated me.

I repeated my plea, and before I knew it, Annie's ample arms surrounded me, supporting me as I teetered off the edge into despair and darkness.

I came to with a start, screamed loudly, and fought against the strong arms that surrounded me. "Shh...shh...it's all right now, honey. I've got you, and you're safe now with us...shh...that's it...relax...I've got you." The balmy voice came from deep within the chest of the person holding me, and thus sounded deeper than it really was; then, I recognized it as the blessed sound of Annie. I instantly stopped struggling and with a whimper cuddled into the bosom of my friend.

When I had rested some, I pulled myself painfully upright, realizing that we were still in the vehicle. The outlines of buildings in the moonlight and small dots of light shining from windows indicated we were nearing Bergen. Moving slowly so the pain would not bring the darkness again, I turned to Annie and thanked her for coming to rescue me, a thought coming to me as I did so, Who was my other rescuer?

As though reading my mind, Annie introduced our companion and driver as Connor Sullivan. In the moonlight, I could see the man had slight curls in his black hair that hung down over his left eye. Although I could not see the color of them, his eyes sparkled, and I could make out a wide brow over a small, slightly upturned nose. His strong jaw jutted toward me in greeting, "Evening, ma'am."

"I thank you kindly, Mr. Sullivan, for coming with Annie." My voice was weak and hollow, so I said no more.

Annie and Mr. Sullivan, though, talked and I gathered that they felt it too dangerous to take me back to Annie's. Because of the late hour, most people in the town would be tucked into their houses for the evening and would not take notice if they were to take me to Mr. Sullivan's residence, a small house three blocks from Annie's.

Once we arrived, Mr. Sullivan and Annie helped me into the house as carefully as they could. Since Mr. Sullivan had no housekeeper, Annie went to the kitchen to prepare a tray of food and hot tea. Mr. Sullivan swooped me into his arms and carried me up the stairs and into one of the spare bedrooms. As though I were breakable, he placed me on the big, soft bed and told me he would return shortly with my valise which he would get from Annie's when he took her car back to her house. I thanked him and then must have fallen asleep.

The next thing I knew, Annie was there placing a tray on a table. She helped me into an upright position, leaning me against soft feather pillows and chattering on about a variety of topics including the pesky drought, this summer's nuptials of two young up and comers, and the latest fashions. Anything except what had happened to me.

Mr. Sullivan arrived with my valise and quickly excused himself. Annie continued her chatter as she helped me into nightclothes. Although I could tell from her wide eyes, and her terse mouth that she was stunned at the lacerations and bruises on my body, she made only one or two "tsk" sounds and tried to do so under her breath. However, I heard her and vowed to look at my body tomorrow; not tonight, though. I was exhausted and too battered to walk to the mirror. Once my nightclothes were on, I settled into the pillows again and pulled the covers up under my arms.

Annie opened the door and spoke softly to Mr. Sullivan, asking him to come into the room for a bite to eat. Only Annie could get away with asking a man to come into a room of his own house so that he could eat his own food. The man's shoulders filled the doorway, and when he entered the room, his presence filled it entirely. The air changed with it, creating a warmth deep in my stomach.

I was surprised that the man appeared to be about my age, with glittery silver streaking his curls. His darkly tanned face had traces of age in it as well: lighter lines ran from his eyes to his hairline, slight bags sat under his eyes, wrinkles curled around his mouth and lined his neck some, too. Hadn't Annie earlier called him a "young man"? Even though his face appeared to be my age, he had retained a youthful figure. My one good eye swept his frame from black boots up his muscular legs that were encased in tightly fitted black trousers, onto his torso over which he wore a loose fitting gray shirt, open just enough to reveal a smattering of silvery-black hair at his neck.

Since I did not wish to be rude, I attempted to eat a sandwich but to no avail. I just could not swallow it past the lump in my throat. The hot tea, though, was soothing and calming.

Again, Annie talked. Now that Mr. Sullivan was there, she began discussing my problems. "We need to do something about this situation, Mr. Sullivan, and quickly. Otherwise, that dreadful man will come back and do who knows what to her. We will be unable to hide here forever, you know. He'll find us, you mark my words. You know what I am saying, don't you?" The desperation was clear in her booming voice.

"Oh, yes, lass. Please, though, call me Sullie. And understand that I know exactly what dangers you and Mrs. Terrell face, but believe me when I say that no chap is gonna harm anyone in this house this evenin' or ever for that matter." He had a lilting accent that sounded Irish. "I think, though, that we need to allow Mrs. Terrell to be getting some sleep right now.

See there?" He nodded toward the bed where I lay with my right eye half closed and my left one swollen shut.

I tried desperately to open my eye when Annie took the cup and saucer from my lap, but it just would not cooperate. The darkness of sleep came over me, and my friend's voice sounded very far away.

"Oh, yes. My manners have just completely left me in all the terror of this night. I am terribly sorry, umm, Mr. Sullie." The fragrance of vanilla filled my nose as she placed the whisper of a kiss on my forehead. There was a quiet rustling as they left with a click of the door.

CHAPTER 6

I became aware of the warm sun on my face first; a breeze of warm spring air brought the chattering of a blue jay to me through an open window. Momentarily forgetting the last evening, I turned on my side to face the fresh air. Pain shot through me, splashing like sparks, and my one good eye sprang wide open. A groan escaped my swollen lips. The events of the night flooded my mind as I lay there, and a tear rolled into a wrinkle in my neck.

Struggling against the pain, I sat upright onto the edge of the bed. Then I stood, gasping as the room spun. After a few seconds, I was able to move to the window where I stared down at the brown yard that in a less dry year would have been sprouting shards of green, flower buds beginning to bloom in the black beds. Now, though, it just appeared desolate and somewhat sad, a mirror to my predicament.

Willing myself to move, I took off my nightgown and stood nude before the full-length mirror. I examined the bruises and abrasions Bob had inflicted on me. I gasped at the reflection. My left eye was completely shut, and around it lines of red streaked across the purple bruise where Bob's fist slammed into it. Nearly my entire face was marred by swellings or bruises. With my right eye, I perused the damage done to the rest of my body. Basically, Bob had left very little of it untouched. The parts that remained free of color and tenderness were those that I was able to protect while curled into the fetal position. I turned to the side and then around, examining my sides, arms, and back. If it were not painted on the canvas of a human body by another's fists and boots, it would be a colorful, pretty, albeit sinister, oil painting of that new type of art, abstract. However, this design was on my back, spilling over onto my sides and arms, and the artist was my husband. The purples were of various depths; the reds were vibrant, throbbing stripes that resembled fingers spread around my arms; there were yellowish green marks, too; and the blues rounded out the palette, meshing the purples and reds with all of the other shades. It was a frightening ensemble.

For some reason, shame overcame me, and a hot redness spread across my chest and up my neck to my face. Somehow, it was my fault this happened. Wanting to cover myself before anyone entered the room, I worked against the pain and dressed.

As I struggled to put stockings on, there was a light tap on the door, and Annie asked if she could enter. I assured her that she could. In the morning sun, Annie appeared drawn and tired. The lines across her round face were more pronounced than they had ever been. And in her eyes, I saw the shadows of horror. The bruising and swelling on my face and neck were the cause, so clear in the morning sunlight, and I was sorry for causing her such pain.

Annie quickly hid her shock, saying, "Well, now, I see you're ready to face the day already. I do have a proposition for you, though. Martha arrived before the sun came up. Would you approve of her coming up here and bathing you and washing your hair for you? I think it would do you good, girl, to get freshened up with more than just clean clothes. What do you say?"

"I don't know about the bath. It was quite a chore getting clothes on this morning. Although, having my hair washed would be okay, but really, you don't have to bother Martha with that. I can do it myself if she just brings me a basin of water." I was only thinking of the embarrassment of having Martha see the bruises on my face and the blood dried in my hair.

"Don't be foolish, Clara. I'll send Martha up right away to wash your hair. I completely understand about the bath, though." And with that, Annie was gone.

A couple of minutes later, Martha arrived with a large basin of steaming water, a white towel draped over its edge. She set the basin on the vanity, and I painfully situated myself on a ladder back chair, tilting my head back into the basin. The lilt of the maid's voice singing an old Irish lullaby as her fingers lightly worked through my hair relaxed me.

Once my hair was towel-dried and put up in a loose twist at the nape of my neck, Annie returned. "You look as pretty as can be now, Clara. This lady is quite the miracle worker with her hands, is she not?" And with that, she reached over and pulled Martha to her, squeezing her with smile. A warm pink blush spotted Martha's cheeks and she smiled at the praise, obviously loving her boss.

"Now, though," Annie continued as she walked gracefully to the door and gestured to the hall with a flourish, "we must go downstairs."

Annie and I went downstairs and settled in the living room while Martha made up my room. Almost immediately, Connor Sullivan was there as well. Just as I opened my mouth to begin thanking them, Annie said, "Isn't he just the most wonderful, kind man ever, Clara?" Not taking a breath to allow me to answer, she rushed on. "Allowing us to stay here at his house where hopefully Bob and his cronies will not find us. Why, he even stayed up all night watching out for us, just in case. No one was going to come into this house uninvited, no siree, not with Sullie here to guard the door!"

At last, I found my voice which sounded stronger this morning. "Yes, Mr. Sullivan, I don't know how to begin to thank you for helping me last night, and now this…" my voice trailed off in shame that this kind man had to have his life so rudely interrupted due to my problems. I was mortified at the thought. Mortified but endlessly grateful as well. How would I ever repay this man? And Annie, too.

Mr. Sullivan's deep voice filled the room, "Whatever it is you are feelin', Mrs. Terrell, is fine with me as long as tis not shame. I cannot abide a woman of your gentleness being abused at any person's hands, and it would pain me no wee bit to think that you feel any shame or remorse for what has happened to you." I shifted uncomfortably, feeling as though he was able to scrutinize my thoughts. How had he known about my feelings of embarrassment earlier this morning?

Mr. Sullivan continued in his lilting accent, "It is intolerable to me, and I will not stand by and watch something that atrocious happen. It's just not in my nature to do so." He relaxed back onto the chair cushion, crossing one ankle over his knee.

I peered at him with my one good eye while he spoke, assessing him. He was a study in opposites. His voice was almost musical, yet it resounded from deep within his chest and exuded power. His reclining posture made him seem relaxed, carefree even; however, his face registered something much different. Its creases had deepened in the night and his blue eyes snapped with anger. Also, I noticed whiteness around his knuckles where his hands clenched together in his lap. This was a powerful man unafraid and angry, yet in full control of his emotions. Goose bumps rose on my arms and legs, the fine hairs raised and scratched on my blouse and stockings. A small tremor went through me.

"Why, Clara, I saw that! Here, put this afghan around you." Annie's voice broke through, and I accepted the soft covering gratefully. Despite the warm morning, I was suddenly chilled.

As I pulled the afghan around my shoulders, I said, "So, what do you think we should do now, Mr. Sullivan?"

"Please, Mrs. Terrell, call me Sullie. It's what I prefer."

"Fine, Sullie," I responded, "but you must then call me Clara, as all of my friends do."

Just then, Martha entered announcing brunch. Obviously, she had set up in the Sullivan household for the time being. We rose and made our way to the dining room where we ate in near silence, avoiding the dilemma I was in until after the meal was finished.

Sullie suggested we move back to the living room to finish our coffee, so we did.

Once we were sitting comfortably, coffee mugs in hand, I broached the delicate subject that seemed to be the elephant in the corner of the room. "So," I began, clearing my throat quietly, "what do you two think I should do to get myself out of this mess?"

The two of them were silent, each looking into the other's eyes as if to find the answers there. Finally, Annie nodded her head slightly to Sullie, indicating that he should speak first.

"Clara, I must admit that I know only a little of your plight, so if you don't mind, I'd like to hear from you what occurred yesterday," Sullie said. Sunlight coming in through the window glinted off the silver in his hair and a soft, welcome breeze rustled the lace curtain.

And so it was that I told my story again. This time was different from yesterday when I bared my soul to Annie, though. It felt better, safer somehow, to tell this strong, confident man my story. Beginning haltingly and tearfully, I soon found myself pulling confidence from Sullie who never took his eyes off my face. My voice gained momentum and volume, and I slowly un-hunched myself. It was uncanny how comfortable he made me feel; how safe, too.

"I see," Sullie said when I finished. "Annie told me a little about your troubles yesterday after your husband left her home with you, and since then I have had some time to think about possible solutions."

"Please, do tell," Annie responded.

"Yes, please do." I was no less anxious than Annie to hear the man's solution.

"I know that there are some very powerful chaps involved in this scheme, as you just said. Judge Valsted who I've had to stand in front of many times-"

I nodded. "Of course, as a lawyer you would have. What do you think of him?"

"He's always made me uncomfortable. Can't really pinpoint any one thing about him, but he just seems too...well, too slick, I guess is the word. And far too self-important for my liking." Sullie pulled his hand through the shock of hair that fell over his eye and took a drink of coffee. "I know Charles Littman really well and it doesn't surprise me at all that he's involved, since he hero worships Valsted. Although Littman has no wife to send away, he is just as despicable to me since he's a man of the law. He knows what these other chaps did, and he helped them do it."

Annie said, "Oh, he is a terrible man, for sure."

Sullie nodded and continued, "Now, Doctor Belzer's involvement does surprise me. He seems like such a gentle man but that just goes to that old idea of wolves in sheep's clothing. The whole thing infuriates me, I'm tellin' you. I want to see them punished!" Sullie's lilting voice boomed, and he set his empty mug on the table in front of him and stood. He walked slowly from one end of the room to the other, hands in his pockets, his shoulders tense.

"Not to mention Judge Valsted and Doctor Belzer's positions in this community. And the influence they have over people...Why it's a travesty of the justice system, I'm tellin' you! They just must pay for what they've done," Sullie's ranting continued.

Suddenly, Sullie's body uncoiled, his voice became softer, and he sat down again. Leaning forward with his elbows on his knees, he said calmly to me, "And you, Clara, you are the key to this whole thing. You'll need to be stronger than you ever have been before. We're gonna be fightin' some powerful people here, and one of them is your husband. Do you think you have it in you to help me put these chaps away where they belong?"

"Will you be there with me, both of you?" I looked hopefully from Annie to Sullie and back again.

"Why, of course I'll be there for you, right by your side," Annie exclaimed. "Where in the world else would I be? I'm just as angry as Sullie is about this, and you know me, I always enjoy a good fight, especially when I know I'm on the right side!"

"And I, too, will be there to guide you and give you advice both as a lawyer and as a friend, if you'd like me to be," Sullie said.

"Thank you, both of you," I said. "Forgive me for saying so, but none of what you've said so far answers my question. What can I, or we, do?"

"You're right. What we need to do is get those women freed. Right?" Sullie said. At our nods he continued, "In order to accomplish that, we need to get those court rulings overturned, which in normal circumstances would mean filin' an appeal to the District Court here in this county. We can't do that though, since the judge is one of the perpetrators. Not to mention it'd have to be the families of the women who filed an appeal anyway, and for sure their husbands aren't gonna do that. It'd have to be their children." Sullie was on his feet again, pacing and

61

pulling his hand through his hair. As I watched him, I marveled at his ability to concentrate. His focus was so intent that he did not seem to notice Annie and me in the room.

"To be honest with you, I think this thing is a wee bit over my head, but I do know a chap who might be able to guide us. I knew him for years back in New York and he's quite a good friend of mine. Maxwell Heinz is his name, and he's in Helena serving as a member of the House of Representatives. I'll give him a call and see what he's got for advice." Sullie's movements quieted again, and his focus came back to the room. "You know, lassies, as I see it, everybody has a boss, someone they must answer to. I intend to find out exactly who Valsted, Littman, and Belzer need to answer to for their actions. Then, we'll get 'em out of business completely."

My voice sounded small and weak. "Their true master is the Good Lord, and He'll give them their due when the time comes."

Both Annie and Sullie turned their attentions to me then, nodding in agreement. Annie touched my hand as she said, "Yes, that's so true, but here on earth they must answer for their crimes as well, and it's our duty to make sure that they do so. Don't you agree?"

"I don't know. It all just sounds like it's too big of a fight for the three of us. This is all so sudden. I just wish I hadn't heard them talking about this and that I was back home with Bob, living my life as I've always done. I'm sorry, but I'm just not strong enough for this." My chin was on my chest and hot tears plopped in my lap.

"Shh, you're just not feeling well is all. You're all beat up both physically and emotionally." Annie's words soothed me, even though she added "by that bastard Bob" under her breath. She continued trying to calm me down. "Naturally, you'd like to be at home. Shh, it's going to be all right. Sullie and I have this handled. All you have to do is tell your story when the time comes, and you have to realize that your safety must come first, if not to you, then to us. We'll make sure you're kept safe, and even though you don't want to hear it right now, that means that you cannot go home. You have to stay here with us."

"Clara, you need to listen to your friend," Sullie added. "Remember what happened the last time you were home? I hate to bring it up, but really, you must keep your head around the severity of your situation. If you're found again, Bob will send you away right off if you're lucky, and if you're not lucky, he'll beat you for sure and perhaps even kill you. Annie and I just cannot allow that to happen, so you're stuck with us, whether you like it or not."

I found the strength to raise my chin again and as I did, I caught the look of concern that passed between them. Sullie nodded subtly to Annie, and she said, "I think it's high time that we put you to bed so that you can heal up. Sullie and I will continue with this work, and you just rest up and don't think about all this for now."

My breath sucked in audibly as I pushed myself from the chair. Sullie took my elbow and led me upstairs and to the bedroom door, where he relinquished me to the care of Annie who all the while she settled me into my nightclothes and the bed, made

63

clucking sounds usually reserved for ill children. These soothing sounds were the last I heard before blackness overtook me.

CHAPTER 7

Periodically, I came into consciousness to find
Sullie bringing me a tray of food or a cup of tea, and
once I thought I saw his shadowy form draped in a
chair which was backlit by a small lamp across the
room. He looked to be writing, but I could not be
sure.

A spring-scented breeze caressing my cheek
awakened me fully, and the cry of a mourning dove
brought me the feeling of home before I realized that I
was not home, that I was at Sullie's house. After
several attempts, I raised from the bed only to have
lightheadedness and weakness sink me abruptly back
down on its edge.

"Well, look who's awake. If it isn't the beautiful
lassie come back to us," Sullie's voice echoed as he
swept in. My head cleared a little, and my cheeks
became hot with embarrassment at his seeing me in my
nightclothes.

"Yes, I'm up, well partly anyway. How long
have I been sleeping, Sullie?"

"Off and on for three days, lass. You've just
been recuperating nicely here and occasionally
awakened to eat a wee bit here and there."

"Three days! Oh my goodness! I'm so sorry
for burdening you so! I certainly never intended to -"

"I know, but it's okay. You needed that rest to
recover from your injuries. Now that you're up,

though, I'll get Annie back over here to help you and then we'll all get a bite to eat. Okay?"

Sullie never saw me nod since he had already turned and left, hurrying to fetch Annie from her home. Somehow, I was able to stand and walk the little ways to the table where there was a pitcher of water and a cloth below a mirror. I gasped at the old, ragged woman with matted hair looking back at me. Once I had washed my face and brushed out my hair, I did not seem to look so much like the forest witch in *Hanzel and Gretel*.

I heard Annie before she appeared. "She's up finally? How is she?"

I could not make out Sullie's muttered reply.

"I'll go up right now and help her. Sullie, you go fix us some breakfast. I know, I know, we've already eaten, too, but we really must get some good food into her, and I know she won't eat alone. And you, Martha, get a bath set up in her bedroom. Now, go, go, you two!" The corners of my mouth turned up as I imagined Annie's arms flapping as she shooshed them to their tasks. Somehow, she calmed herself enough that when she came into the bedroom, her voice and her tread were soft. "Oh, Clara, look at you. Let me see...first, we'll get you into a bath and dressed for the day. Oh, where is that Martha? Then, we'll all sit down and have a bite to eat. That'll help all of us. Now, tell me how you feel."

Before I could utter a word, though, Martha was there, and the rush was on. They somehow got a bath ready for me, gushing all the while over the excitement of my being up. Their words abruptly stopped, though, once I was disrobed. Martha averted her eyes before I could read them, but Annie's face was set and pinched with anger and pain as she peered yet again at my body. Most of the bruises were now greenish yellow, faded yet still visible. Embarrassed, I attempted to cover myself with my hands as I stepped into the tub, and once I was covered with the fragrant bubbly water, I felt less ashamed. Annie was her old self again, too, shouting orders to Martha and setting out my freshly laundered clothes.

"You have no need of shoes, Clara, because they are just too confining for right now. This dress will be just fine, I think and these..." I quickly looked over at Annie as I heard a huge intake of breath from her. She flopped onto the bed, looked at me, and with a small, childlike voice said, "Oh, Clara, I'm so sorry for you. I really am." Once she had shed a few tears and wiped them from her cheeks, she was up and all business once again, helping Martha dry my bruised body. Somehow, with their help, I was ready to face the day, so we walked slowly down the stairs where delightful smells welcomed us.

Once we had eaten and were seated in the living room, Sullie got right down to business. "Okay, then," he said, gently holding his coffee cup. "I talked with Maxwell, my friend in Helena, extensively the past couple of days, and we came up with a plan of sorts. Annie, I've shared some of this with you already but I have some new ideas. Can I share them with you lasses?"

"Of course, Sullie. Go ahead," Annie said.

The hammers were back in my head, making any movement painful, so I was silent.

"This is the way I see it," Sullie continued. "As I said before - -"

"Just a minute," I blurted, my head pounding with the effort. "I'm terribly sorry to interrupt, but I think the first thing I need to do is contact my sons. I really do appreciate all of this, but I'm concerned that Bob will get ahold of the boys, and they'll be worried sick about me."

The big clock in the corner ticked as Sullie and Annie stared at me. A hot flush crept over my cheeks, and I asked, "Don't you agree?"

Annie answered, "This has come up in our conversations, Clara, and the way we see it is this. Your sons do need to know what is happening and that you are safe; however, we can't let them know just yet."

"But, they will –"

"Hush for a minute while I explain," Annie's voice was harsh. "I said 'just yet.' You can contact them when the time is right, and that is not now."

"Why not?"

"Think it through. If you talk to them right now, they will want to know where you are and you would never lie to them, and undoubtedly one of them would tell their dad that you're here. Think about it, Clara. You have to stay in hiding just a little while longer. Then, when it's safer, you can tell your boys. Okay? Does that make sense?"

"Yes, I guess it does, but it doesn't make it any easier." My eyes filled with tears. "I just need them right now. Maybe one of them could come and get me and let me stay with him until all of this goes away." A single hot tear slipped down my cheek, and I swiped it with my hand.

"I understand," Annie said. "But it's just too risky. We can't assume that the boys will feel that your leaving their father is the right thing to do. Your life is at stake." Annie took a deep breath and continued. "I just hope you understand and don't get ahold of them yet."

"Well, when can I contact them?"

"Let's just listen to Sullie's plan and then we can decide that. Okay?"

I gave a short nod and looked at the floor.

"So, as I said earlier, everybody has a boss," Sullie said.

"But not the judge, right, Sullie?" Annie asked. "That son-of-a-bitch -- excuse my language -- is extremely powerful and obviously has not had to answer to anyone at all yet."

"You're right, lass. Since he was voted into his office, he doesn't have a boss per se. And, he's not had to answer for his misdeeds, but I assure you both, he does need to answer for 'em, and I have the feeling we'll be the ones to make him do just that."

"Well, I'd certainly like to see that happen," Annie said and I nodded.

"As I said before," Sullie continued, "normally, we'd have to appeal at least one of these women's cases to the district court. But with Valsted as district judge, we can't do that. So Maxwell said, and I agree with him, that we need to go to the county commissioners with this. They are the men who are mainly concerned with--"

"You don't understand, Sul--" Annie interrupted.

"--the welfare of the people in this county, men and women alike. They'll likely be very interested in hearin' your story, Clara, and will help us go over the judge's head to the state people."

"Sullie," Annie said, trying to get his attention.

"I know most of them and can get ahold of them and get this all started." Sullie boomed. Nausea rose in me as the level of sound reached its peak. The two of them were fairly shouting to be heard above each other. I pressed my forefinger into my temple to quiet the pounding.

"Sullie! You need to listen for a minute. I'm trying to tell you something, and you're doing that lawyer thing and not listening to anyone except yourself!" Annie shouted.

Sullie shrank back at her biting tone but quickly composed himself, apologizing to Annie for his rudeness and smoothing his shirt.

"I'm sorry, too, Sullie, but you're new to this town, so you probably aren't aware that most of the county commissioners are good friends with Judge Valsted and Charles Littman. And Doctor Belzer, for that matter."

"Oh. I see."

Annie's voice was softer. "That's part of the problem around here. These few powerful men control everybody and everything in this town. And we only know the identities of four of the fourteen women who were sent away. Who knows, one or two of the commissioners could be involved in this. In fact, now that I think about it, Richard Clement's wife, Caroline, supposedly went to visit her sister about three years ago and never came back. Word around town was that she ran off with one of the ranch hands who quit about the same time. Hmm…"

"Oh. Now that's interesting. I hadn't thought about that possibility. I'd like to know the identities of all of the other women, but I can't do that because in cases where mental capacity is involved, the records are sealed. Well, I'll need to think this through some more." Sullie let out a deep breath and settled back in his chair, rubbing his left hand over his stubbled cheek.

"Yes, there are so many problems here, aren't there?" Annie said.

Blessedly, the two of them quieted as they each tried to come up with solutions. Annie spoke first.

"You said something about getting the commissioners to help us contact the state, right?"

"Aye, I did," Sullie replied.

"Well, why don't we just go over all their heads and go right to the state, namely your friend Mr. Maxwell Heinz, for help? Wouldn't that be the next logical step? I think so," she answered herself. "And as for the matter of the identities of the other ten women, I can't think of anything we can do with the records sealed, so we need to just leave that for the state to come up with as well." Annie's courage and independent spirit always amazed me, but as she spoke, I felt true admiration for her strength. She was willing to help right an injustice that had nothing to do with her personally, and I felt blessed to be her friend.

"Exactly, lass! That's what we'll do. I'll call Max straightaway, explain our problem with the commissioners being the judge's cronies, and get his help on that end. See what he has to say about all this."

71

Sullie relaxed into his chair. "Also, the way I see it, by goin' straight to the top with this, we'll avoid our little friend here getting into any trouble with her husband and his friends. We'll get her to Helena and keep her safe 'til this mess can be straightened out."

"Going to Helena is a good idea, but Sullie, regardless of how good Mr. Heinz is at getting things accomplished, I don't feel that this is a problem that can be solved overnight. It's going to take a while, and you certainly cannot be gone from your office for as long as all this will take," Annie said.

"Actually, I had no intention of going with you lasses right away. I need to finish up the cases I'm working on first. That'll take, oh, I'd say a good three or four weeks. Now, though, do you think you can handle being gone for as long as this will take, Annie?"

"Most certainly. I just need to make a few arrangements and pack up is all. No problem. I don't know if she's up to the trip quite yet, though. What do you think? Oh, but here we are, Sullie, talking right over Clara. How rude of us. Clara, dear, how are you feeling?" Annie's voice was soft and kind, soothing me.

"I'm doing all right, I guess. I'm still sore and swollen, but I'm getting better all the time. I understand the urgency involved, yet all of this talk about going to Helena is uncomfortable for me, but I'll adjust to the idea. You both are much better at solving problems than I could ever be, and I trust you. Both of you." I looked at Annie and Sullie through my one good eye, seeing the concern in their faces.

Annie's tone was gentle when she replied, "I'd feel so much more at ease if you were checked out by a doctor, but -" A gasp escaped my lips at the mention of the doctor. The only one the town had to offer was that dreadful Doctor Belzer. "Easy now, Clara, let me finish," Annie continued. "I have no intention of letting that sorry excuse for a man anywhere near you. I think we'll get you to a doctor once we get to Helena."

"Oh, no. I don't think I need –" I protested.

"Stop this, now. You've been badly beaten. You might have broken bones even. You need to be looked at. Please, do this for me. Won't you?" Annie said.

"Well, I guess you're right. I'm sure Mr. Heinz can recommend one and set up the appointment for us. Right, Sullie?" I said.

"When I call him here shortly, I'll get Max to set it up directly," Sullie said. "Also, I think you two should catch the train to Helena first thing tomorrow mornin', if you're up to it, lasses."

Annie and I nodded.

Although they did not want to leave me, Annie and Sullie needed to appear as normal as possible so as not to let anyone know they were harboring me, and so we all parted ways. Sullie left for his office to call Maxwell Heinz, Annie and Martha left to tend to travel plans at Annie's house, and I remained at Sullie's. I was nervous about being left alone, but they would all be back, Sullie in a couple of hours and Annie and Martha the next morning. So I sat fidgeting in the living room, praying that my fears were unwarranted. Hoping for the first time in my life that just this once, Bob would drink his way into oblivion where he would stay until we were out of town. Either that or the opposite, that Bob, for once, realized his responsibilities were with the homestead, and he was home taking care of the animals. I especially worried about Champ. He needed to be fed, but he was a survivor and if need be, he would leave the place. Perhaps he would go to our neighbors.' Hopefully, they would take him in. At any rate, I could do nothing to help, could not go back, no matter what.

CHAPTER 8

After an hour of sitting alone, I went upstairs and readied myself for our journey. With every movement that afternoon, I became stronger and my muscles became more flexible. Sullie arrived right before the supper hour.

"I'm so happy to see you up and about, lassie. And you look well, too," his soft voice settled around me, and my cheeks flamed at the compliment.

Once darkness fell, Annie came to the house, which according to Sullie, she had done every night since I arrived, staying until the early morning hours. She fussed over me as though I was a child, he said, anxiously waiting for me to feel better. He failed to mention the fact that Bob had come to Annie's house the day after she and Sullie picked me up on the road.

Annie was the one who told me about his "visit." "It was quite awful, really, Clara, and I'm so thankful that you were safe over here rather than at my house."

"Was he drunk?" I asked.

"I don't think so. But he was irate, shouting for you and calling me names so loudly that I'm sure the whole damned neighborhood could hear. He even forced his way past me to search for you, at which point I informed him that I would fetch the police if he did not leave that instant."

"Oh, no. What did he do when you said that?" I asked.

"He just laughed at me. The look in his eyes was frightening. I remembered that the idiot sheriff would be of no help to me, so I just allowed him to rant and rave and search through my house. Once he was satisfied you weren't there, he stormed out and rode away. Only then could I breathe again. I shut and locked the doors and have kept them locked tightly ever since."

Sullie paced. His hands clenched in his pockets, his brows furrowed, and his eyes snapped. "Annie, tell her the worst. Tell her what Bob said about her."

"I wanted to spare this for you, but you need to hear it, I guess, so you know the severity of your situation. Bob, the bastard--forgive me for my language-- told me, and I quote, 'That woman is mine. I own her, and I'll do whatever I want to with her!' I answered him without thinking, saying, 'Yeah, you'll do whatever you want with her all right! Like send her to Whispering Pines! You have no idea who you're dealing with now, Bob. This whole scheme that you and your buddies have cooked up will be revealed, and you all will be dealt with, I can assure you of that. Yeah, that's right, we know all about how they've been 'dealing' with their wives. You go back to those buddies and tell them that they're dealing with Annie Hazelton and Connor Sullivan and your wife now, and there's no stopping us.' Oh, Clara, I'm so sorry. My big mouth gets me in more trouble than I care to admit." Annie took a ragged breath, and Sullie stopped pacing.

"Oh, my word! How did he react when you said that?"

"It was frightening. He went all still-like but his eyes literally glowed. He looked so evil. I feared he would strike me, but he didn't. He just blew out a huge breath. His breath was awful, I might add. But anyway, he just turned and left right after that. I'm so sorry."

"Don't worry about it," I said. "He's the one to blame for this, and now he knows that we know. What's done is done. However, I think that we are all in danger if we stay here. Sullie, are you sure you can't come with us tomorrow?"

"I wish I could, but it's just not feasible. I have a few cases that need to be finished up, so I just can't. I'm sorry. Please know, though, that I'm perfectly capable of taking care of myself. And I'll be careful, too."

I nodded and asked, "Has Bob or any of the other men come to this house looking for me yet?"

Sullie shook his head. "No, and thankfully so since I surely would be tempted to kill any of 'em that did. After what that man did to you and then darin' to scare Annie-girl that way, why I'd be hard-pressed to hold myself back from him. 'Twas a good thing for him that I wasn't there that day at Annie's."

"Well, I'm certainly happy of that, too, not that I wouldn't want to see him hurt some, but any violence against Bob or those other men would only bring more wrath onto us, and we don't need that right now." I was surprised at how strong and rational I sounded.

"Now, though, since you are feelin' somewhat better, we need to act swiftly. It's my wish that you two be on the train tomorrow morning," Sullie said.

A darkness fell over my soul, and I felt hot tears gather in my eyes, which brought Annie out of her chair and over to mine, her arms around me. "What is it, dear? Shh now. It'll all be okay, you'll see," she cooed to me.

I sniffled. "I'm just so ashamed that you two had to see all of this, and I'm so bothered that you're in danger. Maybe I should just go alone down to Robby's or to Luke's or Pete's. I just don't know what to do!" What happened to my strength?

It was Sullie who answered. "Listen to me, Clara. We just talked about this. You're in imminent danger, lass, and so goin' to the boys' is not an option right now."

–"But my sons love me and will see –" I said.

"Sullie's right," Annie interrupted. "Look, if you want to write to them and let them know what is happening, go right ahead. Write the letters tonight, though, and don't let them know you are going to Helena. They might tell Bob where you are and that would be disastrous. Let them know that they can contact you through Sullie."

A lightness flooded me at the thought of writing to my sons. Although we were no longer as close as we should be, they were my children and they would help me in this time of need. Wouldn't they? I dried my tears and dotted my nose with my handkerchief. Sniffing, I looked with reddened eyes at my friends. All I could do was nod in agreement and shuffle up the stairs to write the letters before I went to bed.

The next morning before I was ready to go downstairs, Annie glided into the room, her cheeks flushed, her smile broad, and her voice low and steady. "I'm all ready to go," she announced. "And as we speak, Martha is readying her things for the trip. My dear, how are you feeling? Do you think you are up to going?" Softness and concern filled her eyes and voice.

"Of course, I am," I replied, surprised that my words came out with so much conviction when inside I felt quite unsure. "I don't have much of a choice now, do I?" And in my heart I knew that was true. After I had written the letters, explaining the best way I could what had happened, I knew deep in my soul that my boys would not understand. But I still had a small morsel of hope.

"Now, then," Annie said as Martha came in the house, "let's get on with our journey."

Sullie rushed out to take our bags to the train depot. Annie, Martha, and I retired to the living room where we filled the time until he returned discussing Martha's plans. She did not desire to travel to Helena with us, but since it was now too dangerous for her to stay at the house alone, Martha was going to her sister and brother-in-law's house in Glendive while we were gone. Martha was looking forward to the reprieve and to playing with her nieces.

Sullie returned and all three of us women relaxed. I really had not known how coiled we were until his arrival. As we left, I gave Sullie the letters to mail, and he handled them like the precious items they were and agreed to send them as soon as we were gone. He also assured me that he would notify me as soon as he heard replies.

To avoid contact with the townspeople and the gossip that would surely ensue if they saw us, we walked the back streets to the depot.

At the train station, however, who should be there waiting but Mrs. Carlson, the banker's wife I had encountered on the street when first arriving in town.

"Why, Mrs. Terrell, what in the world happened to you?" Her shrill voice rang out, turning my cheeks scarlet and causing my eyes to drop. I wrongfully assumed no one would notice the slight swelling of the left side of my face and the residual yellowish bruise that was still slightly visible. The loud woman continued, "Why, I just saw you the other day and you looked fine! Now, tell me what has happened! Where are you all going anyway? I want to know, right this - "

"Mrs. Carlson," Sullie's commanding voice stopped the barrage of words, and the woman's eyes flicked over to his, no doubt seeing the dark threat in them. "Please, now, I don't mean to be rude, but we'd just as soon you mind your own affairs and we mind ours this mornin'. And what a fine mornin' it is here, isn't it? Why, the likes of Ireland couldn't produce a mornin' as fine as Eastern Montana does in the springtime. Wouldn't you agree?"

Mrs. Carlson frowned at the affront and then blinked back her indignation as she began a diatribe on springtime in Montana, commenting on how this dreadful drought had intruded on the best of them. Thankful for Sullie's diverting the woman's attention, I allowed my mind and gaze to wander around to the activity of the station master as he prepared for the incoming train. Annie disappeared with him into the tiny wooden station and returned with our tickets to

Helena, which she discreetly held so Mrs. Carlson could not see them. The last thing we all needed was anyone in town, especially Mrs. Carlson, knowing where we were going. The woman continued her babble. Apparently, she was meeting the train to fetch her sister who hailed from North Dakota and would surely be exhausted; however, she would just have to gather the strength to go to Bea's for lunch with her...and the woman went on and on. If the sister was not exhausted from her trip, she surely would be from having to listen to Mrs. Carlson. I shook my head to remove those unexpected hurtful thoughts and forced myself to think good things. It was quite a feat.

At long last, the train arrived and Mrs. Carlson's sister bounded down the steps and rushed into her sister's arms, talking all the while. How the two women could be so alike astounded me as I imagined what their house must have been like as they grew up, both of them talking non-stop all the time.

When the conductor called for us to board, we handed him our tickets, bid Sullie good-bye, and took seats in the private compartment that was to be ours. The train departed and in a short while Martha left us to be with her sister in Glendive.

CHAPTER 9

The two of us settled in then for the long trip. Annie tried her best to get me to accompany her in socializing with the other passengers, I kept to our compartment, not wishing for anyone to see the slight yet still visible bruises and abrasions on my face. I could not bear to see pity in their eyes and to answer questions they might raise, even though they were strangers. Annie was a gem and sat with me quite a bit so that I would not get too bored or too maudlin.

I did my best not to focus on the fear and uncertainty that surely awaited us in Helena; however, my best was not good enough, so during our afternoon tea, I broached the subject most on my mind. "Annie," I said, "I think we have tiptoed around the purpose of this trip long enough. I want to know what exactly we can expect in Helena. I want to - "

"Oh, Clara," Annie interrupted. "You don't need the stress of it right now. Just concentrate on getting well, and let me worry about Helena. Well, me and Sullie, that is."

"No!" I had not meant to shout, but that was how it came out, so I continued, frustrated with her for treating me as though I was a child. "I need to know. This is my problem, mainly, and it's only right that I be involved in the process. Please, stop coddling me. It's been four days and I'm stronger now and feel that I can handle this. Now, let me!"

"Okay, I guess you're right. I just worry about you is all." Annie said, her eyes almost overflowing. She sniffed delicately into her kerchief and then continued, "Sullie is the one with the expertise in the matter, not me, but I'll do my best to explain what he told me." Her meaty hands enveloped mine and the familiar vanilla filled my nose, calming me. "Since we can't file an appeal from the actual cases against the fourteen women, we need go about it in a different way, and the best way, according to Sullie and Maxwell, is to impeach Judge Valsted which would then bring into question all of his rulings on these cases."

"But, how do we get him impeached?"

Annie squeezed my hands and let them go, giving me a quick smile before continuing. "That's the complicated part. Are you ready for it?"

"Yes. I can handle it, I think."

"Okay. The first thing that needs to happen is the House of Representatives must initiate impeachment proceedings against the judge. That's where Maxwell comes in. He will take your story to the House in Helena right away and see what they think about it. If they think the complaint is viable, then they'll have the Senate convene a hearing to hear actual evidence, and Clara, this is where you come in. It'll be necessary for you to testify in front of a few of the senators about what you heard outside the barn that day. Okay?"

"All right. I can do that." I said, sitting on the edge of my chair, my fingernails biting into my palms.

"Of course you can, dear. Think about it. These women's quality of life is at stake, not to mention righting a horrible, horrible injustice that's been done." Annie was up and pacing the small cabin with her hands fluttering, and her voice, I was sure, carried two or three cabins away. "Not only that, but you can't tell me that any of this will stop happening to women out here in this dried up prairie until judges like Valsted are stopped and made to pay for their miscarriages of justice!" A small smile sneaked its way to the corners of my mouth when I saw my friend's exuberance. She always had been a champion of women's causes.

"Okay, so what happens after I testify?" My voice had captured some of Annie's enthusiasm.

Annie plunked into her chair again, sitting as far forward as she could and continued, "As I understand it, if your testimony convinces them Valsted did wrong, the Senate will impeach the bastar—oh, there I go again." Annie rolled her eyes to the ceiling. "I'm sorry. Anyway, hopefully they impeach him."

"But, what if my testimony isn't enough?"

"Let's just hope it is, but if the senators need more evidence of this tragedy, there's plenty to be had. Right?"

I nodded. "Yes. There are the court transcripts they could read. And hopefully someone will check on the women themselves and see that they are and always have been sane."

"That's right. See? There's nothing to worry about, Clara. These men are guilty and it'll be clear to the senators, I think."

"What do you think will happen to the women?" I asked.

"Well, if Valsted's rulings are found to be flawed, hopefully they'll be freed. I think the Senate and the Supreme Court make that decision. I'm not sure, though."

"Goodness, this all sounds really complicated. Not to mention time-consuming. How long will all of this take? Do you know?"

Annie poured us each a cup of coffee before replying, "I don't know. To be honest, I assume quite a while. Unfortunately, the wheels of government turn slowly. I'm hoping though, that due to the situation these women are in, they will act more quickly than usual."

"Yes. Let's hope. And pray." I took a long drink of coffee as my friend continued.

"Don't forget, that dreadful fool Charles Littman, the lawyer who helps Valsted, needs to be dealt with as well."

"Oh, yes. I almost forgot about the other men. What will happen with them?"

"Nobody can tell for sure, but I guess, if anything is to happen to Littman, it's the State Supreme Court who decides. Mainly, we need to focus on getting Valsted impeached, and then the others will fall like dominos. More than likely, Littman will be disbarred."

"I see. And Doctor Belzer? What will happen to him?" I asked, still stunned that such a seemingly caring man could be involved in this evil.

"Again, none of us know for sure. I hope that his license is revoked. Really, I wish they would all be sent to prison, but that's probably too much to ask." Annie sighed deeply then and said, "First step, though, is to get to Helena and meet with Maxwell. He'll be in charge at least until Sullie can get there. We need to just do this one step at a time."

"You're right, of course. I still wonder, though, how in the world did something of this magnitude happen in this day and age and no one caught it until now? After all, there are fourteen women, fourteen for goodness' sake, sent away in the past four years. I'm just having a really hard time understanding it, is all."

"I can't understand it either, but I've been trying to grasp it. The best I can come up with is that Valsted and his cronies were quite good at keeping their business quiet and secret. People around Bergen are so busy trying to keep their work done and raising their children that they don't have time and energy to worry about other people's doings. And until you overheard those men in the barn, no one was the wiser, is what I think."

"So, it's on me for throwing the doors wide open in our community. I don't know how I feel about all this. It's like I've intruded into everyone's private life. In some part of me, I just wish everything would go back to the way it was before...just me and Bob living on the place like always..." My voice faded and tears started coming. I swiped them off angrily with my handkerchief, leaving hot trails on my cheeks and a fierce pounding in my temples.

"Don't you dare think that way!" Annie stilled my thoughts. "Don't you spin this in your mind to be anything other than what it is. You and Bob weren't living on the place 'like always.' He was a mean drunk who was conspiring to send you away to the insane asylum, and don't you forget that for one minute!"

"But, I can't help it if I still love him," I said so softly that Annie craned forward to hear me. Annie's eyes rolled to the ceiling, so I quickly said, "Look, I'll be all right, believe me. It's just taking me awhile to adjust to all of this. And know that I appreciate what you are doing for me and for all of those other poor women who didn't see what was happening until it was too late for them. Now, if you'll excuse me, I'd like to rest awhile."

"Okay. I'll be just down the way, then, if you need me." Annie rose and squeezed my shoulder as she went to the door, eyes on the floor as she left the compartment.

As I rested, I attempted to make myself feel better by remembering some of the good times from our marriage. Images came to me on the waves of strong emotion. Our small boys playing hide and seek in the yard. Bob leaning back in a chair on the small porch of our house, laughing at something I said. A parade of Christmases, the feel of Bob's callused, warm hand in mine while the boys greedily tore wrapping from the toys and clothes we had bought for them. My heart grew lighter with each memory and at some point, I drifted off to sleep.

I awakened with a clearer mind, the pain in my head just a dull ache. I arose to sit on one of the chairs, staring out the tiny window at the passing scenery allowing my mind to escape into it. Eastern Montana really is a lovely land with its bare naked clay bluffs, scrub pines on the tops making them appear to have unruly hair. A large river ran alongside the tracks; a row of cottonwoods hid it from my view but marked its winding path. With each mile the train clacked westward, the land turned greener and lusher.

A soft tap on the door interrupted my reverie just as I spotted a small herd of antelope grazing in a meadow. It was Annie.

"Are you awake?" Annie asked, poking her round face into the cabin.

"I am, Annie. Please, come in with me. I'm quite over myself now and feel better about what we're doing."

"So you're not angry with me for saying what I did about your marriage?" Annie said as she came in and sat next to me.

"No. How could I be? You were right about it. Partly anyway. It's never been perfect, and it never would've been. But, there were good times too, which cause me to be confused and angry about all of this, so please, forgive me for being short with you."

"Now, now, none of that, Clara," Annie leaned over and wrapped her ample arms around me then, and instantly I felt better.

Soon, the porter announced from the hallway that we were about a half hour from Billings, one of the largest cities in the state. There we would have a two-hour rest stop. It was nearly dark when we debarked from the train; however, the grandeur of the depot was not to be missed. It was a huge brick two-story affair. Rounded doorways dotted its side, and numerous windows allowed us to see inside the spacious reception area.

We walked through one of the rounded doorways and into pandemonium, laughing at ourselves and each other as we attempted to get our land legs back. People scurried everywhere; some were greeted by family or friends there to take them to their final destinations while others, like us, just wanted some time to walk around on solid footing and to go any direction we wished rather than just up or down one narrow aisle. Our break was too quickly over.

Once back on the train, Annie and I talked quietly about a subject we had avoided until now, the identities of the incarcerated women. Of course, we knew four names for sure, and even though it felt a lot like gossiping, we speculated who the others might be. We discussed the women who had left Beaver County for some reason or another and who did not return. They were mainly women we did not know really well. We were able to come up with five more possibilities, and with their names came their faces and with their faces came an urgency to free them such as I had never experienced before.

We also made plans for our arrival in Helena the next morning. We would go immediately to our hotel and freshen up, after which we would go to breakfast and then to my doctor's appointment.

Once we made our plans, Annie went to the dining car to socialize while I remained in our stateroom and got ready for bed. I took my hair out of its bun and brushed it with the silver brush my mother had given me when I turned sixteen years old. A wave of nostalgia overcame me as I remembered that delightful day.

I was in Green Bay again, in the huge house I grew up in next door to Annie. It was March 11, 1885, and the day graced us with sunshine and warmth. I was allowed to sleep late and arose to the sounds of preparations for my special party. The maids and extra help my parents had hired for the day rushed around making sure every inch of the house gleamed. Some helped the cook in the kitchen while others set up chairs and tables on the porches and in the ballroom. Still others bustled around arranging large bouquets of flowers into vases. Wonderful aromas of baked meats, fresh bread, and fruit pies wafted up the stairs to greet me.

     Annie could not be kept away from the excitement of the day and arrived early to help. She, Mama, and a maid came to help with my hair and dress. Ah, what a gown that was...a magical piece of fine workmanship and multiple layers of pale pink silk which transformed my lanky, boyish lines into soft feminine curves. Starched crinolines shaped the floor-length skirt into a bell and rustled softly against my legs when I walked and danced. The rouched, pleated silk underskirt was decorated with row after row of embroidered flowers. Dark red roses, if I remembered correctly. Swirling and twinkling around them were thousands of beads. A stiffer, smoother, much shorter overskirt fell elegantly from a high waist and formed three broad scallops at its base which my fingertips could just reach. Mama kept scolding me about fingering it, but I just could not still my hands that day. A bustle made it feminine and fashionable and quite grown up. The embroidered roses and sparkly beadwork also embellished the short sleeves and the bodice, which were tight over my newly budding bosom. Short gloves and the softest kid leather slippers completed the ensemble.

The ladies swooped my long, wavy golden chestnut tresses into a high knot atop my head, leaving clusters of ringlets to frame my face. I literally gasped at my reflection when I looked in the mirror, which caused the four of us to break into such giggling that Father came into the room to see what was happening. The look on his face, a strange mix of pride and terror, only caused the giggling to turn to outright raucous laughter.

Later, once all of the guests had arrived, Annie escorted me as I glided down the gleaming staircase in this beautiful gown and was announced to everyone as a young woman. That day was one of the most important of my life, and now I smiled remembering all of the fun banter, the dancing, the succulent food, and the attention I received. For months after the party, I held those feelings of love and acceptance in my heart and knew that all was well in my world. Little did I know what the future held in store for me.

After the party ended and all the guests had left, my beautiful mother came to me with one final gift just from her. It was this stunning silver mirror and hair brush. Now, as I caressed the intricate rose trellis patterns on the back of each piece and turned the brush over to feel its bristles whispering over my palm, Mama's presence came to me.

How special she was: kind, loving, friendly, truly a lover of all living things. At one time I prided myself on being very like her. One of the many things I learned from her was that a warm, friendly smile makes everyone feel at ease. Even in the darkest times, my mama found the strength to smile. Funny, sometimes days would go by out here on the prairie without my face breaking into that smile she had given me. Some days, especially lately, I just could not summon the strength to be happy or to pretend to be happy. For some reason, I just could not. Oh, how I missed Mama.

Everything was so different now. Even the color of my hair, more silver than chestnut. And my clothes, no silks for me anymore. I shook my head to clear away the negative thoughts and self-pity. With a sigh, I placed the brush on the night table, said my prayers, laid myself in the bed, and slept.

The next morning I awoke with a foggy head, sand-filled eyes, and cruddy mouth. Once the porter arrived and the smooth aroma of coffee reached me, I felt more human. Brushing my teeth, doing my hair, and dressing while listening to Annie's boisterous, comic recall of last night's gossip also helped. I laughed and smiled more that morning than I had in a long while.

CHAPTER 10

It was a little after seven o'clock in the morning when we stepped off the train into the Helena depot, a sprawling building with a tall spire at the top of its steeply pitched roof. Annie arranged for a car to take us to the hotel where she had made reservations before we left Bergen.

Sometime in the night, the coulees, bluffs, and sagebrush of the east had transformed into lush pine-covered mountains which now surrounded us. The smell was heavenly as I breathed deeply of the crisp morning air, only partly stained by the smoke coming from the train, and I looked around at the colors of the flowers trying to start their blooms in pots on the depot porch.

At last, we were loaded into the car. My hands nervously worked the handle of my purse as Annie carried on an animated conversation with the driver. Traveling through Helena, the largest city I had been in since my return to Green Bay when Mama passed, excited and unnerved me. Three-story brick buildings lined most of the streets in the downtown area, and our driver pointed out the Merchants Hotel, a huge, gabled brick building that encompassed nearly an entire block. According to our driver, that was the place which held the first meeting of both houses of the state legislature in 1895. I was awed at the important decisions that had been made and the laws that were created in that building. People were everywhere, scurrying down the walkways hurrying toward who knew what.

Smoothing down the thin cotton of my old-fashioned prairie dress, the second best one I owned, I noticed the women wore dresses similar to Annie's, which was form-fitting and fell only to the middle of her calf. So different from mine. Oddly enough, Annie's attention to fashion set her apart in Bergen and made her look out of place there. Here, she fit right in. The women in Helena were even more fashionable than Annie, though. They wore shoes that had higher heels than I had ever seen, and some of them had bobbed hair that merely peeked out from beneath hats of all shapes and sizes. Since coming west, I had not paid much attention to these things, opting for comfort instead, but now it was clear that my attire would, in these people's minds anyway, place me in a shack right in the middle of the eastern prairies. I pulled at the edge of my bonnet, the best one I owned, in embarrassment. Not one of these people will listen to someone like me and take what I have to say seriously.

Annie's warm, meaty fingers suddenly entwined mine, and as she met my gaze, I knew she understood as only a woman could. "It'll be all right, Clara," she said. "You'll see. Everything will be just fine. Calm down, now, and enjoy the view. It really is a lovely city, is it not?"

"Oh, I agree with you completely. Look at that!" I exclaimed and pointed out the window at the largest building I had seen yet. It stood three stories high with a single white granite column appearing to hold up the entire corner of the building. That corner was stunning, built out from the rest of the building

94

with a covered observation cupola at the top. The flat roof was bordered by a beautiful railing behind which I assumed folks could stand and look out at the city.

"Yes, it is even more beautiful than I had heard," Annie said. "And guess what, my dear?"

"What?" I said not taking my eyes off the building as we were nearing the front of it.

"That is the Grandon Hotel, and it is our home for the next however long."

I was stunned. I quickly turned to face my friend, my hands gripping hers. "No, Annie, really. It's much too fancy for someone like me to - "

"Nonsense. We're here on the most important of business, and we will stay in none other than the finest hotel in the city. Plus, it'll be fun, won't it? Have you ever seen such a place?"

"Oh, I'm so excited," I gushed and let go of Annie's hand since mine was damp. "I really can't wait to see what it's like inside. If the outside is this lovely, can you imagine its inside?"

As we chattered, the driver pulled in front of the hotel and helped Annie and me onto the sidewalk next to the grand column. A porter, who introduced himself as Mr. Kershaw, rushed to help us into the hotel. Once clear of the front doors, I entered another world. The reception area was immense, with pillars standing like sentries down the center of the room. Dark panels adorned the bottom of the walls, and patterned wall paper lightened the tops. Electric lights illuminated the desk area which covered one entire wall of the room where Annie checked us in. Numerous lamps lent a softer glow to the various sitting areas scattered throughout the room. An elaborate staircase glowed in front of us.

Mr. Kershaw led us up the stairs and showed us our rooms. Annie and I were sharing a suite which was opulent yet comforting, with deeply cushioned chairs and lounges in the sitting room which was decorated in golden and burgundy tones. My bedroom was almost as large as our entire home, complete with its own sitting area and huge feather bed that I could hardly wait to sink into. Annie had a separate bedroom, just as beautiful as mine, although hers was done in shades of green whereas mine was burgundy and pink.

The most exciting part of the entire suite, though, was the indoor bathroom, complete with hot and cold running water that went directly into the large porcelain bathtub that stood on clawed feet in the corner of the room. Soft, thick towels were folded neatly over a rack next to the tub.

"Oh, Annie." I whispered as she showed me the bathroom. "It's delightful. I can hardly wait to return here this evening and take a long, hot bath. That will be a dream come true."

"Why do you have to wait, Clara? Just jump in there right now. I'll have our hostess draw you a bath, okay? Just wait right here, and I'll fetch her." Despite my protests, Annie returned in only a couple of minutes with a tiny young woman with a sprite's face who she introduced as Gretchen, our hostess.

Gretchen went directly to work drawing a warm bath, and once it was ready, I quickly undressed and immersed myself in it, actually giggling in delight at one point. It felt so wonderful. The heat eased the aches in my joints and muscles, and the citrus-scented bubbles that the water made when Gretchen poured some beads into it tickled my face. I could hardly force myself out of it, but I knew that Annie wanted to bathe before we started our day, too, so I told myself that this was not the last bath I would take here, and thus was better spirited about getting out and wrapping myself in a towel.

Plodding into my bedroom, I gasped. There, spread on the bed, was a fashionable pale blue walking dress, stockings, black shoes with a bit of a heel, and a straw hat with its brim held up in front with a blue flower. "Annie!" I yelled and my friend appeared, grinning and rubbing her hands together. She came to stand next to me, staring at the outfit. "Oh, Annie, what have you done?" Hot tears ran down my cheeks, and I tried to brush them away.

"Now, now, you deserve this. I want to do this for you, my friend. I just want you to feel comfortable today. However, I hope I haven't overstepped my boundaries. Is it okay?"

"Oh, Annie, yes! It's fine. It's just been so many, many years since anyone has done something this nice for me. I can't imagine how I'll ever repay you."

"Nonsense! Allow me to treat you. Please, now, just try it on. I must confess that I called and ordered it from a boutique before leaving home and just guessed at your size, so I hope that it fits you and suits your taste. If it doesn't, we'll return it and get a different one. While you do that, I'll bathe and ready myself for the day."

"Oh, Annie. It suits me just fine!" I exclaimed and as soon as Annie closed the bedroom door, I dropped the towel onto a chair and dressed quickly. The dress was the softest fabric that draped snugly over my hips to mid-calf, and a row of buttons hidden by a placket ran the entire length of it. Once I had the dress on, I stood in front of the full-length oval mirror, admiring it. A small round collar framed my face perfectly when I pulled my hair back. Thankfully, my face was less swollen and only a little greenish-yellow encircled my left eye and trailed down my cheek.

Once I finished putting my hair into a loose roll that suited the small hat, I put on the fine stockings and the shoes, which were a tiny bit loose, but that was fine with me since I knew my feet would swell some throughout the day. With one last satisfied glance in the mirror, I joined Annie in the sitting room.

Annie gasped as I walked in. Her hands flew to her mouth as she exclaimed in her boisterous voice, "By golly, Clara, you're absolutely stunning! I remember your being a stylish girl when we were growing up, and here that girl is again! How does it feel?"

"Heavenly, absolutely wondrous. I cannot thank you enough, Annie. It's strange, though, that for years I have given no thought whatsoever to fashion or style, and then once we were off the prairie and on our way here, I noticed how backwards I looked. I felt I wouldn't fit in with the people here. I was embarrassed and feared no one would take me seriously. But now that you've done this for me, I'm confident for the first time that someone will really hear us and will help us solve this mess. Oh, look at me, blubbering away." I swiped the tears with my handkerchief. "At any rate," I continued, "vanity has returned to me, and I'm not sure if that's a good thing or not."

"Just let it all be. In the next day or two, since these clothes appear to fit you well, I'll have the boutique send over a few more items for you, so you're not stuck with only one set of clothes. Let vanity prevail! I say!"

"Oh no, I can't allow you to—"

"Nonsense! Now, let's go downstairs for breakfast," Annie said.

After breakfast, we left for my appointment with a Doctor Mitchell. Once we were in our hired car, Annie took my hand, warming it with her own. "Now, you need to just relax and know that we're in good hands, God's hands."

"God's hands, His care, and His will. Those are what I've been praying for all my life, Annie. Now, I can see that this is all part of His master plan for me. Getting these women freed could very well be my life's work, well this and raising my boys to be good men." Tension ran out of me as if it was syrup out of a pitcher. It was sweet and good to be with my friend and to know that I was being of service to the poor souls who were unlawfully locked away, having who knows what done to them in that horrid place.

I turned to look out the car window at the city buildings rushing by, people scampering around doing their business, seriousness on most of their faces. At one point, we stopped as a group of children ran in front of us, each carrying a load of books strapped together. Their twinkling light voices and the occasional high-pitched scream made my heart soar a little higher. They were headed for a large building with a dirt yard filled with swings and a makeshift baseball diamond set up in front of it. Ah, a school day today for them.

"Oh my goodness, will you look at that!" Annie pointed, startling me. Her eyes trained on a huge white building with a dome on top, its lawns impeccably green. Flowers and bushes bloomed everywhere, and numerous windows reflected the morning sun. "That must be the capitol building. Right, driver?"

"Yes, ma'am. It is at that. Isn't it a beauty, though?"

"Stunning, absolutely stunning," was all that I could mutter. It was breathtaking to think about all of the important business that went on behind those huge doors.

CHAPTER 11

Annie and I continued to watch and exclaim about various buildings and parks we passed, until suddenly our driver parked in front of a nondescript office building in which I presumed Doctor Mitchell conducted his business.

I presumed correctly. The thought of seeing a doctor whisked away my bright mood and my rediscovered confidence. What if he diagnosed me as insane? I stared absently as Annie steered me into the doctor's office. I heard only my shallow breaths. Trying to recover, I took deeper ones, but the smells of the disinfectant and sickness wadded up and caught in my throat. Bitterness burned the back of my tongue, so I grabbed a handkerchief and held it as inconspicuously as possible under my nose.

We sat in a small waiting area until a uniformed nurse who introduced herself as Nurse Compton ushered us into an examination room. The nurse's gray hair was in a tight bun that sat below the rim of her white cap, and her curt manner was disconcerting.

"Mrs. Terrell, as is my duty, I must ask you a few questions and then do a brief preliminary examination before the doctor arrives," she said, her voice matching her mannerisms. I started at the directness of her voice but finally lowered the handkerchief and focused on the process of readying myself to see the doctor. Once she had taken notes in a precise hand about my reasons for the visit, she efficiently took my blood pressure, temperature, and pulse. While she worked, I studied her face and found it to be attractively lined yet harsh; her lips pursed constantly and her brown eyes snapped as she looked at my still-bruised face. Surprisingly, though, her hands were warm and comforting. Before she clipped out of the room, she ordered me to disrobe and dress in a light cotton garment the likes of which I had never seen before. The thing tied at my chin but was otherwise open. Annie and I both chuckled a little at the sight I made in it. So much for vanity.

Finally, there was a light knock on the door and a white-coated Doctor Mitchell entered, bringing with him an aura of comfort and the pleasing scent of sawdust and pipe tobacco. Was he a carpenter as well as a doctor? He was tall and younger than I imagined, near the age of my sons. When he introduced himself, his voice resonated kindness from deep within his chest, and, despite the cotton garment, I was comfortable. His hand completely enveloped mine when he gently shook it.

"Doctor Mitchell, this is Annie Hazelton. She is my dear friend, and if it is all right with you, I'd like her to stay with me during your visit."

"Sure, no problem," he said as he slumped into a chair at the desk. "Sit, sit, you two." And so we sat in the other two chairs as the doctor continued, "I hope you don't mind, but I asked Maxwell to tell me why you were coming all the way from Bergen to see me, and he told me the story of what you heard in the barn, Mrs. Terrell, and also that your husband had beaten you. Please, accept my apology for being so curious and realize that both Maxwell and I just want to help you do what needs to be done to help yourself and those other women. Okay?"

I nodded and looked down at my hands, blushing at the thought of these two strangers discussing my problems.

"No need to be embarrassed, Mrs. Terrell," the doctor said as he gently patted my clenched hands. "I'm just here to help you. Now, on to the business at hand. Please, why don't you describe for me how you've been feeling lately. You know, emotionally and physically. Okay?"

Nurse Compton came in then. I glanced at her, and she nodded curtly.

"Well, I just haven't felt like myself, I guess. Usually, I'm fairly happy, going about my days without much concern for my troubles, but lately - -"

"You must forgive me for interrupting, but what do you mean by 'lately'?" the doctor asked.

"Well, I'd say for probably the last six months or so I've been out of sorts, crabby even, and clumsy. I'll drop things that I'm carrying and then I get so mad at myself that I can feel my heart pounding in my throat. And, I'm ashamed to admit it, but I've also been short-tempered and angry with Bob – that's my husband - during all of this, even going so far as to raise my voice to him, which I never have done before."

"Okay. Can you tell me more about your relationship with your husband? How does he react to you raising your voice to him?" The doctor's eyes narrowed as he looked at the bruising around my left eye.

I flushed at the thought of him judging me, and tears welled up and threatened to overflow. "He, umm," I cleared my throat and quickly swiped at my eyes, regaining my composure. "He has spent more and more time away from home, leaving me alone for the most part, but then I accidentally overheard the conversation Mr. Heinz told you about." My mind veered back to that morning, and I could not go on.

The doctor's hand covered mine, and Annie's arm circled my shoulders. She patted the top of my arm with her meaty warm hand. My head fell to my chest and the tears began in earnest.

"It's all right. Really, it's all right. You can tell me anything and it won't go any farther, I promise you. Now, please, though, I would appreciate you telling me what you overheard the men in the barn saying. I'd like to hear it from you." The doctor's voice was barely a whisper.

"Can I tell you, doctor?" Annie spoke for the first time since the doctor's arrival.

"I suppose you can. You are familiar with what transpired the other day, are you?"

"Yes, I am. Clara told me everything. We have no secrets." At the doctor's nod, Annie told the entire story. When I had the strength, I looked up to find the doctor on the edge of his chair, elbows on his widespread knees. His narrowed eyes had darkened almost black, and when they met mine, I saw anger clearly evident in them. He nodded occasionally and his smooth forehead now had two horizontal lines across it. His hands were clenched tightly between his knees.

Once Annie finished, Doctor Mitchell took a deep breath, unclenched his hands, relaxed back into a slump, and looked directly at me. "Well, that is quite the story, is it not? Yes, quite the story."

Suddenly, fear that the doctor thought I was making all this up and his apparent anger was for me started to overcome me. All I wanted was to leave, even if it meant doing so in that dumb cotton thing. I started to get up, and Nurse Compton took a step toward me. I shrank back into the chair and said, "You don't believe me, do you, Doctor?"

"Believe you?" A gentle chuckle erupted from him. "Of course, I believe you, Mrs. Terrell. Why in the world would I not? People don't generally travel hundreds of miles bruised and broken to come and tell me lies, you know?" Another chuckle, this one louder. "Oh, Mrs. Terrell, you are a dear, dear lady. Please, don't be uncomfortable with me. I'm just soaking in all the details and to be honest, I'm terribly angry at your husband. Now, I want to hear more about your symptoms. Tell me, are you sleeping well?"

Relief flooded me and I found my voice to be fairly strong. "Honestly, I haven't slept well for quite a few months. I have strange nightmares and wake up with paralyzing headaches, soaked clear through my nightclothes. Because I haven't been sleeping well at night, I find myself napping during the day, sometimes up to a couple of hours, which I never used to do. Then I don't get my work done and get frustrated with myself which brings on more headaches."

"I see. Now, tell me about your moods. You mentioned frustration and anger, but what about sadness? Do you feel sad at times?"

"Oh, yes. Quite often the sadness comes right out of nowhere and hits me like a wave. It's so bad that at times I cannot function; all I can do is sit and cry. A few times I've even laid on the floor sobbing for no good reason. I don't understand what is wrong with me."

"I'm starting to understand more, but there's just a couple more things I want to know about your symptoms. How about your ability to concentrate? Are you able to do that pretty consistently?"

"Well, I've always had a pretty good head on my shoulders and can think things through pretty well, but lately that's changed, too. There've been times when my mind just goes blank, and it takes a while for me to remember what I was doing or where something is. I lose my train of thought quite often, I guess." My voice trailed off.

The ticking clock was the only sound for a moment or two. Finally, Doctor Mitchell cleared his throat, sighed, and looked deeply at me, his eyes now a light brown. His voice was soft. "You may think it's none of my business to ask this, but remember that I'm your doctor, and I want you to be honest here, Mrs. Terrell. How about your interest in, well, intimacy?"

"What do you mean?" I asked, blushing at the partial understanding of his question.

Annie's commanding voice answered for the doctor who was staring uncomfortably at the floor now. "Clara, don't be so dense. The good doctor is asking about sex. You know, are you interested in sex?" She nudged me with her elbow and I blushed deeper.

I somehow was able to tell them all that no, I really had no interest in it and had not for quite some time, perhaps a year or so. I explained that Bob and I had intercourse occasionally, but it seemed to be chore-like for both of us, so the episodes became fewer and farther between, usually due to me making an excuse. In the past couple of months, though, Bob stopped asking and just took advantage of me, rape-like and angry in his drunkenness. He had even stopped apologizing afterward, muttering to me about his rights as a husband.

Once I finished, the doctor raked a hand through his short hair, looked closely at me, and said, "Well, Mrs. Terrell, thank you. I know that wasn't easy for you to talk about, and I appreciate your honesty. I really do. I'm pretty sure I know what ails you, but let me think on it a little while. Right now, though, I need to examine the injuries your husband inflicted on you, so I need you to get up on that table there. Mrs. Compton, please help Mrs. Terrell, will you? And Mrs. Hazelton, I think it'd be best for Mrs. Terrell if you waited in the other room while we do this. All right?"

I glanced and nodded at Annie that I would be all right, and she walked out leaving traces of vanilla behind. Once Annie was gone and I was laying on the cold table, I tried to think about anything other than where I was, but to no avail. The sawdust, pipe tobacco scent was stronger now and kept me in the present place and time. Nurse Compton pulled back both sides of the cotton gown, exposing my body for the doctor to examine, which he did, prodding here and there and asking me what hurt the most. My face was hot and red as no one, not even Bob, had ever looked so closely at my body. Both the doctor and the nurse, however, worked efficiently and professionally, never once talking to each other; although, I did see a serious, pity-filled look pass between them once which only made me more embarrassed.

Once the examination was complete, they left me alone in the room to dress, and after a few minutes, they came back with Annie.

"Now, Mrs. Terrell. Let me begin with your bodily injuries," Doctor Mitchell began. "You sustained quite a beating. I'm surprised and thankful for you that no bones are broken; however, there is substantial bruising, both that you can see and also where you cannot see, so I really need you to take it easy. Make sure that you do not bump into anything or get jostled around for the next week or so. Rest as often as you can, too. Your body will heal itself with time and rest."

I let out a deep breath. No broken bones. Just rest and heal. That sounded good.

The doctor took a deep breath and continued, "Now, for what is happening inside you. I assure you, you are not insane, nor are you going insane. Your symptoms, combined with knowledge of your age, lead me to diagnose you as menopausal."

I was silent, could not for my life create a sentence. I knew what menopause was and thought perhaps that was what I was going through, but to hear the word spoken aloud by a doctor, or by any man for that matter, was overwhelming.

Thankfully, Annie spoke for me, "So, what does that mean for her, doctor?"

"Well, the way I see it is that your symptoms will persist for a while, even a year or so, and then, once the menopause has run its course, you will feel better, more like yourself again. It is, though, called The Change for a reason. After menopause, you will be unable to have children, and you will notice changes in your body. But the good news is that you will not have menses every month and you will regain your self. It is a long process, but one that women do have to go through."

"So, Doctor, you're saying that I'll be just fine in about a year?" I said shakily.

"Yes, you should be. And if you're not, then come right on back here, and we'll see what the problem is. For now, I'm going to give you some medication to help with those headaches you've been having. Hopefully, it will help. If it doesn't, feel free to come and see me again. All right? Mrs. Compton, would you mind getting this for Mrs. Terrell, please?" Doctor Mitchell said, leaning forward and passing a small piece of paper to his nurse.

"Certainly, Doctor," she said and left the room.

"So what about those women from Bergen who were sent to Whispering Pines? Were they just going through The Change, too?" Annie asked.

"Without actually seeing and examining them, I can't say for sure, but my guess is that yes, they were. Unfortunately, the subject is not one that is openly discussed in our culture. It is misunderstood, and that misunderstanding can, and I suspect has in this case, led to dire consequences for the women going through menopause. Men often don't understand the changes a woman goes through during this time of her life and therefore can over-react to the symptoms, thinking they are permanent. Therefore, in the husband's mind at least, he is justified in declaring her insane. I don't understand it all, but I think that is exactly what transpired in Bergen. I also suspect that once one woman was sent to Whispering Pines, it became like a contagion, and the men of the town saw a way to get rid of their wives, even in some cases giving them the right to take a new wife, a much younger wife. "

I gasped at his bluntness.

"I know, it's harsh. I'm terribly sorry, but I'm also thankful that you overheard that conversation and took the proper steps to escape. Also, that you have the courage to come forward and try to right this wrong."

"Is there anything that you are willing to do to help us make this right and get those women out of that horrible place, Doctor?" Annie's confident voice asked the question I was forming in my head.

"Oh, yes. I'd be honored to help. When you figure out what I can do or if you need me to testify or anything, I'm willing."

Nurse Compton came on silent feet into the room and handed a small white bottle to Doctor Mitchell who smiled at her and invited her to stay and listen.

"Also, this Doctor Belzer needs to be dealt with, swiftly and finally, if indeed his wife is only menopausal and not mentally ill. He should know better as a physician, and I intend to have him reviewed by the state medical board."

"That's a good idea," Annie said. "Can you do that? Have him reviewed, I mean?"

"Yes, I can and I'd like to start the proceedings right away. However, it probably would be wise to wait until they decide whether or not to impeach Judge Valsted. I haven't made up my mind when to get started on it; however, I assure you that I will do whatever is necessary to ensure that the man doesn't practice medicine again, at least not in this state." Doctor Mitchell was again sitting forward, hands clenched between his knees.

"Doctor, we appreciate that more than anything else, honestly. You are a God-send," Annie said as she stood and reached to help me up.

"Yes," I said, reaching for her hand. "You truly have been a great help. Thank you." I turned to Nurse Compton and touched her hand as well.

The nurse said, "Blessings be with you, ladies. What you are doing is extremely courageous, and as an older woman already through The Change, I appreciate what you are doing. Thank you both," Nurse Compton said, her face and eyes no longer pinched and snapping.

When Annie and I got to the front door, I turned and said, "Thank you both, and if you can do anything to get that awful Doctor Belzer to not practice medicine ever again, I will be eternally grateful."

Doctor Mitchell said, "Don't worry, Mrs. Terrell, I'll see to it."

And with that Annie and I were back on the sidewalk, walking toward our car and driver. My steps were light and my back was straight. I felt at least twenty pounds lighter and ten years younger.

CHAPTER 12

We swept into the hotel lobby in a cloud of banter, recalling every word the doctor said and were stopped by Mr. Kershaw, the young porter who had settled us into our suite the night before.

"Madams, excuse me," he said. "A gentleman is waiting for you in the sitting area."

"What? A man you say? Why, who is it?"

Annie's voice raised the heads of the people behind the check-in counter.

"Please, just this way, madams," the porter said, leading us to a sitting area that appeared empty.

"Is this some kind of joke, sir? Why, there's no one..." Annie's voice trailed off as a tiny man stepped into sight. My breath caught as I took in the bespeckled man whose white shaggy hair created a spiky halo around his round face. As we drew up to him, he bowed at the waist which caused his glasses to fall to the end of his nose. He caught them and pushed them up as he righted himself.

"Ladies, I am Maxwell Heinz and pleased to make your acquaintance."

This strange-looking man was to be in charge of righting all of this wrong? I glanced at Annie whose mouth was gaping.

I found my voice first, "Thank you, I am Clara Terrell, and this is—"

"Annie Hazelton. Pleased to make your acquaintance as well, sir," Annie's voice was quieter than usual.

We all sat, Maxwell giving us each a cup of coffee, which I perched on my knees. I dared not sit back in the puffy chair for fear of not being able to get out of it. Annie, though, flopped back in hers which apparently caused her great relief as she blew an enormous amount of air from her mouth. An uncomfortable silence surrounded us for a little while, and then.

"So how do you--"

"I hope I am not--"

Maxwell and Annie spoke at the same time, tinkled out a laugh, and then, with a gesture from Maxwell, Annie asked, "So how do you know Mr. Sullivan?"

Maxwell briefly described their friendship which began in New York where they both were attorneys who tried in vain to right the injustices in the city, which infuriated them both. Maxwell turned to civil law to relieve his frustration; whereas, Sullie kept up the fight. The two men were nearly inseparable until Maxwell decided to move west, where his vast knowledge of the law, both civil and criminal, made him a successful, wealthy man. He soon was in politics and was elected to be a representative. I was stunned at this man's ambitious drive which belied his rumpled appearance.

"So what happened after you came out here? I mean, with your friendship and all," Annie asked, sitting forward in her chair.

"Sullie stayed in New York after I left, but we kept in touch as much as possible. Finally, he became tired of the city and came west, too. He visited me here, but he really liked the open spaces of Eastern Montana better, so that is where he settled and started his practice just a couple of months ago, as you know." Maxwell's round face turned to each of us.

"We feel quite lucky that he did, too," Annie said as I nodded.

Maxwell said, "If I may, I would like to change the subject. I hope I am not overstepping my boundaries by asking, but I am curious to hear how the appointment with Doctor Mitchell went."

Annie regaled the man with the details of the doctor's appointment, and when she told him that I was going through The Change and that likely the other women were as well, I flushed hotly and looked down at my hands in embarrassment. Although I knew in my heart that Maxwell needed to know this information, my mind screamed at such personal information being discussed, and with a man nonetheless. A woman just did not talk about this.

After a while, though, they moved on in their conversation. I tried hard not to stare, but I could not take my eyes from the man. Under that spiky mess of white hair was the strangest face I had ever seen. He had only one lip: a bottom one, which somehow managed to suck into his mouth every few seconds, emerging damp and pink. Directly above the lip was a hooked nose upon which hung thick round spectacles, his silver-dollar-sized gray eyes bulging out from behind them. They blinked but little, staring intently at Annie when she spoke.

Finally, Annie asked what Maxwell thought our course of action should be.

"Okay. Here it is as I see it. If you will allow me, I would like to take this case to my fellow representatives who hopefully will see the urgency and initiate an immediate hearing on the matter." Maxwell's voice was surprisingly deep, resonant, and articulate for coming out of such a tiny man with only a bottom lip. "Once they do that, then they should schedule a hearing with the Senate. I am thinking that it will just be a small number of senators, a committee actually, who attend to this hearing. Did Sullie tell you about any of this?"

"Oh, yes. He did, but it's good to hear it again now that we're here. Right, Clara?" Annie said, her hands fluttering around her bosom.

I nodded and said, "Please continue, Mr. Heinz."

Annie broke in and said, "Can we dispense with the formalities, please? Let's just all call each other by our first names. Agreed?"

"Okay," Maxwell and I said in unison.

"Now Clara, you will have to testify to what you heard in your barn that morning. You can do that, correct?"

Maxwell, who had been glancing around as he spoke, focused his eyes on mine, waiting for my response.

At my nod, he continued, "Good. So I believe it will be up to the committee of senators to either decide right then and there to impeach Judge Valsted or to convene a Judicial Committee to hear the case, and then, you might have to testify again. Does this make sense to you?" Maxwell pushed his glasses up and sucked in his bottom lip, letting it out with a 'pffft.'

I hid my disgust and said, "I think so, but how long do you think all this will take?"

"Quite some time and you will be needed from time to time, so if it is possible, you had best stay in Helena if you can."

I started to protest, but Annie interrupted.

"Oh, yes. We've already arranged to be here for as long as need be," Annie said with a pointed look that silenced me.

"Good. So that is how this whole process will start."

"What about Charles Littman, that dirty bast---. Oh, excuse me," Annie said, covering her mouth to keep from swearing.

"We need to see what the senate committee decides before we worry about Mr. Littman. The senators will order the next course of action. For now, let us just take it as far as that. Then, we will see."

I glanced at Annie, and saw that although her body remained trapped in the viselike grip of her chair, her eyes were riveted to Maxwell's face and her index finger lazily stroked her coffee cup.

"What do you want us to do first?" I asked, anxious to start the proceedings.

"Nothing right now except get settled here in Helena. I hope you do not mind, but I already have told a couple of my colleagues in the House about this, and they have agreed to back me as I go to the entire group. If you will agree, Clara, I will officially begin the proceedings tomorrow."

Maxwell's huge round eyes bored into mine. Focusing on the wire bow of Maxwell's eyeglasses that imbedded itself into the side of his round cheek, I said, "Yes, thank you so much. I appreciate your believing me and helping us in this. These women need our help desperately, and if you can get those awful men punished at the same time, then more power to you."

Maxwell nodded his thanks and explained that he must be on his way. And so it was that we all rose. I did so quite easily. Maxwell fairly slipped off his perch and scurried over to help Annie who was struggling to release herself from the bondage of those chair arms. Finally, we were all upright and said our good-byes, Maxwell promising to meet with us soon. As he walked away, it hit me that the little man had become less unattractive to me. Perhaps it was just a passing mood of mine that saw such ugliness upon first meeting him.

That evening Annie was exceptionally quiet as we sat reading in our suite, so I voiced my concern, "Is there something bothering you today?"

"Hmmm, that's a good question. Is there something bothering me?" she repeated, getting up to nervously pace the room. "Well, to be honest, I'm not sure."

"You can tell me anything. You know that, don't you?"

"Of course I know that. It's just that I'm unsure of what it is that's affecting me so. It's Mr. Heinz, I think." And then she opened up to me like an oyster showing off its pearl. "The damnedest thing happened. A strange feeling overcame me when we were introduced, and then when he helped me out of that dreadfully small chair, I actually felt a tingling all through my body. It started at my hair and ended in my toes. I just passed it off as another new thing that happens to us old people, but ever since then, I cannot for the life of me concentrate on anything except Mr. Heinz." Annie flumped down into the quilted burgundy chair that was the twin to the one I sat in.

I am sure my face registered the shock I felt at her confession. She was falling in love with this awkward little man! And her naiveté and lack of knowledge about herself intrigued me. How could an intuitive, independent woman of her age not know when love's arrow struck her own heart? Should I tell her, or should I let this sweater unravel to reveal what lay underneath?

Annie sniffed into her handkerchief. "I just don't know what's come over me. Maybe I've caught some sort of ailment. I felt flushed most of the day today. I just can't understand it." Annie puffed her cheeks out as she wound down and relaxed back into the soft chair. I could not help but worry about her getting stuck in the chair, as it had engulfed her completely it seemed.

"So, what are your thoughts, Clara?"

I hoped the shaking of my head was imperceptible, and it appeared to be as she just stared into my eyes, waiting for a reply. "Well, it seems to me that..." my voice trailed off, and I could not meet her eyes. "...I'm not too sure what it is, but one thing is for sure. You will recover from this, so don't worry too much about it. Really, it's probably just a flu like you said." I could not believe how easily the lie came out of me, but I had always felt that matters concerning love were to be handled by the two who were parties to the feelings, not by an outsider such as myself. At least that was how I justified the lie.

Annie sighed heavily and announced that she needed to get some sleep. So, after several attempts and with the help of my arm, she heaved her ample self upright and glided to her bedroom door, where she turned and said, "Thank you for listening. I appreciate you so much and just knowing that you're here and safely away from that awful husband of yours is a blessing."

"No, I'm the one who's grateful. Honestly, I don't know what would have happened to me had you not taken me in. Well, I have a vague idea of what would've happened…" I shook my head.

"You have a good night's sleep, Clara."

"You, too."

Annie's round eyes misted as she turned and walked into her room, her head bobbing with the effort. Alone in the quiet of my room, I pondered Annie's last words, and tears tore hot trails down my cheeks and threatened to soil the beautiful dress Annie had bought me, so as a diversion I changed into my nightclothes and sat at the edge of the soft bed, taking the pins from my hair and then brushing it out with the precious silver brush, my hand feeling the rose design on its back.

Thoughts began to swirl like cottonwood leaves in the fall winds. If I had stayed in my home, I would be on my way to Whispering Pines, arrested and deemed insane by Judge Valsted and Bob. But how could a man be so cruel to a woman who had taken such good care of him, raised his children, and loved him with such ferocity? I shook my head to clear it and forced myself to think more pleasant thoughts. Finally, I settled into a deep sleep.

CHAPTER 13

And so our stay in Helena continued. Maxwell, true to his word, began working the next day on the case, taking it to the House of Representatives first. He met with us on several occasions, keeping us abreast of what was happening both in Helena and at home as he frequently talked with Sullie. Annie and I went sightseeing and giggled and talked as we shopped and watched the people of Helena hurrying here and there. Annie insisted on purchasing me five stylish dresses and all the accessories to go with them. My friend was back to her old gregarious self, and we had a great deal of fun.

Occasionally, fear traced its icy finger up my back and into my mind. Fear that Bob would find out where I was and come to do us harm, but Annie always assured me that he had no way of finding out my whereabouts as Sullie was the only person in Bergen who knew we were in Helena and he was trustworthy. She laughed as she told me that we need not fear making the news since we certainly were not socialites. As the days passed, my feeling of backwardness disappeared almost completely, and I felt independent, strong, and free.

We had been in Helena for a little over two weeks when I was called to the telephone at the main desk.

At the sound of Sullie's deep lilting voice, my heart swelled and pounded. I placed a hand on my chest in some strange gesture of protection. "Clara? Is that you? Can you hear me?" he asked.

"Yes, Sullie. I can hear you fine. How are you?"

"Just fine. I called, though, with news from your sons. They've all three responded to your letters." There was silence on the line and a pounding in my head. My cheeks flooded with heat.

"What did they say? You can tell me, even if it's bad news."

Silence again. Finally, Sullie sighed loudly and I envisioned him swiping his hair out of his eyes.

"It's not good, I'm afraid. They all were upset at the news you sent 'em, Robby most of all. He called. Luke and Peter wrote back."

"What did Robby say?" I heard the pitiful hopefulness in my voice.

"This is hard for me to say, I'm afraid, but here it is," Sullie hesitated and then continued. "He basically said that he thinks there must be somethin' wrong with you to have left his dad. I'm sorry, lass, but he said he feels you've betrayed the family with your actions."

I caught a loud sob with my hand, tears welling. I could not talk.

"There's more. Luke and Peter's letters said much the same. I'm goin' to be blunt here, and I'm sorry for it. None of 'em offered to take you in, not now or after this is finished. And none of 'em expressed sympathy or understandin' for you. Essentially, they sided with their father."

My neck and bodice were soaked, and my head hung down on my chest, too heavy for me to hold up.

122

I scarcely had the strength to hold the telephone receiver.

"Clara? Are you there? Did you hear me?"

Somehow I squeaked out, "Yes."

"Is Annie there with you, lass?"

"Yes. Upstairs."

"Okay. I'm goin' to let you go and I want you to go to Annie now. All right? And again, I'm sorry."

"Yes. Good-bye."

My legs wobbled so badly that I had to hold onto the desk, and as I stumbled toward the stair railing, Mr. Kershaw grabbed my elbow.

"Ma'am, may I help you to your room?"

I looked up and nodded, causing more tears to fall. The young porter held me up and gently helped me to our suite. Annie was at my side in an instant and dismissed Kershaw with a tart "thank you." Somehow she got me on to the settee and placed a pillow behind my head. She pulled a chair over to me and sat on the edge of it as she held my hands.

"Was it Sullie?" She asked softly and I nodded. "Tell me what he said." I closed my eyes and relayed to her what my boys had done.

Annie stood and began pacing, "Those ungrateful little --- Well, they're not so little, but oh! Am I ever mad!" Annie's face was scarlet and her hands were flapping.

I reached a hand out to her and quietly asked her to calm down.

"Oh, but I am so angry!"

"I know, but please don't be. They're still my sons. Although I'm disappointed, I can't be angry.

They have the right to think and feel any way they want. Right?"

"Yeah, right!" Annie huffed and sat down again. "You might not be mad, but I sure as hell am!" Annie suddenly became still. "Hey, what about their wives? Did Sullie say the boys' wives felt the same way? Maybe –"

"No. He said nothing about their wives. And you know how they are, except for Robby's Lillian. Let's just say it, Pete and Luke didn't marry so well-"

"Oh, no doubt about that one! Those two girls are so spoiled and snooty! You're right. They'd do nothing to help anyone except themselves."

"Lillian, though, surprises me. Well, if she knows, that is."

"My bet is that Robby never told her a thing," Annie sniffed and rolled her eyes. "I wonder if you should contact Lillian directly."

"Oh, no. I can't do that. Robby feels betrayed by me anyway, and I'm certainly not going to go behind his back and cause trouble in his marriage. I'll just have to manage on my own and hope and pray that the boys see the truth at some point and have a change of heart."

"Are you all right with that?" Annie fell back into her chair and we locked eyes.

"I have to be, I guess. So yes, I am." And I was. My heart had mended with the sharing of its betrayal, and I felt stronger as the reality set in. I would have to learn to be more independent and find a new way to live now.

Another week passed before Sullie called again. This time with news that he had finished his urgent cases in Bergen and had turned over his other work to his assistant so that he could come to Helena for the remainder of our stay. Annie fairly flew around the hotel, making arrangements for a car to take us to the depot to pick Sullie up and reserving a suite for him just down the hall from ours. Her excitement was contagious, and two days later when Sullie stepped off the train, my heart leapt. At least I thought it was just Annie's emotions permeating my own. It couldn't be my own, could it? But when Sullie's deep blue eyes found mine, my stomach trembled and I grabbed it with one hand.

"Are you all right, Clara lass?" He asked, dwarfing my hands in his.

"Oh, yes. Just a little jittery is all," I said looking into his tanned face. "You look good, Sullie. How was your trip?"

He dropped my hands, pushed back a lock of hair, and began regaling us with stories of Bergen and his trip. I was especially interested in news from home, wondering if there was any gossip about our whereabouts, but Sullie assured me that he had heard nothing concerning our leaving town, which was odd if I had thought about it, but I longed for safety, so my mind engulfed only the news that no one knew where we were.

We settled into a routine of sorts. Maxwell and Sullie worked on getting our case heard and reported the progress to Annie and me. The wheels of the government did indeed turn slowly. Impatient as I was, I understood that convening a committee to hear the case took time, and so I tried my best to stay busy and not dwell on the time passing.

A couple of evenings, Maxwell had us come to his home on the east side of Helena. Actually, his house was more palatial than homey. It sprawled across an acreage filled with pine trees and exquisite gardens whose flowers emitted scents that I had never experienced before. Paths spotted with small stone benches meandered around the landscape, so one could enjoy the peacefulness of nature. Whenever one of us commented about its opulence, Maxwell would make a circular wave in the air with his pale hand and claim that it was nothing and that he could not take credit for any of it since he had "people who managed all that."

Although Maxwell seldom ventured into his gardens, the second night we were there he asked Annie to join him on a walk after dinner, and she agreed, only glancing slightly at me before taking his arm. As the two walked away, I was struck by how matched they were to each other, stride for stride, the same height, both looking straight ahead.

Suddenly, I was quite aware of Sullie's presence, and when I moved my eyes to his face, I was surprised that he was staring intently at me, his blue eyes framed by dark black feathery lashes. Blushing, I walked on surer feet than I felt to the parlor and Sullie followed. Settling ourselves into two big cushioned chairs, we were served coffee by one of Maxwell's wait staff. Our conversation seemed stilted as we purposely avoided talking about the couple out for a walk in the starlit gardens. Our eyes gave us away, though, as neither of us could keep from gazing out the huge open window where a soft springtime breeze carried in fragrances and an occasional soft voice from where our friends walked.

Finally, they returned. Annie's flushed cheeks and sparkling eyes told me all I needed to know, and my heart gladdened at her happiness. Maxwell, however, did not raise his eyes to meet ours, but the round spots of pink on his cheeks gave his feelings away. Sullie and I pretended not to notice the long gazes between the two and continued conversing as though nothing had changed.

"So, Clara lass, do you think you'll be up to testifyin' in front of the senate committee soon? Max here figures that there'll likely be a hearing in the next few days."

At the mention of the hearing, I went cold and then hot, the flush rising from my stomach to the top of my head. "Oh, goodness, I certainly hope so, but I'm just so nervous about it."

"There's nothing for you to worry about," Annie said.

"We'll all be right there with you and will help you through it. The men in the committee just want to hear the story of what you heard so they can make the right decision. Also, if I understand correctly what Maxwell's told me, it's not the whole Senate. Right?" Sullie said turning to Maxwell.

"Right," Maxwell nodded. "The committee consists of five senators is all, and there is nothing to fear from them."

"I know that in my head but it's my heart that troubles me. It's just that I can't imagine these important people taking anything I have to say seriously. They're so much more powerful than I am."

"Which is exactly why we're here. They have the power to make change, and so do you, Clara. You need to be strong and tell your story just like you told it to all of us." Annie's soft voice calmed me and the flush abated. I touched her chubby hand and smiled my gratitude.

"Lasses, we'd best take our leave now and get some sleep. Okay?" Sullie interrupted us. "And if I may say so myself, a wonderful evenin' it's been. I thank you, Max."

We rose and made our way to the door where Thomas, a large quiet man who worked as Maxwell's personal assistant, helped us out, our host standing behind gazing longingly at Annie as she glided to the car.

Once we were back at our hotel, I changed into my nightclothes and was kneeling beside the bed to pray when there was a tentative knock on my bedroom door. It was a flustered Annie, still dressed, obviously in need of an ear.

"Come in, Annie," I said, my knees creaking as I rose.

"I hate to disturb you at this late hour and during your prayer time and all, but I just can't settle down right now. My mind races with so many thoughts. I just can't get any control and it's driving me batty," Annie said, fingers flying from her hair to her mouth to her bodice and then to smooth her skirt.

"Here, sit down, and tell me what's bothering you so," I said moving to a pink armchair near the fireplace.

"I can't sit. I'm too flustered."

"Okay, so why don't you tell me what it is. Maybe just talking it out will help you to settle down some," I responded.

"Well, maybe you're right. Where should I start; where should I start?" The familiar scent of vanilla filled my room as she paced back and forth clucking and tsk-ing, her fingers still fluttering around her.

I could not help but smile as I knew already what was troubling my friend. Love has a way of creeping up on a person when least expected, taking one off guard like nothing else can.

"It's all these feelings and these thoughts...oh, Lord, the thoughts. I just get all hot inside when I think these thoughts."

"What thoughts? Please, just slow down and tell me. It'll help."

"Okay," she said as she stopped pacing and plopped into a chair across from me, once again making me wonder if and how she would ever get out of it. "Here it is. I think...I think...well, I think I'm falling in love with Max! How's that for an old foolish woman. To fall in love at this age! Why, it's preposterous. Isn't it? Please, tell me how wrong this is so it'll stop!" She was fairly shouting.

"Just take a few deep breaths and calm yourself down a little. Okay?" Once she had calmed herself with a few heaving breaths, I continued. "I'm going to offer you some advice, and you can take it or leave it, but know that I love you either way. Okay?"

She bobbed her head in agreement, curls shaking loose from the bun at the base of her neck.

"Now, here it is. Age doesn't matter much in matters of the heart, I'm afraid, and really, you are not that old, so dismiss that thought from your mind. If you feel the beginnings of love for Maxwell, then I think that's just fine."

"But what about Walter?" she asked.

"Well, based on what I knew about him, Walter lived to make you happy. Now though, he's gone."

"I know, but I'd be betraying-" Annie's voice caught and one lone tear trailed down her round cheek.

"Shh," I interrupted, patting her hand. "That's nonsense. He'd be happy just knowing you're moving on in this life. In fact, he'd think like I do -- that it's about time you found someone to love again."

"Do you really think so?" Annie leaned as far forward as the chair would allow, her eyes round and her mouth tense.

"Yes, I do. Now though, I think it'd be wise for you to search your heart for God's blessing in this. If this is part of His plan for your life, you'll feel a whole lot better about it. Then, just allow yourself to enjoy all of those wonderful emotions that only romance can give you. Okay?"

"Oh! I knew you would know just the words to calm me down about this. You're so wise and caring. Do you know that?"

"Well, I'm not so wise in romantic love, I'm afraid. Look at the fix I'm in with Bob. I do know, though, that trusting in God's plan is the only way to true happiness and peace. Goodness, I've come to a realization myself. All that's happening must be part of His great plan for my life. He wants me to do His work for these other women, and that's why He placed me outside the barn that day. I can feel it." And I could. Gloom lifted from me, and a lightness caught me off guard. It was usefulness. I now knew my purpose and much of the trepidation dissipated as I allowed myself to stop fighting these feelings and just accepted them.

"Your eyes are twinkling again, Clara, and it's good to see that again. And yes, we must both trust in the Lord's plans for us and allow Him to work through us, too. Now, though, I'll let you get your sleep and I'll return to my room to pray and search my heart." At that, Annie heaved herself from the chair and was nearly out the door before I managed to get myself upright.

The next afternoon, Sullie and Maxwell came to our suite.

"Lassies," Sullie said, a gentle smile on his full lips, "we've some news about the hearing. It appears the senators are at last ready to hear your story, Clara, and would like you to come before them officially tomorrow mornin'."

"Oh, Sullie, that's good news indeed!" Annie boomed. "And Maxwell, you are my hero for getting this to their attention," she gushed. Maxwell's cheeks turned pink, and he sucked in his lip.

My heart pounded as anxiety filled me. I fought it, though, grabbing hold of the sense of purpose I found the night before. The time had come to right this wrong, and I would be strong for the Bergen women.

I cleared my throat and said, "That is good news. It's time we get this underway, and although I'm afraid—"

"Afraid of what?" Annie interrupted.

"What if I say the wrong thing, or what if they don't believe me? What if I fail?" I answered.

Maxwell's clear baritone commanded my attention. "Clara, look at me," he said, so I turned to the rumpled little man. "These senators are people just like you and me, and they are just and caring men. Well, a couple of them are at least."

"What do you mean, a couple of them are?" Annie asked. "There are five of them, aren't there?"

Maxwell took a deep breath, looked up at Sullie, and asked, "Should I tell them?"

"Tell us what? What the hell are you talking about? What's going on?" Annie's voice was hard.

Sullie gave Maxwell a slight nod and stood with his strong jaw clenched staring at me.

"Okay. Here it is. The senators who are on the committee –," Maxwell began.

"What about them?" Annie interrupted.

"Let me speak, Annie," Maxwell said curtly. "I know most of the senators who are on the committee, and I have seen them work and know that they are good, but I am concerned."

"Why?" Annie asked.

"Well, I know for sure that two of them will be receptive to what you have to say, Clara, but I am not sure about the other three. You see," Maxwell's tiny hands fluttered around his face as he said, "there are two of them, Mills and Palmetto, who could cause us some problems. I am just not sure how they will see it. The two of them are very close friends. And although it is not right, the two of them always vote the same way. Mills is the stronger of the two and he makes the decision, it seems to me, and then Palmetto goes along with him."

"But, that's not fair! Get those two assholes off the committee!" Annie said, her face red.

"We cannot do that," Maxwell said. "Once the committee is created, there is no way to change it. I am sorry, but that is how the justice system works."

"Let me explain the good news, though." Sullie said, sitting down and pulling his hand through his hair. "There only needs to be a majority vote from this committee for a formal decision. That means three, so even if Mills and Palmetto vote against us, the other three could vote in favor. The problem, though, is that Maxwell knows only two of the other senators. One is Brink. He's the chairman of the committee, so that's good. The other is Gable, and Max knows him really well. Right?"

"That is correct. I feel confident that those two will be on our side, but the other one, Senator Dandridge I think his name is, I do not know at all. It would be impossible to predict the outcome of all this because of him. He will be the deciding vote, I think."

The room fell silent for a moment before I found my voice.

"So, we could lose?" My pulse pounded in my neck.

"Well, we just don't know, lassie," Sullie said.

"But, what will happen to the women if we lose?" I got to my feet, needing to pace and wiped sweat from my forehead. "What will I do for that matter?" Hysteria rose in my chest.

"Dammit, Sullie!" Annie was on her feet, too, standing in front of Sullie waving a fist. "Did you know about this?"

"I'm sorry." Sullie nodded. "Maxwell told me a couple of days ago."

"And you didn't see fit to tell us?"

"We did not want to worry you both without cause," Maxwell said, taking Annie's fist in his hand. "We wanted to avoid this type of thing."

"You wanted to protect us, is that it? Treating us as though we are a couple of simpy little...Of all things!" Annie huffed and shouted at him.

"Well, I guess so. Not that we wanted to treat you as though you are...what did you say? A couple of little simpies? Not at all. I did not intend to offend you. I can see how wrong I was not to include you both in the discussion. You had a right to know the entire story, and I am sorry. To you both." Maxwell's bulging gray eyes looked at Annie and me.

"And I, too, am sorry. It won't happen again," Sullie said, looking sheepish.

"Really, ladies, there is nothing to fear. All five of these men already know what happened in Bergen. My colleagues and I made sure of that. They just want to hear it from you, Clara. Then, they will make their decision and we will have to accept it."

I could only nod my head slightly as I sat back down. Maxwell was right.

"I'm just nervous is all. I don't know what to expect," I said smoothing my skirt.

"Allow me to explain," Maxwell replied, sucking in his bottom lip. "First, once you are called to testify, you will be sworn in. After that, the senators will have you tell the whole story first. When you are finished, they will probably ask clarifying questions, so that they can completely understand what happened to the women. You have nothing to be concerned about. All you have to do is be perfectly honest and tell your story completely, and they will do the rest. Okay? Does that alleviate some of your fears?"

"I guess it does," I answered in a small voice. "I'll just do my best."

"That's all that's expected of you, lassie," Sullie said.

CHAPTER 14

The next morning was a rushed one, getting ready for such a big day. After my morning prayers, I bathed and pulled my hair into a loose bun at the nape of my neck, as I always did. Upon re-entering my bedchamber, I gasped and nearly lost my balance when I found the most elegant suit and blouse lying on my bed.

"Annie," I whispered as I reached out to touch the baby-soft gray wool fabric. My hand trembled as I fingered the sleeve of a pale pink silk blouse which lay next to the suit. It was the most exquisite fabric. I blushed at the thought of an old country woman such as myself in these garments. Like a child on Christmas morning, though, I hurriedly put my underclothes on, having to re-do my chemise, which I had put on inside-out due to sheer excitement. Then, I put on the silken blouse, closing my eyes as I moved my hands down my arms, the fabric kissing my skin ever so softly. The skirt fit neatly, hugging my hips in the most delicate wool I had ever seen, let alone worn. The jacket was also a perfect fit, and confidence filled me as I buttoned it.

Once completely dressed, I rushed into Annie's room, forgetting to knock. "Oh, Annie, thank you, thank you, thank you," I gushed as my friend gaped at me.

"It's more stunning on you than I thought it'd be. I'm speechless, which is a huge feat, if you think about it."

I twirled around like a little girl in a party dress, allowing a slight giggle to emerge, momentarily forgetting about the nerve-racking affair we had to go to this morning.

Annie's laughter came from deep within, loud and low. "It's good to finally hear you laugh again," she said.

"Thank you, Annie. You really did outdo yourself this time. I have no idea how to ever repay your kindness and generosity."

"You don't have to repay me, not ever. Your being my confidante and friend is payment enough. I just want you to feel confident and I know how shallow this will sound, but I think the right outfit can make a woman feel that way."

"Oh, this suit does just that, Annie. I feel like I can do anything today." I smiled and warmth flooded me at the thought of finally being heard and believed.

"Okay, then," Annie broke into my thoughts, "let's go downstairs and meet Sullie for breakfast."

Sullie was having coffee in the restaurant, and when he glanced up from the morning newspaper, his eyes swept over me, capturing me with a look that I had never seen before. It was fleeting, though, and hard as I tried, I could not decipher it. I noticed a slight tremor in his long fingers as he folded the newspaper and laid it on the table. Only then did he come to his feet, giving each of us a slight hug and holding out our chairs.

"My, my, my, lassie," he said, his voice trembling a little and his blue eyes glittering, "you do take a man's breath away, I'm tellin' you." A light chuckle escaped his chest, and he raked one hand through his hair, never taking his eyes off me. I blushed and looked down.

"Thank you, Sullie," I managed, feeling self-conscious under his scrutiny.

Annie lightened the mood by announcing that we had better get ourselves fed and off or we would be late.

On the drive to the capitol building, I fought to find that sense of usefulness again, but my mind swirled with insecurities. A rivulet of sweat formed on my chest and my back, my underarms became damp, and concerns of ruining the silk blouse came to me. Annie took my wet hand in her meaty cool one, and some of my apprehension faded. She cooed to me while Sullie tried to calm me with words of assurance, telling me once again that I just had to tell the truth and let the senators make their decision. By the time we arrived at the entrance to the huge stone building, I was a mess.

Annie's strong arm guided me through the foyer, which was cool and bustling with people that I felt more than I saw. We arrived all too soon at the high wooden double doors of the room where I would testify. Sullie swung the door open, and we were greeted by Maxwell who took one look at me with his huge bespeckled eyes and must have known how rattled I was. He quickly brushed Annie's arm aside and took my arm in his, steering me to a table and chairs near the front of the huge room. His deep baritone was soothing; however, I could not make out his exact words due to a loud ringing that had taken up residence in my head. Finally, I managed to calm myself and turned to find Annie and Sullie.

There were rows and rows of seats for spectators, with very few people in them. Annie and Sullie sat in the front row directly behind Maxwell and me. There were two other men in the front row, too. They were slumped in their chairs, leisurely visiting with each other. Lined notebooks of the type I used in school lay open to blank pages on their laps. One of them had a pencil perched behind his ear, while the other tapped his on his notebook.

I turned to the front of the room again and took in the long row of dark wooden tables. Padded chairs were spaced evenly behind the tables, facing us. This was where the senators would sit, Maxwell explained and then directed my attention to the polished oak podium which stood like a sentry a little bit forward and to the right of us, facing the senators' table. I would tell my story from behind that podium.

"Take a deep breath. It will help calm you," Maxwell said into my ear. "That's right," he said as my chest swelled and my shoulders raised with a deep breath. "Now, take as many of these breaths as you need to as you testify. Take your time and be as detailed as possible. Try to remember that these are just men, and they are here to listen to your story. Okay?"

Again, a small nod. I stared straight ahead, feeling my fingernails bite into the palms of my hands.

"Can you stay with me, Maxwell, please?" I asked in a voice barely above a whisper.

"I will ask once the senators come in, but they have the final say. And I must stay here at this table, not be with you at the podium. Okay?"

Again, the small nod.

Suddenly, a door to the right of the senators' tables opened, and a man in a gray suit stood with his hands folded in front of him as he announced that everyone was to come to their feet. We all stood. The men came into the room then, black robes fluttering as they walked. The first senator to come in stood behind the middle chair, and I could not help but smile curiously at the blue denim jeans and boots with either mud or manure smeared on them peeking out from under his robe. He had an abundance of thick white hair that he combed straight back off his high, tanned forehead. His face was deeply lined with leather-like skin that told me he would rather be on the back of his horse in the sunshine than in this room listening to these proceedings. Despite that, his round eyes, the color of the summer sky, twinkled. The other senators stood behind their seats on either side of this cowboy senator who I correctly assumed was Chairman Brink.

We all recited the Pledge of Allegiance, and sometime during the recitation, the flannel blanket of peace returned. I took a deep breath and thanked Him.

Once the senators were perched on their chairs like a troop of crows, Chairman Brink went down the line taking a roll call. I took them all in. I remembered what Maxwell had said about each of them earlier. To my far right was Senator Dandridge, a thin man with a pinched look. He could be the deciding vote. My palms became damp. Next to him was Senator Gable, a grandfatherly man with bushy white eyebrows that

Maxwell knew to be a fair, open-minded man. On the other side of the chairman were the two men who always voted the same. They also looked the same except that Mills was older than Palmetto. Black glasses overpowered their pale faces. At that moment they had their heads together and their hands cupped over their mouths having a private conversation. Identical blue bow ties protruded from their robes and bobbed up and down as they chuckled together before lowering their hands and staring straight ahead, still smirking. I hoped they voted in favor of us.

Maxwell stood and addressed Chairman Brink, asking for permission to sit at the table while I testified, just for support. Brink agreed, so Maxwell sat next to me and touched my forearm, giving me a nodding smile with his one lip.

The man in the gray suit directed me to the podium, and my gaze caught on my friends. Annie smiled encouragement; Sullie gave a subtle wink.

Once sworn in, I turned to face the senators, and Chairman Brink's gravelly, deep voice calmed me as he read from a paper he pulled from his stack. "The purpose of this hearing, on this the twenty-fifth day of May in the year 1920, is to hear testimony regarding the possible misconduct of officials, namely Judge Edward Valsted and County Attorney Charles Littman, in Beaver County, State of Montana. The claim of misconduct comes from Mrs. Robert Terrell, who is here to testify today and who has been duly sworn to uphold the truth in her testimony. Mrs. Terrell claims that fourteen women in Beaver County were falsely arrested and subsequently sentenced to spend the remainder of their lives in Whispering Pines, the

Montana State Insane Asylum. We will now begin the proceedings by hearing Mrs. Terrell's account of the aforementioned events which led her to bring these allegations against these officials. Gentlemen, please hold any questions you might have for Mrs. Terrell until after she has completed her account. Thank you. Mrs. Terrell, you may begin. Please be as thorough as you possibly can and remember that you are sworn to tell the whole truth. Please, state your name and where you reside first."

Chairman Brink sighed loudly and pushed his chair noisily back from the table, allowing him room to stretch out his long length, boots crossed under the table. He undid his robe, flinging it open to reveal a blue chambray shirt open at the neck, a few white hairs curling around the edges as though attempting to escape into the open air. The brown end of a large cigar peeked out of his shirt pocket.

"My name is Clara Terr--"

"You need to speak much louder, Mrs. Terrell. I can hardly hear you," Brink interrupted me. The man now had the cigar between his teeth, somehow not hindering his speech in the least.

So I began again, this time forcing my voice to be stronger. "My name is Clara Terrell. I am the wife of Robert Terrell, and we live on a small farm outside of Bergen, a little town in Beaver County," I began, looking down the line of black robed men to make sure they could all hear me. It appeared they could, so I forced my attention to the story I needed to tell, straightened my shoulders and back, and began.

"It was in the morning about a month ago, April twenty-fifth to be exact, and I was in the kitchen finishing up a stew I was making for lunch when I heard the dog making a ruckus outside. When I looked out -"

"Thwuck!" My attention shot to where the sound came from just in time to see a chunk of cigar fly through the air and into a spittoon which sat on the floor beside Chairman Brink. I flinched and noticed the man beside the spittoon, Senator Gable, did as well, scooting his chair a bit farther away. Of their own volition, the edges of my lips curled upward as I tried my best not to giggle. Certainly, these serious men would not allow giggling in this chamber.

I regained my composure, not looking at Chairman Brink who was now loudly sucking on the unlit cigar, and continued, "When I looked outside, I saw Joshua Miller - he's a farmer in the area - riding away from our place quite fast. I knew there were other men in the barn with my husband and became concerned for Bob's well-being. Joshua's manner and the dog's barking made me apprehensive, so I went down to the barn and hid near the open door, eavesdropping on the men, just to make sure Bob was okay. That's when I heard what they were talking about."

Gable leaned back and folded his hands over his paunch as he listened intently. Dandridge, though, appeared to be glaring at me. As his narrow dark eyes intently focused on mine, his head swayed to the right and then to the left, his greased black hair not moving at all. I wondered what I had said to perturb him. A slight shiver ran down my body. I looked down at the smooth surface of the podium top as if to find courage on it.

143

"Mrs. Terrell?" Chairman Brink's voice brought me back to the present, and I focused once again. "Are you all right? May we get you anything? Something to drink, perhaps?" Without waiting for my answer, he ordered, "Lucas, get the woman a glass of water, will ya?" And the man who swore me in skittered out the door, barely making a sound. "You may continue, Mrs. Terrell."

"Okay, this is what I heard. First, I heard Judge Valsted saying how they needed to be careful what they said to Joshua Miller - that's the man I saw ride away so quickly - from now on. Then, he addressed Bob directly and told him that Joshua's story was no different than any of the other men's stories in that they all had had troubles with their wives. Basically, that their wives had become unbearable, I think he said…." My voice trailed off when I noticed Mills and Palmetto scribbling in their notebooks and passing them to each other like a couple of schoolgirls. Luckily, my water arrived just then. Lucas scampered to the podium, placed the glass on it, and quickly moved back to his place by the door.

I took a quick swallow of water and re-focused. "Then, Frank Larson, another farmer friend of Bob's, a man who scares me half to death, told about how he beat his wife Sarah for all of their marriage because she was dumb and lazy. He said that she'd always been so good about it, learning from her mistakes and such, but that about two years ago she'd started to act funny, talking back to him and taking her punishments silently and then in private crying and screaming. He called her pitiful and crazy, someone he didn't recognize any

144

more. He put up with it for about a year and a half, and then..."

"Excuse me, Mrs. Terrell, but I must interrupt for just a moment," Chairman Brink said taking the cigar from his mouth. He turned to his left and waved the cigar at Mills and Palmetto. "Gentlemen, stop that incessant scribbling. It's unnerving for Mrs. Terrell and is rude. Please remember why we are here." The two put their pencils down and frowned at me as though it was my fault they were chastised. Brink asked me to go on, stretched out again, and began sucking on the cigar.

I took a deep breath and continued, "Well, Frank said he heard that Judge Valsted and Doctor Belzer had had the same problems with their wives and that they had their wives sent to Whispering Pines, so he went to them and got their help in sending Sarah there, too. He also admitted that shortly after getting rid of Sarah, he re-married and started over with Laura, a much younger and nicer woman than Sarah.

"I thought at that point Bob would throw these men off his property with their far-fetched stories right along with them, just as he had done to Joshua Miller, but I was wrong. When Bob spoke, I realized that he was drunk, and the questions he asked were about their wives." I sneaked another look down the line of senators and found Dandridge still glaring, the slow wobble of his head unnerving me. Deep vertical lines formed a Y between his thin black eyebrows, and his nose pointed directly at the thin line his red lips formed. I could not help but think of the rattle snakes I so hated back home. Mills and Palmetto were looking around the room as though they were bored.

I looked at Brink and continued. "The judge admitted that all of their wives and ten others as well were sent to Whispering Pines in the past four or four and a half years. That's fourteen women sent there, and then the judge said that I was to be number fifteen. Why, I nearly fainted at that, but somehow I managed to stay where I was hidden by the barn door." I took another deep breath and a big drink of water.

"Bob then asked how to go about getting me committed to the insane asylum, and the judge explained that all Bob needed to do was to go to the courthouse and get a complaint sworn against me. Then, the sheriff would write up an arrest warrant, come to our house, and bring me to town and put me in jail. He told Bob that there would be a trial the next day and that Bob would have to be there. A trial that would last no longer than a half hour. He said that Charles Littman - he's the attorney for Beaver County - would be there and would ask Bob to tell of my behaviors and that I don't own any property and that I am a danger to myself or other people. Bob put up a little fuss about having to say that I am dangerous, but Doctor Belzer spoke up and I realized that he was the other man in the barn, which surprised me since I always thought he was a good man."

"Thwuck!" Another huge wad of cigar hit the spittoon.

"Doctor Belzer said that the judge was speaking the truth and that Bob would need to say those things about me if he wanted me sent to Whispering Pines so that he wouldn't have to put up with my craziness any more. Bob told them that he understood and that it sounded easy enough and that he thought he just might do that to be rid of me. That's when I somehow managed to walk back up to the house without them hearing me."

I figured I was finished, so I took a long deep breath, concentrating on loosening the muscles in my neck and shoulders and unclenching my fingers which threatened to make my palms bleed.

Chairman Brink pulled himself up in his chair and said, "And then what, Mrs. Terrell?"

"Pardon, me, sir?"

"What did you do then, ma'am?" I was not finished after all.

"Sir, I was so frightened that I couldn't think what to do. So I, umm, I..." My voice faded as I wondered what these men would think about my actions.

"You what, Mrs. Terrell?" That gravelly, soothing voice again. I took another deep breath and continued.

"Well, I cleaned the house is what I did." My nerves tightened as Brink's eyebrows created two half-moons high above his eyes. Dandridge's head stopped moving and he slithered back into his chair, smirking. I finally had the attention of Mills and Palmetto. They both frowned at me. Gable drew in a quick breath. I clearly needed to explain myself, so I rushed, "Mind you, I do my best thinking when my hands are busy, and that's what I needed to do just then, think about what I could do to save myself."

"And what decision did you make while you – uhh – while you cleaned?" Brink asked, relaxing back in his slumped state, chewing on the cigar which by now was only about two inches long.

147

"Well, I needed to get some advice and thought my best friend, Annie Hazelton, could help me so I decided to go to her. I was nervous and confused and wanted to leave right away, but I couldn't because those men were still in the barn. Finally though, they left and thankfully Bob went with them. I feared they went to get an arrest warrant for me, so I got out of there as quickly as I could. I walked the five miles to Bergen to Annie's house, explained to her what I heard, and asked for her advice. She's been a great help in all this. She and Sullie, I mean Connor Sullivan, have been so helpful and understanding. Mr. Sullivan is an attorney in Bergen. He arranged for me to come here and meet with Mr. Heinz who in turn arranged for this hearing." There! I had done it. That was all there was to tell. A sigh escaped my lips.

CHAPTER 15

Brink took the cigar from his mouth, and said, "Okay, Mrs. Terrell, very good. Now, I'm certain that these fine men sitting up here with me," he surprised me with a brilliantly white smile, "have a few questions for you. Isn't that right, sirs?" Gable nodded and smiled, Mills and Palmetto were back to scribbling, and Dandridge glared and moved his head.

"Okay, I guess we'll just start over here on my far left with Senator Mills and then move down the line. Joe, do you have any questions for Mrs. Terrell?" Senator Mills plunked his pen down on top of his notebook and looked up.

"Thank you, Chairman Brink. Yes, I do have a question for her. How many years have you and Mr. Terrell been married?" Mills's voice was syrupy-sweet. Dull, lifeless, brown eyes looked into mine from behind his glasses before they slowly trailed down my upper body and back up again. A blush spread over me and the hairs on the back of my neck raised.

"Twenty-four." My voice was tight and small again, so I cleared my throat and repeated the answer more loudly. "Twenty-four, sir."

"Okay, and do you and Mr. Terrell have any children from this marriage?" The man stared, unblinking, his heavy dark brows furrowed.

"Yes, we have three boys. Well, they're men now. They no longer live in Montana and have families of their own. We also had a daughter, Julia, but she passed to Heaven as a toddler."

"Okay. That's all – for now anyway." The man smirked, swept me with his eyes again, and returned to his scribbling.

Brink then asked for questions from Palmetto.

"Mrs. Terrell, perhaps it is no business of mine, but I'd like to know your age, please," he said, glancing at me and then turning to give Senator Mills a quick smile.

"I am fifty-one," I replied.

"That's all I have – for now." Again the odd smile at Mills before he returned to his notepad.

It was difficult to concentrate on the other questions asked of me due to Mills and Palmetto who were once again sharing notes with each other. And the snake staring at me from the other end of the table was equally disconcerting. However, I did the best that I could, praying all the while that my answers would impress upon these men the importance of what had happened to these other women.

Senator Gable asked the most questions. His voice was soft and polite and he was engaged in my answers, smiling and nodding at times.

He asked, "What caused you to go to the barn in the first place?"

"I heard our dog Champ barking in a way that I recognized as upsetting, so I looked out the door of our house and saw him running from the barn to the house, and then I saw Joshua Miller riding away on his horse. He was riding very fast and appeared angry. So, I became worried for Bob's well-being and went to see what was happening in the barn, just to make sure Bob was okay. That's when I overheard the men talking."

He then followed up by asking me why the men did not hear me approaching the barn, and I replied that I made certain my steps were quiet just in case there was danger.

Gable nodded and continued, "How well do you know these men? Namely Charles Littman, Judge Valsted, and Doctor Belzer."

I took a deep breath and began, "I know Doctor Belzer very well since he is, or at least he always had been, our family doctor. He and Mary - that's his wife - helped my daughter Julia quite a bit until she died of poor lungs. Julia I mean, not Mary. Judge Valsted I only know from seeing in town a few times. He lives in Glendive but is in Bergen often on business. His wife Lucretia lived with him in Glendive until she was sent to Whispering Pines...." At the mention of that awful place, my voice failed me, and I had to stop and breathe to compose myself before I could continue.

"Charles Littman is our county's lawyer who people say just seems to follow Judge Valsted around when he's in town. Really though, I've never seen the man, not even with Judge Valsted. Mind you, I'm not in town much either, so I really can't say what the man is like. Joshua Miller, the man who rode away in such a rush, is a farmer who lives quite a ways from us, so I know him only from seeing him in town over the years, too. I know his wife Rebecca, a sweet woman about my age, from our quilting circles. And Frank Larson I know by his reputation as a terrible, violent man. He farms, too, and has been at our house occasionally, but I never did like or trust him, so I always steered clear of

151

him. He and Bob usually just stayed out in the barn drinking and talking whenever he came to our place. I never did get to meet his wife. Rumor was that Frank wouldn't allow her to join our quilting groups or to visit neighbors and such, so no one really knew her very well. I saw her a few times in town buying grocery items and such, but we never spoke as she was always skittish and shy, keeping to herself. I heard that he beat and hit her all the time but really never put much stock in it until I heard what he said in the barn about her not being able to 'learn' unless he 'taught' her with his belt or fist. That's really all I know about the men. But if you have more specific questions about them, I'll try my best to answer them for you."

"Thank you, Mrs. Terrell. You were quite thorough in your answer, and I appreciate it," Senator Gable said.

"Mrs. Terrell, I have some questions for you." My head swung around at Dandridge's loud voice. My eyes met his snappy little black ones and then flew to Chairman Brink, who was relaxed back in his chair, boots crossed, chewing on his cigar.

"Okay, Senator Dandridge. Even though I haven't called on you yet, go ahead," Brink said around his cigar.

The pale, gaunt man asked, his head no longer weaving, "How did you know who the men in the barn were? You clearly stated that you were hidden from their view, so I assume you could not see them, either. Correct?" He sat back and sent me an evil little grin. I knew then that this man did not believe what I had said and that he would need some convincing, so I sent a silent prayer up to God to help me form the words needed to make him believe the severity of this situation. Then, I was able to look directly in his eyes and answer him.

"I did not actually see any of the men. However, I heard them call each other by name or by 'Judge' or 'Doc.' Also, I recognized the voices of Doctor Belzer and Frank Larson because I've had dealings with them for years."

Dandridge tapped his pencil on his notepad while I talked, but then he stopped, licked his full red lips and said, "Okay, so you recognized two of the voices other than your husband's. How about the one they called 'Judge'? How do you know this judge in your barn was Judge Valsted specifically?"

I said with certainty, "I know it was him because he is the only judge in the area. The only one it could be. Also, I've heard him talking in various businesses around town, so I know his voice. I've just never actually met the man, but I'm certain that it was him."

"Hmm..." The tapping continued and the man's staring made me uncomfortable, so I took another sip of water, preparing myself for his next question. "So why do you think these what - fourteen - women were not reported as missing? Fourteen is an awful lot of women to go missing out of a small place like Bergen. And no one reported them missing? I'm confused about that, Mrs. Terrell." His voice dripped sarcasm.

"I only know about Mary, Doctor Belzer's wife, for sure. Supposedly, she went to Illinois to care for her elderly mother. Nobody questioned that and when she didn't return, I guess I just never questioned that either. The other women I didn't know as well and so I

wasn't aware that they'd disappeared or why they
weren't around any longer. Senator, people on the
prairie are very busy just making ends meet. Many of
us are quite isolated and don't keep up with the
comings and goings of others."

"So, you only know about one of the women,
this Mary Belzer, and she could very well be tending to
an ailing mother in Illinois. Correct?"

"No, she is NOT in Illinois," I fairly shouted at
the man. I had the full attention of all five men now.
"I clearly heard her name and each of the other men in
the barn that day talking about their own wives
specifically. They said directly that they had their
wives, and that includes Mary Belzer, and ten others
sent to Whispering Pines. These are very powerful
men in our community, Senator Dandridge, and people
simply do not question them about anything, so if they
say their wives are here or there or wherever, people
just believe them and never voice their concerns. I
heard what I heard in the barn that day, though.
Clearly, I did."

"I just have one more question for you, Mrs.
Terrell." His lips curled back without showing any
teeth, and he asked, "Why did these women's children
not report them missing? After all, these are their
mothers?"

"I only know of the Belzer children. They have
their own families and live in Arizona and New York
now. I assume they were told their mother went to
care for their grandmother, and after that I have no
idea what they were told. I have no knowledge of the
children of the other women, but I assume they were

told similar stories by their fathers. I think that Sarah Larson, Frank's wife, never did have any children."

Senator Dandridge nodded his head and said, "That is all for now, Chairman Brink."

The air fairly puffed out of my lungs, and my shoulders relaxed a little.

Brink leaned forward, tucked his boots under his chair, and said, "Senators, do you have any follow up questions for Mrs. Terrell?"

"I do." Senator Mills raked me with his eyes again and asked, "Mrs. Terrell, do you know the names and circumstances surrounding the other ten women who were allegedly sent to Whispering Pines by their husbands?"

"No, I understand the court records of their trials are sealed, but I would think that men in your positions could gain access to them."

Mills nodded and said, "I have no more questions, Mr. Chairman."

Senator Palmetto also had one final line of questions for me that began with what caused Bob to want to send me to Whispering Pines. Heat and color spread from my bosom to my face at having to answer this personal question. Perhaps these men would deem me insane and send me to Whispering Pines themselves after they heard what I had done to perpetuate all of this. But I had to answer, and so I did.

"In the past year or so, I just haven't felt like myself. Normally, I am a loving and caring person who works hard and never complains about anything, but lately I've often been angry, which felt strange to me when it first began, so I worked hard to keep my emotions to myself, especially the anger. But then it would come out in strange actions like me screaming at Bob, calling him names, accusing him of improper behavior when he was gone a few days into town. Once, I said I wished I'd never married him. After I would say these awful things to him, I'd apologize and go back to being more myself, but then the anger and the headaches would just build up again until they spilled out of me. I've been terribly moody, going from cheerful to crying like a baby in no time at all. I'm sure Bob was confused by it all."

"So, with all of this moodiness and anger and crying, did you ever go to a doctor to see what might be wrong with you?"

That is when I remembered Doctor Mitchell. "Oh, yes! Well, not while I was in Bergen. I didn't see a doctor until I came here to Helena. Then, I went to see a Doctor Mitchell. He told me that if you need to talk to him, he'd be willing to come here and tell you what his opinion is."

"Okay, so just what did the doctor say is wrong with you?"

I blushed due to the extreme personal nature of my answer. I looked down at my hands which lay on the podium and said in as strong a voice as I could, "He said that I am in menopause." As hard as it was, I looked up and continued, "And he also said that more than likely those women who were sent to Whispering Pines were only menopausal, too, and that the symptoms pass in time. Senators, please, you must believe me. These women are not insane. They were just suffering through what every woman who lives to be my age does...they were going through The Change. Most of them are probably already back to their old selves and yet they are sitting there in Whispering Pines wondering how in the world they can get their lives back!" My voice echoed off the walls of the great chamber. Every eye was on me, and my conviction did not allow my eyes to fall or my voice to fail.

Brink took the cigar from his mouth and addressed me, "All right, Mrs. Terrell, is there anything else you would like to add to these proceedings?"

"No, sir, but I thank you all for allowing me to testify today on behalf of the women of Beaver County."

"Senators, any more questions for Mrs. Terrell?" Brink asked.

The moment's silence was deafening, and I was relieved when Brink said, "As I stated earlier, the purpose of this hearing is to determine whether Judge Edward Valsted and County Attorney Charles Littman might have conducted themselves inappropriately or acted outside the limits of the law. Gentlemen..." His head nodded to his left and to his right, "we need to adjourn for now and reconvene in one hour to make our decision. Mrs. Terrell, you are free to leave. However, I would appreciate it if you would return in one hour, in case we have any further questions."

I managed a slight nod and remained at the podium until the senators had all left the chambers, and the man in the gray suit said that I was dismissed. Immediately, I ran to Annie and Sullie, completely forgetting poor Maxwell.

"Oh, Annie, how did I do?"

"You did just fine," Annie said, putting her fleshy arms around me.

"You did better than fine if you ask me. You couldn't have done better, lass," Sullie's deep voice resonated with emotion. Pulling out of Annie's embrace, I smiled into his eyes and squeezed his arm.

I then turned to Maxwell and thanked him for being there for me.

"Not a problem at all," he said. "Now, though, we had best go get something to eat as the lunch hour is upon us, and we only have an hour before we must return."

CHAPTER 16

And so we had lunch at a restaurant about a block from the capitol. We tried to predict how the senators would vote, and I expressed my concern about Mills and Palmetto's sharing of notes and lack of attention and Dandridge's apparent anger at me. Maxwell said it was nothing to worry about, so I tried to relax, the worst part over. Although we acted nonchalant and kept our conversations light, I could tell my friends felt the same tension I did by the way Maxwell squirmed in his seat, Sullie kept running his hand through his hair, and Annie sighed often. I tried to will the muscles in my neck and back to relax, but to no avail, so finally, I just allowed them to be tight, hoping this would not cause a headache.

When we returned to the chambers, we sat in the same places. Once the senators were seated, Chairman Brink announced in his gravelly voice that proceedings would continue and would be concluded that afternoon.

Brink, a fresh long cigar in his hand, said, "Gentlemen, I believe that first we should vote on the matter of County Attorney Charles Littman. We will do this with a simple 'nay' or 'aye' verbal vote. All those who believe Charles Littman acted outside the boundaries of the law in these cases, please say 'aye.'"

I held my breath so I could hear over the pounding in my ears.

"Aye," Dandridge and Gable said simultaneously. I grabbed Maxwell's arm as my eyes flew to the right side of the table. Silent smirks from both Mills and Palmetto.

Chairman Brink continued with, "Opposed, please say 'nay.'"

"Nay," Mills and Palmetto chimed.

My breath caught. Dandridge voted in our favor. It was a tie. Maxwell placed one small cool hand on mine and whispered, "It will be okay. Just wait."

"Thank you, gentlemen," Brink said. "Thwuck." He spit the first piece of his afternoon cigar into the spittoon. "When the committee is equally divided, as this one is, the deciding vote resides with the chairman. That is me." He smiled. "Before I make my decision, though, I would like Senators Mills and Palmetto to voice their reasons for the 'nay' vote." He looked to his left and nodded at the senators.

Mills cleared his throat. "I just don't want to rush this judgment. I feel we need more evidence. All we have to go on is this woman's testimony." He waved a hand in my direction. "And for me that just isn't enough. How do we know Mrs. Terrell here is not really insane and just trying to escape being sent to the asylum? Or, how do we know she isn't just trying to stir up trouble for the judge and county attorney? In my opinion, we need more evidence." He glanced at Senator Palmetto who was nodding and staring at him as he spoke.

"Yes," Palmetto said, looking at the table in front of him. "I agree completely with Joe – err, Senator Mills. We need more evidence."

My heart skipped a beat and then took up pounding in my throat at the thought that Judge Valsted and Charles Littman could actually be declared within their rights and thus allowed to continue to practice law in Bergen.

Brink stared blankly at the back of the room for a full minute before he sat up straight in his chair, clutched his cigar, and said, "Okay. I understand your reasoning, and I agree that we need to see more evidence. However, we are just here today to decide whether or not to send the cases against Valsted and Littman on to the next level, so my ruling is that sometime before June thirtieth of this year, County Attorney Charles Littman must appear in front of the Montana State Supreme Court, where the power to disbar attorneys resides, for proceedings against him." A whoosh of air came out of me, and I was suddenly lightheaded.

"But, Chairman Brink –" Mills's voice held a knife's edge.

"You are out of order, Senator Mills." Brink's was equally hard as he glared at the man. Mills fell back in his chair, rolled his eyes, and huffed as he threw his pencil onto the table and rubbed a hand over his face. "Let's continue," Brink said as he set aside a small pile of papers which I assume were those regarding Littman and pulled another pile closer to him.

"Now then, we also must vote whether or not to conduct a hearing to determine whether District Judge Edward Valsted should be impeached due to his conduct in the matter told to us in this hearing. Again, we will do an 'aye' or 'nay' vote verbally. After which, if need be, we will have more discussion about the matter. The question you will answer with a 'nay' or an 'aye' is, Do you feel this committee should conduct a hearing, with Judge Valsted appearing before us, to determine if the judge should be impeached? All in favor, please state 'aye.'"

This time I was not surprised as the vote was the same as for Littman. A tie. Virtually the same objections were made by Mills and Palmetto, and Brink made his ruling, which was the same as for Littman. Judge Valsted would have to come before this committee. I was able to breathe again.

Chairman Brink caught my attention when he cleared his throat and sank back into his chair, his long, denim-clad legs outstretched. "Okay, these two matters are settled for now. I will have my assistant arrange a suitable date for the hearing with Judge Valsted, so if any of you have dates that are unacceptable, please get them to my office as soon as possible. Upon further thought, I would like to address Senators Mills and Palmetto's concern about lack of evidence. As I said earlier, I agree that we need more evidence before we make any official ruling on the impeachment of Judge Valsted. Also, the Supreme Court will need the same evidence in order to make their decision about Charles Littman." He paused. "So, as soon as possible, I will order copies of the Beaver County court transcripts of the fourteen cases in question be sent to me. Due to the sensitive nature of the cases and the importance of protecting the anonymity of the women, I will black out their names. Then, I will get copies of these documents to each of you and to the Chief Justice. All in favor of my doing this, please indicate with an 'aye'."
My shoulders tensed.

162

"Aye," all the senators said.

"Please indicate with a 'nay' if you are not in agreement."

Silence. I breathed softly through my teeth.

Chairman Brink shifted in his seat before he continued. "Now, I think it would be beneficial for us to know if the fourteen women are truly insane or not. So what I would like to see happen is to have Doctor Mitchell, who according to Mrs. Terrell, has offered his services in this case, go to Whispering Pines and examine the women. He can then report to us and to the Supreme Court, both in writing and through testimony. I think a vote about this is in order, though. So, the question you will answer is, Should I release, to Doctor Edward Mitchell only, the names of the fourteen women who were allegedly unlawfully sent to Whispering Pines?"

The senators voted unanimously for Brink to do this, and my tension eased. Having Doctor Mitchell examine the women was exactly what needed to happen.

Brink continued, "I will ask Doctor Mitchell to examine the women to determine if they are clinically insane or a danger to themselves or others or if they are merely menopausal. I feel it would be beneficial to allow him to work with one other physician of his choosing. Now, I would like to hear concerns from you all about this matter, so I open the floor to you." Brink leaned back in his chair and looked from side to side at the other men.

"My only concern," Senator Gable said, "is that the names of the women must be kept confidential, even from the second physician. The fewer people

163

who know these women's names, the better, as far as I'm concerned."

"Yes, I concur. Absolute anonymity must be upheld for the sake of these women, regardless of the outcome of the examinations," Dandridge responded.

Silence echoed in the room as everyone sat perfectly still. The senators were deep in thought, it seemed. Finally, Brink leaned forward and said, "I feel it is time to take a vote. The question you will answer is, Should I allow Doctor Mitchell to appoint an assistant to help him examine the women, keeping their names confidential? All in favor please say 'aye.'"

Their "ayes" were loud and clear.

"Opposed, please say 'nay.'"

Silence.

"All right. I will order Doctor Mitchell and another doctor of his own choosing to complete these examinations and give a written report of his findings to my office some time before June eighteenth. Once I get the doctors' reports, my assistant will copy and get them to each of you and to the Chief Justice so he can pass them along to the other Supreme Court Justices. Also, if Doctor Mitchell is willing, I will have him appear at both hearings where he can explain his findings and answer questions we all might have. I hope this will give you all the evidence you need." All of the senators nodded so he continued. "Now, Mrs. Terrell?" His blue eyes twinkled at me.

"Yes, sir?"

"I must advise that you might be required to testify in front of the Supreme Court when they hold their proceedings against Mr. Littman, so I ask you to remain in Helena. Understood?"

I slumped in my chair and felt a slow heat rise to my face. Maxwell looked at Brink and placed his cool hand on my forearm. "Excuse me, Mr. Chairman, is that really necessary? After all, the Justices could read Mrs. Terrell's testimony she gave here today and have all they would need."

Brink answered in a tight voice, "Mr. Heinz, you know the law well enough to know that an accused person has the right to face his accuser. Surely, the Justices will have a copy of Mrs. Terrell's testimony she gave today. In fact, I will make sure they have copies of it tomorrow. However, they may require her to appear and testify in person." With that, he placed the cigar in his mouth once again, his lips tight around it.

"Yes, sir," was all Maxwell said as he patted my arm.

Brink remained still and silent for at least a full minute.

"Mrs. Terrell," the gravelly voice made me jump. "More bad news, I'm afraid. You will also need to testify once again in front of this committee at Judge Valsted's hearing."

Under my breath, the words that were bouncing in my head came out, "What have I done? What have I done?" Maxwell's hand gripped my arm tightly. Apparently, he had heard me.

"Chairman Brink, again I must speak for Mrs. Terrell. She has already testified in front of this committee. I do not see the need for her to tell her story yet again. It was difficult enough for her to come here and to accuse these men of wrongdoing. Must she do it time and time again? For what purpose?" Maxwell said.

"Once again, Mr. Heinz, must I remind you that an accused has rights, too?" Brink said.

"Well--"

"May I interrupt, please?" This from Dandridge. My thoughts were tumbling over each other like small children at play. How can I do this? What's next? Somehow, I broke into their play and focused on Dandridge.

"Mr. Chairman, I agree with Mr. Heinz on this matter. We have already heard Mrs. Terrell's testimony, we understand it completely, and we only need to read Doctor Mitchell's report and the trial transcripts and to hear Judge Valsted's side of the story in order to make a ruling. I know that he has a right to face his accuser and all that, but for the sake of saving some time on this, I feel that giving Judge Valsted a copy of Mrs. Terrell's testimony well in advance of his hearing is good enough. That way he can prepare his answer to her accusations, come in front of us and state his case, and then we can make a ruling. I move that we conduct one final vote to determine whether or not Mrs. Terrell needs to testify in front of this committee again." With that, he pulled his lips back in a smile that showed no teeth, sat back in his chair, and appeared to relax.

My mouth literally gaped at him, and I had to purposely shut it. Then, I nodded thanks to him and focused my attention back on Brink who was now sitting straight in his chair, the cigar hanging forlorn and soggy between his fingers.

"Well, this is a turn of events, to be sure," Brink began. "I guess it wouldn't hurt to vote to see what you all have to say about this. So, all in favor of Mrs.

Terrell coming once again to testify in person at Judge Valsted's hearing, please indicate with an 'aye' vote."

My heart was thudding and a pillow was in my chest as I waited for their replies, especially for Mills's and Palmetto's. My insides quaked and my hands shook even though they were clenched tightly together.

Silence! Just what I wanted to hear!

"Those of you opposed, please indicate with a 'nay' vote."

"Nay," from all of them. Did I understand correctly? Was my mind playing tricks on me?

"Max," I said, touching his hand that still gripped my forearm, "what does this mean?"

"Shh, he replied. "Listen now."

"Motion denied. Mrs. Terrell, you will not have to testify in front of us again during Judge Valsted's hearing. However, I would like you to be present at said hearing, in case we have any further questions for you. We will advise Mr. Heinz of the dates and times that you are to appear at these hearings, and he can relay those to you. Understood?"

"Yes, sir."

As the meeting came to a close, we all rose for the senators to leave. I was able to stand only because Maxwell supported me with his thin arm around my waist. He somehow moved me to Annie and Sullie who were excitedly talking at once. Their lips moved, but the words got lost in the foggy tunnel of my mind.

"Oh, my, we'd best get this lass to the hotel, immediately it looks like," Sullie said, noticing my ragged, unstable appearance.

With Sullie's strong supporting arm around me, I made it to the car and then to the hotel suite. Annie had Gretchen, our suite-maid, fetch me a cool rag and some tea, which helped me feel more like myself. At least the foggy tunnel cleared a little.

Maxwell perched on a chair next to Annie and began the inevitable conversation about the hearing and what was to happen next.

He sucked in his lip, "pfft," and began, "The hearing went well –"

"For the love of God, Maxwell, it did not!" Annie exclaimed. "Those two ass-, pardon me, Mills and Palmetto infuriated me! They voted against us! Why, they weren't even paying attention. Maxwell, surely you can get them off this committee, can't you?"

"We have discussed this before, Annie, and no. There is nothing that can be done about them."

"Max is right, lass. The committee can't be changed. All we can do is hope that the evidence ordered by Brink'll sway their votes," Sullie said as he paced.

Annie's cheeks bloomed red. "Yes, but we also need to prepare ourselves just in case they don't change their vote."

I found my voice and expressed what lay heaviest on my mind. "And they could even persuade Dandridge to change his vote. That would be three against us. And –"

"Stop this, all of you!" Sullie's tight voice stilled us. "Really, we can't do anything about Dandridge or Mills or Palmetto. We need to concentrate on the next step and just hope and pray for the best outcome."

"Sullie is right," Maxwell said.

"Okay, so what is the next step and how can we prepare?" I asked Maxwell.

"First of all, you should just relax and rest as much as possible until I hear word from Brink about the dates and times of the hearings. Littman's will occur first, more than likely, and by the sounds of it, his could be as late as the end of June," Maxwell said.

I sucked in a breath as the realization that we would be here for another month, even longer perhaps, came to me. "That's right," I whispered.

Maxwell continued, "Now, as was ruled, Clara, you will need to tell your story again to the Supreme Court justices. The hearing will be very much the same as the one today, so all you have to do is repeat what you said today. Okay?"

I managed a small nod and smiled because he reminded me of an old owl perched on his chair with his white hair sticking up like pickets in a fence and his nose nearly reaching where his top lip should be. I adored him. He had a huge servant's heart, and he loved my best friend and treated her like a princess.

"Then, at Valsted's hearing in front of the committee, you will just need to be in the chamber with us, so that will be quite easy for you, I would imagine," Maxwell said.

"I will be just fine," I said.

"Great, lass," Sullie's deep voice resonated in the room and pulled my attention to him. "No worries, then."

"Well, I do have one fairly big problem on my mind," I said. I looked down at my clenched hands, and heat spread across my chest and up into my neck and face.

"What is it?" Annie asked and then she guessed. "It's having to face those terrible monsters, isn't it?" She leaned as far forward as her chair would allow.

"Yes. Although I've known all along that at some point I'd have to come face-to-face with them, I'm scared half to death of it."

"Don't you dare be frightened, lassie. We'll all be right there for you and won't let anything bad happen, I swear it," Sullie said.

"That's right. Maxwell will be right beside you, and Sullie and I will be in the spectator seats, just as we all were today," Annie said.

I nodded and felt a little better about it all.

"Speakin' of the spectators today," Sullie said quietly. "We need to talk about the reporters who were there."

"Reporters! What –" I said, and blood pulsed in my neck.

"Now, don't get upset, lass. Did you see those two men in the front row?"

I nodded and he continued, "They were news men there to report about the hearing."

"Oh, no." I grabbed the arm of my chair as I realized that once the newspapers came out, Bob would find out where I was. Dark edges of fear crowded my vision.

"It's okay –" Sullie began.

"She's scared, Sullie, can't you tell that? It's not okay." Annie said, reaching for me.

"I just mean that there's nothin' that can be done about it. People have the right to know what's happening, even if we don't want them to. Even if it creates danger for us. Besides, you didn't think we could keep this a secret, did you?" Sullie said, his wide brow furrowed.

"No, and you're right, Sullie," I said quietly. "But I admit I'm afraid. Bob will know where I am now and what we're doing here. He'll be furious and who knows what he'll do."

"That's just it. We don't know what he'll do, so let's not borrow trouble. Instead, let's just be very vigilant, on the lookout as they say," Sullie said.

"Sullie's right. We need to be careful," Maxwell said. "And Bob is not the only danger we might face in the next month or so. Valsted, Littman, Belzer, or any of the men who sent their wives away could react badly and come here to do us harm. I think we all need to be careful, and you ladies," he said, his gray bulging eyes landing on each of us, "should not go anywhere alone. Make sure you always let someone know where you are if you leave the hotel, too. Just to be safe."

We all agreed that this would be best and that we needed to just accept what we could not change. Maxwell had business to attend to at his office, so he bid Sullie and me farewell and asked Annie to escort him out, which she did.

"So, lass, are you really feelin' better now?" Sullie said, his blue eyes dark with concern.

"I guess so. I just have to remember that fear can actually keep me safe. Not safe, but vigilant. I do feel safe with you, though, Sullie. Thank you for that." Changing the subject, I said, "And I'm so happy that

Annie and Maxwell found love in each other. Funny how things work, isn't it?"

Sullie's laugh came from deep in his chest as he said, "Aye, it surely is. It surely is...." His voice trailed off and he clasped his long fingers together between his knees and looked at the carpet in front of him, his dark fringe of lashes feathering along his cheekbones.

Uncomfortable at his sudden seriousness, I rose from my chair and busied myself until Annie returned, at which time Sullie dismissed himself to go to his suite.

Two days later, the newspapers in Billings and Helena contained articles about the hearing, and fear with tension as its companion settled over me. We all moved about with hyper-awareness, expecting Bob or the others to appear at any moment.

Chairman Brink worked as quickly as the news reporters, it seemed. In the next two days, Maxwell told us that Judge Valsted's Senate hearing was scheduled for August third, and that a copy of my testimony had been sent to Valsted immediately after the hearing at which I testified. Littman had been served orders to appear in front of the State Supreme Court on June twenty-ninth. My orders to appear came the very next day. The tension grew and we became, as Sullie advised, vigilant.

Doctor Mitchell had also been served papers ordering him to testify at Valsted's hearing in front of the senators and at Littman's trial at the Supreme Court. The doctor agreed to examine all of the women sent to Whispering Pines from Bergen and report his findings in writing to the senate committee and to the Supreme Court before June eighteenth. I wanted more than anything to go and talk to him, but Sullie advised me not to do that as it might appear that I was influencing his testimony in some way. I had to agree.

CHAPTER 17

Our short stay in Helena was turning into quite a lengthy one, and it was going to extend into August by the looks of things, so I decided to broach the subject of going home for a while.

"Annie, Sullie, I have something I'd like to talk to you about," I began, trying to keep a smile in my voice. My eyes, however, strayed to the carpet and remained there. "By the end of all of this, Annie, you will have been away from home for over three months, and, Sullie, you will have been away for almost as long. I think that's a terribly long time for you both to have spent away, and I'm worried that I'm keeping you from your businesses. What I'm trying to say is, if you want to, we can go back to Bergen." There, I had said it. A whoosh of air gushed from my lungs. My shoulders and neck remained tense; however, because I truly did not know what I would do if they wanted to return. I had no home to go back to. Not to mention the fact that Bob was there, and I had a pretty good idea of what he would do to me now.

The thick, long silence caused me to look up to see both of them gaping at me. Suddenly, Sullie was on his feet, pacing and running his hand through his hair.

It was Annie who broke through the silence. "How can you even suggest a thing like that!" Her voice boomed and she threw herself back into her chair. I jumped at her tone and my eyes immediately went to the carpet again. Now, what had I done?

"Lass, you've actually brought up a really good point, so don't go gettin' all upset on us here. I've thought about this myself, and really see no reason at all to go back there right now," Sullie said and folded his lanky form into a chair next to Annie. He clasped his hands between his knees, leaned forward, and continued in his deep soothing voice that brought my eyes up to his, "I took care of my cases before I came to join you here, and with the help of my assistant, Mr. O'Malley, I'm able to conduct business over the telephone. So, I'm free to stay here as long as is necessary to see this thing through."

"Oh, Sullie, are you sure?" I said.

"Aye, I'm certain of it. There's nothin' at all to be concerned with there. What's important right now is what we're doin' here."

Annie's voice was a little softer, but she was still obviously upset. "Yes, that's right. I have no business in Bergen right now. Our houses will take care of themselves and be damned with everything else in that town! Why, just the thought of going back there right now just makes me wanna spit!" Ironically, saliva sprayed from her with her last word. "Goodness, why am I upset? There's nothing to be upset about, and Clara, I'm sorry. It's just that you need to understand that it is just not safe there for you...or for any of us for that matter. At least here, the law will protect us."

At first it was difficult to get used to moving about with hyper-awareness and the sense of danger we were in now that the key players knew what could happen to them. I soon found out that Helena was not immune to gossip as I endured the stares and whispers of people in the hotel and on the streets. Word spread quickly about who we were and what we were in town to do. Although I was constantly aware of the potential danger, I also came to realize that many of the people of Helena supported what we were doing. In fact, some of them expressed their appreciation and wished us luck. I was especially touched when Mr. Kershaw, the porter, approached Annie and me one morning on our way out of the hotel.

"Mrs. Terrell?" he said. "May I have a word?"

"Of course," I answered, smoothing my skirt as I stood in front of him.

"Well, I just want to tell you that I…" The man was wringing his hands, his gaze on the floor. "Well, my wife and I…" He finally looked me in the eye. "…we admire you for what you're doing to help those women."

"Mr. Kershaw," I gently touched his arm. "That means a lot to me. To us," and I gestured to Annie. "And I thank you for all of the help you've given us, too. You have a big heart."

"I thank you for that, but it's you who has the big heart. Anyway, we just wanted you to know how we feel about you is all." The corners of his mouth turned up a little, and my heart lightened as Annie and I went on our way.

Two days later I was summoned to the hotel desk for a telephone call. Who could it be? Maybe it's Robby. Maybe he's had a change of heart. My pulse quickened as I picked up the receiver and said hello.

"Is this Clara Terrell?" A man, not Robby, asked.

"Yes. Who is this?" My fingers tightened on the phone.

Click. The phone went dead. My hand shook as I replaced the receiver. Sweat beaded on my forehead and tickled my scalp. Somehow I made it back to our suite. Annie immediately took my hands and led me to the settee.

"Was it Robby?" I shook my head. "Who was it? What's happened?" she asked frantically. "You're pale and sweating, Clara. Now talk to me!"

"I think they know that we're here," I managed, "not just in Helena but in this hotel."

"Who does? What are you talking about?"

I took a deep breath and told her about the call.

"Oh, no!" She ran a hand down her face which reminded me of Sullie. I suddenly wanted him with me.

"Annie, I'm frightened."

"I know. Me, too." She got up and checked the locks on the door. "Calm down and think this through," she said more to herself than to me, pacing the floor. "You know, it might not be them. It might have just been a prank caller, someone trying to scare us." Her voice trailed off.

"You could be right, but let's not take any chances. Let's just stay here behind locked doors until Sullie and Maxwell come over later. Okay?"

"Oh, definitely," she said.

We waited in near silence for hours, jumping at every noise and holding our breaths at footfalls in the hallway. Finally, the men arrived. We flung ourselves at them, both talking at once.

"One at a time, lassies," Sullie said, catching my hands in his, concern rippling his brow. Annie nodded to me, so I told them about the telephone call. They looked shocked.

"You did the right thing in staying here with the door locked." Maxwell said.

"I think it'd be best if we all were a bit more vigilant from now on," Sullie said. "This is just the reminder we needed. Valsted and Littman are not men who'll take these charges lightly. Their livelihood and their pride are at stake, and they'll defend themselves, for sure."

"You're right, Sullie," I said. "We'll just have to be more aware of our surroundings until the trials are over." The other three nodded.

The next day I received another telephone call. This time Annie came with me. Just as I said hello, Sullie and Maxwell came in the front door of the hotel and saw us. They rushed over.

"Who is it? What's happened?" Sullie said. I held a hand up to quiet him so I could hear the caller.

I immediately recognized Judge Valsted's deep voice. "You need to drop all of these ridiculous charges against me or else, little lady. You hear me?" I gasped and began to shake.

"Or else what?" I managed.

"Or else I will come to you and stab you as you sleep. You and your friends, too, Sullie and Annie and that Maxwell character. I'll kill all of you, one at a time and slowly. I'll slice you up into little pieces and scatter your parts all over the mountains is what I'll do. Don't think I can't get away with it –"

Sullie grabbed the phone from me and shouted, "Who is this?"

The phone went dead in his hand. Darkness came at me from all sides, and I reached for the hotel desk. Somehow, Sullie and Maxwell pulled me up the stairs and into the suite where they placed me in a chair, got me a glass of water, and began asking me questions. I managed to tell them that it was Valsted, and I told them what he said. They all talked at once which made me lightheaded.

"Stop it! All of you!" I shouted. They were silent and still, startled at my sudden outburst. "All of this –" I gestured at them. "All of this won't accomplish a thing. We need to be rational. And we need to work this out together, and one at a time."

"You're right, lass. Of course." Sullie said as he stopped pacing and sat next to me. "Maxwell, you go first." He gestured to Maxwell and clenched his hands between his knees.

"Okay. Clearly, Valsted is not stable and poses a great danger to us. That is obvious. Let's go through our options." Silence filled the room as we thought. Maxwell spoke first, "One of them is for you three to move to a different hotel."

Sullie said, "More than likely, that call yesterday was someone makin' calls to all of the hotels here for Valsted. You know, to find out which one we're staying in. If we move to another one, he'll just find us again. Sorry, Max. That won't work."

"How about we leave Helena? Go somewhere else until the trials," I said, wanting just to run from this place.

"No!" Annie exclaimed. "Max's work is important. He has people counting on him. Right, dear?"

"That is correct. Yes. I would not be able to go anywhere with you right now, I am afraid."

"So, no. I can't leave Max here alone. I won't," Annie said.

"Oh, I agree," I said. "I won't leave without him, either. I just hadn't thought that through, I guess."

"You could all move into my place. I have plenty of room." This from Maxwell. "It is not proper for you ladies, I know, but under the circumstances I think morality could be put aside."

"That's a wonderful –" Annie said, flapping her hands.

"No, we can't." Annie stopped flapping and gaped at Sullie.

"Why not?"

"Because it's far too isolated. We need to have people around who can help us if need be. Here in this hotel, all of the personnel know us and can be told of the danger we're in so they can watch out for us. I think we need to stay here," Sullie said. We all sat silently pondering that.

Maxwell spoke first again. "I agree. However, I will hire guards for us all. I will call around immediately and find men to be with you around the clock. And one for myself as well."

"I think that's a good idea, dear," Annie said, and Sullie and I nodded.

"Thanks, Max," Sullie said. "And, lasses, I don't care about propriety under these circumstances. I'll spend all of my time here with you except for when I have to go to Maxwell's office to conduct business.

I'll sleep on the settee in here and just leave you to bathe and dress in my own room."

Maxwell said, "Sullie, I know you have your pistol with you. I think you should put it here in the suite for the ladies. Do you know how to use a gun?" His gray eyes bulged at Annie and me. When we both nodded, he said, "Good. Then, Sullie, just leave it here for them to use. Put it in that desk drawer over there."

"I'd already decided to do just that, Max. Thanks, though, for asking the lasses first," Sullie said.

"Yes, thank you, Maxwell. And you, too, Sullie," I said.

This was the only option that was feasible, so we had no choice but to accept it. Maxwell left to contact the police and to hire guards for us. I was nervous for him and wished Sullie would go with him, but at the same time, I needed Sullie to stay with Annie and me. Maxwell arrived safely back to us in about three hours. He informed us that the police refused to do anything to help since they were too understaffed to help us with what they called "just a telephone threat." My blood heated at that, but there was nothing for me to do about it, so I accepted it. I gratefully accepted the guards Maxwell hired, too. One was posted outside our door at all times, and if we needed to go anywhere, he went with us.

So we settled in to our new life of isolation, which was difficult for me but must have been excruciating for Annie. Mostly, we talked about the hearings and added more names to our list of who we thought the women might be. Sullie still had business in Bergen, so once a week he went to Maxwell's office to conduct it over the telephone with Patrick. He

181

would relay the news of Bergen to us, which Annie and I enjoyed. We also talked about ourselves. Annie and I shared funny stories of our growing up together in Green Bay, and Annie talked about her work with the Suffragettes in Chicago. Sullie shared as well, telling us about his family and life in Dublin and about his and Maxwell's time in New York. Annie showered him with questions and glowed whenever he spoke of Maxwell. I added what I could about my life on the prairie, which seemed incredibly boring compared to Annie's and Sullie's lives. The reminiscing was good; the deepening friendship with Sullie was better.

One night, Sullie and I sat up talking long after Annie went to bed.

I tentatively asked, "Why did you leave Ireland, Sullie? If you don't mind my asking." I flushed as his eyes burrowed into mine. Then, just as I saw a glimmer of something, I knew not what, he looked away.

He gazed past me as he answered. "I came to this country because there was a bit too much unrest in Ireland at the time. For a few years before I left, the country felt uneasy. I attempted to convince my parents to come to the United States with me, but to no avail. They were too entrenched in their life there, and besides, they were elderly. So, in 1915, I left without 'em. As you probably already know, in 1916 during Easter Week, of all things, a bloody uprising occurred, leavin' thousands of people dead in my hometown."

"Why, that must have been just awful. Were your parents harmed?" I sat forward in my chair.

"Thank the good Lord, they weren't. However, since then, they've both passed on of old age. Actually, within a few months of each other. Perhaps there is somethin' to that 'dying of a broken heart' theory. I hope that my leavin' did not precipitate their deaths in any way, though."

"I'm sure not, Sullie, but I am sorry to hear of your country's misfortunes. So, when you came to the United States --"

"Yes, I sailed to New York City where I was able to work as a lawyer. That's what I did back in Dublin, too. I met Maxwell there and we became fast friends, doing everything together. After he moved west, though, I began feelin' strangled by the city, so I decided to travel out this way and see where the tracks would lead me. Anyway, they led me to Bergen and you know the rest, I guess. I've only lived there a couple of months but already I feel like it's my true home." Sullie sighed at his own long-windedness and dragged in a long breath, pulling his lanky form upright.

"I'm happy to hear you think of Bergen as your home, Sullie. It's a fine place to live, and you are certainly an asset to our community."

Sullie blushed and his eyes shot to mine. "Clara, I need –" He stopped himself, pushed his hair from his eyes, and stood.

"You need what, Sullie?" I asked.

"Never you mind, lassie. It's nothing. Now, we'd best be gettin' to bed before the sun comes up."

I lay awake that night pondering what it was that Sullie needed.

CHAPTER 18

It was the middle of June, a couple of weeks before Littman's trial. Sullie had gone to Maxwell's office. Annie and I were napping when Sullie burst into the suite, shouting for Annie and me to come out of our bedrooms. I hurriedly smoothed my clothes and hair and came into the living room just as Annie came out of her bedroom.

"What in the world is the problem, Sullie?" she exclaimed. Sullie rushed to me, taking my arms in his strong hands. His hair was mussed and he was nearly breathless.

"Oh, the best news. The best news indeed!" He looked deeply into my eyes, and I saw a twinkling such as I had not seen from him before. It was captivating.

"What is it? Share this news with us right now!" Annie fairly shouted at him. "Something good has happened? Really?"

"Really, really good," Sullie replied. He dropped his hold on my arms and my eyes, and I felt a hollow void in my chest. "I've got to tell you straight away!" He paced as his words tumbled out. "I talked to Patrick this morning, and he told me that Joshua Miller, you know the man who raced away from your barn, Clara?"

I was able to get a quick nod in before he continued. "Well, Patrick told me that Joshua wanted to discuss something very important with me, so I had

Patrick go out and fetch the chap from his farm and then call me back at three o'clock."

"So, what did Joshua have to say?" I asked.

Sullie's hand raked his hair and then his face and stopped pacing. He took a deep breath while he looked at the ceiling and said, "I just got off the telephone with Joshua, and he wants to help us. He told me that he saw the article in the newspaper about what we're doing over here to help those women and he wants to help!"

"But, what in the world can he do to help?" I asked, nervously fingering the collar on my dress.

Annie said loudly, "Yes. That asshole sent his wife to Whispering Pines, after all. What does he think he can do now, and why in the world would he want to help anyway?"

"Let me finish. He said that he did indeed send Rebecca to Whispering Pines because he truly was convinced she was lunatic, but once he heard about all the other women bein' sent there, he started to wonder what was really goin' on. Doubt and guilt started pecking away at him so badly that he decided to go to the asylum to see if she was better and if she was, then he'd bring her back home with him if he could." Sullie paced again. Annie flumped down into an armchair, and since my legs shook, I did the same, my hands clenched between my knees.

"What happened at Whispering Pines, Sullie?" Annie asked quietly.

"Well, when he got there, he asked to see her and they told him...they told him that she'd passed away not but three months earlier." We gasped. "Lasses, that was three years ago, less than a year after he sent her away. He said he was one of the first men to send his wife off to that place and that he'd regretted it ever since. The guilt got to him pretty quickly but he was still too late to save her."

Annie wiped tears from her round, red cheeks, and I swallowed hard around the lump that had formed in my throat.

"Oh, my Heavens, Sullie. That's terrible, just tragic," Annie said in a husky voice.

"Aye, it is at that."

"How did she die?" I asked.

"I'm sorry. I didn't have the heart to ask him that."

"So, how is it that he can help us? What is he offering to do?" This from Annie, her voice stronger now.

"He said that he's willin' to come here to testify to who was in your barn that day, Clara, and also he'll tell all that he knows about Valsted and Littman and the other men, too."

"But he'll get himself in trouble right along with them. And he might be in danger. Does he know that?" Annie said.

"Aye, he knows that but he's willin' to help anyway, just so that maybe some of the other women can be freed. Personally, I think he's hopin' to alleviate some of his guilt."

"Well, he damned well should feel guilty! He's nothing but a low-down, good-for-nothing---"

I interrupted Annie's tirade. "Now, Annie, he says he didn't know really what was happening at the time, so let's give him the benefit of the doubt here. He is, after all, willing to help now."

186

"I guess you're right. I'll try my best to stay calm," Annie replied with a sniff. "So what happens now, Sullie?"

"Well, Maxwell needs to arrange it all, but he was out of the office when I talked to Joshua. I left him a message to make the arrangements and call Patrick with them. Then, Patrick can get the details to Joshua. That's all I could do, so I came up here to tell you the news. Now, I guess we'll just have to wait for Maxwell to tell us what's going to happen next."

And so we waited, Annie at the edge of the armchair, Sullie alternately pacing and lounging on the settee, and me attempting to calm the fluttering in my midsection by breathing as deeply as possible.

Finally, Maxwell burst into the room, his round face flushed. "This is the best news! The very best news!"

"What did you find out, dear?" Annie hefted herself out of the armchair and went to Maxwell. We all looked expectantly at the tiny man.

"I did as you asked and made the arrangements with Chairman Brink for Joshua to testify. He believes the Court will be in favor of hearing his testimony, too, and will relay the information to the Chief Justice for us. When I called your office, Sullie, Joshua was still there, so I was able to give him the details right away. He is willing to tell his story at both Littman's and Valsted's trials. I told him to be here by the twenty-eighth since Littman's trial is the twenty-ninth. Oh, this is so good!" A cloak of assuredness fell over me as I realized that both Joshua Miller and Doctor Mitchell would be supporting my testimony at the hearings. Just the evidence we needed.

Maxwell informed us when Joshua Miller arrived in Helena on the evening of the twenty-eighth. I wanted desperately to talk to him and to hear what he was going to say at the hearings; however, I was quite afraid of the man, too. After all, he was one of the men who sent their wives off to Whispering Pines. No matter, though, as Maxwell forbade me from seeing him, claiming that a meeting between us could be construed as unfair to Valsted and Littman. Not only that but it was far too dangerous for two witnesses to be in the same place right now. Who knew what Valsted and Littman were capable of.

Sleep was impossible that night.

The morning of Littman's trial dawned overcast and gray with rain streaking my bedroom window, and I got stiffly up from the bed and made my way to the window to look down at the damp street below. Black bobbing circles indicated the few people making their ways to who-knows-where and for what purpose. Even the dull sunlight made my head pound, so I turned away, feeling queasy and weak.

The stress that was my constant companion in the past weeks had eaten hungrily at my body, I noticed when I donned the soft gray suit and pink blouse I wore to the hearing in May. Stinging tears sprang to my eyes when I looked in the mirror and saw the way the suit now hung off my hips and gapped at the shoulders and chest. Midnight black half-moons under my eyes had spread lower on my cheeks every day and the lines on my face had become more deeply carved. I took some of the medicine for the headache, smoothed my skirt, and joined Annie and Sullie in the sitting room.

Annie let out a small gasp. "Oh my goodness! You look just wonderful! That suit really does flatter you!" She lied as she pulled on the skirt, smoothed the jacket, and glanced at Sullie. "Although, my gracious, you have lost a lot of weight. Well, you look good nonetheless." Her chins quivered as she laughed nervously, and directed me out the door before I could say a word.

Then, with a guard accompanying us, we made our way to the capitol building for Littman's trial. A very large umbrella, which Sullie held for us, kept us dry as we raced up the wet walkway to the capitol doors where Maxwell met us, his suit even more rumpled than normal due to the high humidity, I supposed. I was amazed that his white spiky halo of hair had not flattened one bit in the rain, though.

He grabbed Annie's arm and Sullie's warmth soothed me as he held my arm tightly, and we made our way to the room in which the Montana State Supreme Court held its proceedings, the beauty of which stopped me so suddenly that Sullie's arm in mine nearly toppled me over.

I pulled in a little breath and Sullie reached down and whispered, "Beautiful, isn't it?"

"Oh, yes it is," I replied as I stared at the four cream-colored marble pillars at the front of the room, heavy velvet curtains behind them. They seemed to reach to Heaven, but as my gaze swept upwards, I noticed that they ended, and gorgeous scenes carved in a shiny ivory marble wall reached to the ceiling. An American flag hung on each side of the front of the room. I closed my gaping mouth and told myself to breathe. Facing us, there were five huge leather chairs behind a long dark table where I assumed the justices would sit. In front of the table, a podium stood between two smaller tables. As Sullie moved me forward, down rows of dark oak seats that looked an awful lot like pews in a church, he said that he, Annie, and I would sit in the front "pew" as part of the audience. A long oak partition separated these seats from the tables and podium.

Our guards sat near the door, and Doctor Mitchell also sat near the back. He gave us a smile and a short wave as we passed by.

Joshua Miller was there, too, twirling his cowboy hat between his knees and looking straight ahead at the justices' table. I detected a slight trembling in his head and shoulders. He never looked our way.

Finally, we made it to our seats, where I sat between Sullie and Annie. We all watched as Maxwell marched confidently to his seat at one of the small tables. The doors swung open behind us and a chill rushed over me. I recognized Charles Littman's voice as he talked loudly to another man who I assumed was his lawyer. I stared straight ahead, trying to concentrate on the opulent marble pillars. Sullie and Annie each grabbed my hand as the man and his lawyer strutted to their seats at the other small table. I trembled as he passed.

"It's okay, Clara," Annie soothed. "We're right here. Don't you worry about a thing. He cannot harm you in any way...." I realized she was trying to keep the man's voice from reaching me. When I got enough courage, I looked at Littman and was surprised at how small he was, tiny actually. His shoulders were narrow in his coal black suit jacket, which hung looser than my own and appeared to have flecks of white fuzz on it. His feet, I noticed, barely reached the floor and were encased in small dull black shoes. He had sandy hair that was so recently cut that I could see where the scissors had gouged into it. When he turned to face his attorney, a hugely overweight man who was quite well-dressed in a dark blue suit, his face was marked with pock scars and he had squinty eyes that were of a non-descript color. He was so homely, I actually felt pity for him for a moment. Then, I remembered the awful things he perpetrated in Bergen, and heat coursed through me again.

Suddenly, it was time to begin. A marshal came into the courtroom from a side door, called the court to order, and asked us to stand. Shuffling feet and rustling garments indicated that we were not the only spectators. Five men in swirling midnight black robes, shiny white collars sitting like slipped haloes around their necks, entered from the same door the marshal had used.

Sullie bent his head and breathed into my ear, "The Chief Justice is in the center like Brink was. He'll probably ask most of the questions, but all of the justices will have read the transcripts from Beaver County and will have studied the briefs about the case. Now, though, Maxwell will tell your side of the story, and he'll probably call you up to verify what he says. Okay?"

I managed a small nod and felt better just knowing Sullie was beside me. A small rivulet of sweat formed between my breasts and ran down to the waistband of my skirt. I felt the back of my neck dampening as well.

The Chief Justice straightened the stack of papers in front of him and looked up and around the entire room. He cleared his throat, his hand cupped over his mouth, and said, "This special session of the Montana Supreme Court has now come to order. I will begin with a quick preview of this case. The defendant, Mr. Charles Littman, County Attorney for Beaver County in Montana, is accused of ethical misconduct. We are here today to hear arguments from the accusers, Mrs. Robert Terrell and Mr. Joshua Miller, and from the defendant." A lightheaded relief flooded me at mention of two accusers. I was no longer alone in this.

The Chief Justice continued, "For the record, all five of us justices received and read the court records from Beaver County that are pertinent to this case. We also received and read the report of Doctor Mitchell's findings and agree to hear his testimony about them." The Chief Justice paused while he perused the papers in front of him and then asked that the hearing begin with oral arguments starting with my side of the story.

I prayed silently as Maxwell stood and began to argue our case, stressing the role that Littman had in all of the proceedings against the women in Bergen.

After about five minutes, he asked the justices if they would allow me to corroborate his story, and the Chief Justice said, "By all means. Please, bring her up." Maxwell turned and motioned for me to come forward, nodding his head at me as he hurriedly opened a short gate in the partition which separated us. As I rose, Sullie and Annie came to their feet as well.

Annie grabbed my sleeve as I passed by, so I stopped and looked into her round face as she whispered, "Don't you dare even look over at that evil little son of a bitch, you hear me?" Then, she gave my arm a squeeze and winked.

I made my way through the gate and stood next to Maxwell facing the Justices, realizing for the first time that they were all kindly-looking older men with shiny heads bald or nearly so. They all had round, wire-rimmed eyeglasses settled on their round cheeks just below bushy white eyebrows as though these were some requisite to their wardrobe. I could not believe how alike they all were, subtly smiling and nodding at me. None of this soothed my quaking; however, and I clutched my hands together in front of me. The dampness at the base of my skull let loose with droplets of moisture which trickled down my spine. My forehead and upper lip also felt damp. I refused to look over at the little man whose glare I could feel deep in my soul.

After I was sworn in, the Chief Justice said, "Please, Mrs. Terrell, briefly tell this Court what it was that you overheard in the barn the morning of April twenty-fifth of this year."

And so it was that I once again told the story of what I heard that dreadful morning. I tried to be as short and yet complete as possible. You would think that with each telling, it would get easier; however, it did not. In fact, each telling seemed to rip the scab off my wounded heart which was so desperately attempting to heal itself. As I oozed out the details of what I heard that morning, even more clarity was lent to the fact that my own husband, the man I vowed to love and cherish every day of my life and who vowed to do the same for me, wanted to rid his life of me and had the power to do just that, with the help of men like Valsted and Littman.

Once I finished, I took a ragged breath and looked up at the Chief Justice who asked, "I am wondering, Mrs. Terrell, specifically what did you hear in the barn that morning that makes you think Mr. Charles Littman had any part in the travesty of justice that occurred in Bergen?" He leaned forward, clasping his hands on the table in front of him, as he waited for my reply.

I took a deep breath, collected my thoughts, and said, "Sir, I heard Judge Valsted say that Mr. Littman was at each of the women's trials in Bergen after they were arrested. His job, according to Judge Valsted, was to act as the prosecutor and to ask the husband about his wife's actions and about financial matters. Mr. Littman was to ask questions that would make it clear that the woman owned nothing and that she was a danger to herself and others."

"Thank you, Mrs. Terrell."

"I have one more thing to add, if you please," I said and looked at all of the Justices. "There is no doubt in my mind that Mr. Littman knew exactly what was happening to the women who were on trial since they were sentenced to Whispering Pines right there in the courtroom with him present."

The Chief Justice then leaned back, scowled at Littman, and said, "Again, thank you so much. You may be seated, and we will call you again if need be." I hurriedly sat down between Sullie and Annie, accepting their warm pats on my arms.

Maxwell cleared his throat and said, "Your Honors, I would now like to call Mr. Joshua Miller."

And so Joshua rose, walked forward, and was sworn in. The Chief Justice had to ask him to look up from the ground. Joshua's entire body trembled and he drew a deep breath as he looked at the Chief Justice.

"Mr. Miller, I understand that you are appearing before us today to corroborate Mrs. Terrell's story of what she overheard in the barn on the morning of April twenty-fifth of this year. Is that correct?" The Chief Justice asked.

When Joshua merely nodded, the Chief Justice told him that all of his answers had to be audible, so Joshua shakily said, "Yes, that's correct, sir."

"Very good. You may commence."

"Well, I want y'all to know that I'm here because I wanna be here," Joshua began and turned his head to Maxwell who encouraged him with a nod. "I wanna tell my story to y'all so that you can understand what's been happening in Bergen in the last four years." He paused, looked down at his hands outspread on the podium, and continued, "It was about three years ago when Rebecca, my wife, was acting all funny like. She was out of her head most of the time, crying and carrying on about nothing and sometimes yelling and screamin' at me about things I knew nothing of. Anyway, this went on for a few months when I'd had enough of it. One night, I was drunk and telling everyone in the bar in town about her fits, and Judge Valsted was in there and took me off by myself. He told me that he could help me with my problem, meaning Rebecca, so I listened. He told me that he, along with Doctor Belzer and Mr. Littman, could have Rebecca sent to Whispering Pines where she could get the help that she needed." Joshua's voice had gotten progressively lower and finally started to break, so he took a few ragged breaths.

"I believed the man and did what he told me to do which was to have Rebecca arrested and brought before him and Littman. They only took about half an hour to convict her of bein' a lunatic and sent her to Whispering Pines. I just let it happen." Joshua's shoulders shook, and he swiped at tears running down his face.

"Mr. Miller," the Chief Justice said, "is that all you have to tell us?"

"No, sir. There's more." He covered his mouth with one fist and cleared his throat before he continued, his composure regained, "After she was taken away, for a while I felt relieved and thought that she was gettin' the help she needed. That only lasted a few months, though, before the guilt started in on me. About that time, I was gettin' wind of some other women who the judge and Littman sent off to that insane asylum, same as Rebecca. It just didn't seem right to me, so about then, I decided to go and see my wife to see if she was well and ready to come home. So, I went there, and sir, it was horrible. The way that place was, or is I should say, is awfully bad. I could hear the cryin' and saw some of the patients from where they left me while they looked to see where my Rebecca was. It was terrible, I'm tellin' you. Anyway, finally a man came and took me into an office where he told me that my Rebecca was dead. She'd died just a month or two earlier. She killed herself, hung herself with a bed sheet, she did." Again, Joshua stopped to compose himself, wiping his face and looking up at the ceiling to squelch his tears.

"Continue, please, Mr. Miller," the Chief Justice said in a loud, forceful voice.

"Yes, sir. So, like I already said, that was three years ago and since then, there's been lots of Bergen women sent to that place in the same way Rebecca was.

"Anyway, it was on April twenty-fifth that Judge Valsted came to my farm and told me that there was some trouble over at Bob Terrell's place and that he needed me to come and help him with it. I know Bob pretty well, so I went with the judge. Me, the judge, Doc Belzer, and Frank Larson met with Bob in his barn that morning. I thought they were gonna talk about a legal or a money problem or something like that, but all of a sudden I realized they were talkin' about the problem being Clara, his wife. I knew then that they wanted Bob to do what I'd done and have Clara sent away to Whispering Pines. Once I realized that, why, it felt like the walls came in around me. I left in one big hurry, I can tell you. That's all I know about, and I guess I'm done." Joshua's bony shoulders drooped, and he let his chin rest on his chest. My heart nearly broke for him, yet I was so grateful for his help.

"Any questions for Mr. Miller before he is dismissed?" The Chief Justice asked. The other Justices shook their heads. Joshua sighed loudly and slowly made his way to his seat, his shoulders and his head drooping.

CHAPTER 19

The Chief Justice looked out at the spectators and said, "We will now hear testimony from Doctor Mitchell. Doctor, please come and be sworn in." As Doctor Mitchell walked to the podium, the Chief Justice continued, "Although we have already read the doctor's report regarding this matter, it is important that he testify here so that it is on the record officially." I sat up straighter in anticipation of what Doctor Mitchell would say about the condition of the asylum and about the women being held there.

After the doctor was sworn in, the Chief Justice said, "Doctor, please feel free to tell us anything that you think is pertinent to this case against Mr. Littman. We also wish to know the conditions of the fourteen, errr pardon me, the thirteen women you examined at Whispering Pines." He glanced at Joshua Miller and continued, "Feel free to explain to us the living conditions at the asylum, too, but perhaps telling us your credentials first would be helpful." And with a curt nod to Doctor Mitchell, whose broad straight shoulders were relaxed under his dark brown suit jacket, the Chief Justice leaned back in his chair to listen.

Doctor Mitchell cleared his throat and began, his soft voice resonating kindness and concern. "Well, I have had a medical practice here in Helena for the past ten years and have seen numerous menopausal women during that time. I am not an expert by any means; however, I have researched menopause extensively. It is a condition that most women must go through, and in my opinion, their families must be patient and understanding as they transition into the next phase of life.

"Also, let me add that once I was assigned the role of examining the women from Beaver County, I brushed up on the newest research about menopause and female hormones so that I could better diagnose the women I was to see. I found there are no known 'cures' for it." Doctor Mitchell made quotation marks in the air with his fingers.

He took a deep breath, rolled his shoulders, and continued. "The symptoms can be quite frightening to the women and their families, often coming on suddenly. Menopausal women can experience restlessness, extreme irritability, forgetfulness, hot flashes, night sweats, headaches, erratic menses, and such things. The symptoms come and go on a whim, so there is no way to know from one moment to the next what she will be feeling like."

I stole a glance up at Sullie who stared straight ahead, his heavy brows furrowed. My neck grew warm and my cheeks flushed as I recognized my own symptoms on the list. Without looking at me, Sullie took my sweating hand in his, entwining our fingers together. Immediately, I calmed as I realized his understanding and compassion.

"Compounding the problem is our society," Doctor Mitchell continued. "Menopause is simply not discussed openly; therefore, it is misunderstood which can lead to dire consequences such as what happened to the women of Beaver County. I feel strongly that

199

the husbands of these women overreacted to their symptoms and felt, as Joshua Miller testified, that they were justified in sending their wives for help. Also, a pack mentality settled over Beaver County, I think, in that once a few men had gotten rid of their wives, many more lined up to do the same." I heard the ticking of a clock which hung on the back wall of the room as Doctor Mitchell took a deep breath.

"Now, with that said, I also would like it on record that I believe that without the 'help'," again Doctor Mitchell made quotation marks with his fingers, "of Judge Valsted, Mr. Littman, and Doctor Belzer the fourteen women from Beaver County would never have been sent to Whispering Pines in the first place. Most of the blame for this travesty must be placed on these three professionals.

"Now, if I may, please allow me to describe for you the conditions at Whispering Pines, and I apologize if I offend anyone's sensibilities here. The outside of the buildings and the grounds surrounding them are relatively nice. As is the receiving area. Clean, bright, and well-maintained, which is in direct contrast to the wards the director took me into. When I entered the women's ward, I was immediately assaulted by the smell of feces and urine mixed with some sort of disinfectant that was obviously not doing its job. The entire place was filthy. Some of the walls were smeared with something, who knows what, brown or rust in color. I even observed handprints on some of the walls." Sullie's fingers clenched like a vise around mine, so I wiggled mine, and he relaxed his grip, glancing down at me briefly. His eyes were dark.

"The sounds in the ward were incessant. A low moan permeated throughout my entire stay there. Occasionally, a scream or sobs rose above it, but the moan was most present. At first I thought it was the ventilation system, but then I realized that it was the inmates themselves. It was sad for me as I fully believe that people need some silence in their lives in order to heal. Without it, one can go truly insane, I think. Anyway, that is a quick overview of the physical location."

A glass of water was placed on the podium, and Doctor Mitchell nodded and thanked the man who brought it for him. He drank deeply, nearly draining the glass before continuing, "Now, for the patients. The director took my colleague and me into two separate rooms where we each examined the women from Beaver County one at a time over the course of two days. I saw seven of them, my colleague saw five, and we went together to the room of one of the women who had been rendered incapacitated when a nurse administered an incorrect dosage of her medication about two years into her incarceration. To my knowledge there is nothing that can be done for her, unfortunately. My colleague and I agree with the Whispering Pines doctors in that she must remain where she is.

"About the other twelve women...what I noticed most and was most stunned at was that all of them had just received baths and had their hair washed and combed right before they came in to see me. When I conferred with my colleague, he said the same thing about his patients. We found it odd, and so did the patients, it seemed. They kept patting their hair and rubbing their hands on their faces and then looking at their hands as though they didn't recognize them. I came to the conclusion that they had not been bathed in a long, long while. One poor woman would not close her lips together. She just kept running her tongue over her teeth, eyes closed as she said 'mmm'." I felt Annie look over at me, but I could not meet her eyes, fearing I might shed the hot tears welling in my eyes. Instead, I tipped my chin toward the ceiling, willing the tears back.

"My colleague and I asked the women a series of predetermined questions which were mainly about their mental and physical health before they were convicted and sentenced to Whispering Pines. Then, we just visited with each woman for a while, making observations about her well-being. We then conferred about our findings before meeting with the Whispering Pines doctors.

"By the way, the doctors and nurses at the asylum are quite caring, professional people who are basically in a bad situation. The facility is managed by state officials who will not give them enough money to operate a clean, orderly health care facility. The state officials, according to the doctors and nurses I visited with, view the asylum as a dumping ground for disturbed prisoners and the incurably insane, and therefore think that any money put into the care of these people is a waste of funds. It is a sad state of affairs to say the least.

"When we sat down with the asylum director and doctors, they were quite cooperative and were, if not happy, then perhaps relieved, that we were assigned the task of helping to get these women released. Now, what I have to say next might shock a great many of you, as it did me." Doctor Mitchell took a deep breath and rubbed his face before continuing. "The director and doctors told my colleague and me that Beaver County might not be the only county to commit menopausal women to the asylum. Numerous other counties may have done so as well."

I froze. Annie grabbed my hand. The Justices squirmed and fidgeted with their pens and notebooks and eyeglasses. The spectators erupted into loud conversations, and the Chief Justice rapped his gavel and shouted for silence. When the courtroom settled again into relative quiet, he said, "You may continue Doctor Mitchell."

"Thank you, Your Honor. Naturally, I asked to see the women or at least read their files, but the asylum could not allow me to do that. A court order is needed for the other women to be examined. I beg of you to consider them and to issue such an order. I am willing to examine them if you are so inclined. Or feel free to assign another doctor to the task, but please, make the order."

The Justices looked at each other. Only the Chief Justice stared straight ahead at Doctor Mitchell who continued, "Now though, back to the Beaver County women. The director and the doctors at the asylum also feel the women are merely menopausal and will recover completely on their own if given time. A few of the women have already, I feel, gone completely through menopause and are one hundred percent well. That being said, though, my colleague and I reviewed the medical records on the women and feel the doctors there are doing a huge disservice to these women in that they are medicating them to keep them quiet and passive, almost to the point where the women are unconscious at times. Of course, on the days we were at the asylum, the women were given only partial doses of their medication and therefore were more alert for our visits.

"Anyway, my colleague, the asylum doctors, and I reviewed each patient's case individually and came up with the following recommendations. Keep in mind that for the sake of the women's privacy I cannot say their names here today; however, in the written report you Justices received, I did state the names. Okay, so on to our conclusions. The woman who was given the accidental overdose two years ago must remain in Whispering Pines since she is mentally and physically unable to care for herself. One other woman was deemed truly mentally ill and must also stay in Whispering Pines. The other eleven women should be released as soon as possible. The director assured me that if you order the women released, he will gladly comply and give the women instructions prior to their release about how to better live out their post-menopausal years.

"And so, those are our conclusions. I thank you all for allowing me the time to state my opinions, and I ask you to consider investigating other counties to determine if travesties of justice occurred in places other than Beaver County." Doctor Mitchell nodded to the Justices.

"Gentlemen, any questions for Doctor Mitchell before he sits down? Please, keep in mind that this trial is to determine the guilt or innocence of Mr. Charles Littman. Your questions at this time must be in regard to this case only. We will deal with the alleged misconduct in other counties later. Is that clear?" The Chief Justice asked, looking at his tablemates who nodded their white heads. "Again, do any of you have any questions for the doctor?" None of the Justices had questions, so the Chief Justice looked at Maxwell.

"Anything further, Mr. Heinz?" the Chief Justice asked.

"No, sir, we will rest for now," Maxwell replied.

The Chief Justice nodded curtly before he continued, "We will now hear from the respondent, please. Mr. Appleton, you are up."

The huge ball of navy blue rose to its feet with a grunt and walked a few feet to the podium and faced the Justices. "Your Honors, my client, Mr. Charles Littman--" He gestured toward the tiny man. "--is an upstanding citizen of Beaver County, and I am here as legal counsel to speak on his behalf. His credibility as an attorney has never before come into question, and he had absolutely no knowledge that he was doing anything wrong when he prosecuted the women who supposedly were unjustly sent to Whispering Pines. In fact, he was merely doing what was required of him in his position as County Attorney." The huge man barely moved as he spoke.

"As you well know, a County Attorney's job is to prosecute offenders once they are arrested, regardless of who they are. My client was only acting for the good of the community, as far as he knew. He was aware these women were arrested for acting insane and prosecuted them for being a danger to themselves or others." Appleton turned and smiled at Littman.

Appleton continued, "This case centers around a conversation which occurred in the Terrell barn, and my client has *never* been in that barn, has no idea what, if anything, was actually said in that barn about himself, and he has done nothing except his job, which is to prosecute offenders who are arrested in his county. As for Mr. Miller here--" Appleton gestured back toward Joshua. "--he is the one to blame for Rebecca's fate, not my client. It is his guilty conscience reaching out for someone else to blame for his own actions that brings him to this courtroom today. I hope you can see that Mr. Littman has done no wrong here and that you will act according to the law and vote that he retain his license to practice law in this state. That is all I have to say unless any of you have questions of me." The huge man smoothed his suit coat with a chubby hand.

The Chief Justice once again leaned forward, clasped his hands, and spoke, "Yes, as a matter of fact, I do have a question or two for Mr. Littman. Mr. Littman, please rise and come forward. I would like for you to answer the questions yourself."

I could not stop myself from watching as Littman slid off his chair and walked to the center of the room where the marshal swore him in. The disheveled little man held his chin up and his shoulders square as he stood next to his huge lawyer.

"Mr. Littman, the accusations against you are quite serious, and so I want to hear you answer them in your own words. Did you, or did you not, have knowledge that the fourteen women whose husbands had them arrested and who you prosecuted were being unjustly sent to the Montana State Insane Asylum, Whispering Pines?"

Littman's answer was a croak, hardly audible, "No, I did not, Your Honor," was all he said.

The Justice waited for more from the little man, but when no further reply came, his eyebrows raised and he continued, "I guess I need to ask if Mr. Appleton or you, Mr. Littman, have anything else to add to your argument?"

"No, Your Honor," Appleton said, and the two men shuffled to their seats.

"Mr. Heinz, you are entitled to a short rebuttal, if you wish to have one. Do you want rebuttal?"

Maxwell gave me a quick glance and rose from his chair in front of us. "Yes, I most certainly do," he said.

"Proceed, please."

"I would first like to address the conversation in the barn. The fact that Mr. Littman was not in the barn has no bearing on this case. What was said about his actions does. Mrs. Terrell overheard the men discussing Mr. Littman's involvement, and Mr. Miller's testimony supports what she heard. Also, I believe that each of you have received and read the court transcripts from Beaver County which clearly show Mr. Littman's involvement in prosecuting the fourteen women over the past four years, and if I may say so myself, that is an awfully high number of women to suddenly become insane in one small county in our state.

"Mr. Miller's testimony also helps substantiate the allegations against Mr. Littman. Mr. Miller was present in the courtroom when Littman, er- Mr.

Littman convicted his wife, having her sentenced to
Whispering Pines for the remainder of her life. Mr.
Littman knew full well what he was doing and that it
was unethical, if not illegal. He is the man who had
these women sent to Whispering Pines at the request of
their husbands. And as Doctor Mitchell so clearly
stated, thirteen of the women he sent away are perfectly
sane. They are in a normal, biological part of life called
menopause and should never have been sent to an
insane asylum. Mr. Littman is to blame for this, Your
Honors, and he broke ethical practice laws doing it.
Mr. Littman should never be allowed to practice law in
the state of Montana again!" And with that, a red-faced
Maxwell turned and strode to his seat, giving the
Justices a small bow before sitting down.

The Chief Justice cleared his throat and said,
"Now that the oral arguments have been stated and
heard, we Justices will confer about the case and will
draft an opinion. Each Justice has the right to revise it
according to his own individual opinion. This opinion
will then be filed with the Clerk of Courts and will be
released to the public at that time. One final note,
though, if I may." The Chief Justice looked to both
sides as the other justices nodded for him to continue.

"This case is unusual in a number of ways. Our
deciding to hear it at a time when we are not in session
is just one. I see its outcome affecting many, many
lives, which is of great concern to me, and because of
this, I would like to have a decision made and filed in a
timely manner. Let's say... no later than July twenty-
sixth. Is that acceptable to you other Justices? All in
agreement, please say 'aye.'"

The room echoed the "aye" response.

"All those opposed, please say 'nay.'"

Silence.

"And so it is. Our decision with regard to Mr. Littman's retaining his license to practice law in the state of Montana will be filed with the Court no later than July twenty-sixth.

"Now, with regard to the possibility of other Montana women being unlawfully committed to Whispering Pines. Let us take a vote. The question you will answer is, 'Should we initiate a complete investigation into all cases of women at Whispering Pines who are over the age of forty to determine if any of them were unlawfully incarcerated?' All in favor, please say 'aye.'"

All of the Justices responded. My heart jumped.

"All opposed, please say 'nay.'"

Silence.

"It is unanimous. I will write an order for the women at Whispering Pines over the age of forty to be examined by Doctor Mitchell and the colleague who assisted him with the Beaver County women. The women's files will be released to the doctors, too."

Whispers and shuffling ensued from behind and around us.

"Thank you, fellow Justices. I appreciate you taking your time to hear this case with me. Doctor Mitchell, Mrs. Terrell, Mr. Miller, Mr. Heinz, Mr. Littman, Mr. Appleton, we appreciate your being here, and you all will receive our opinion on the same day it is filed with the Court. We are adjourned." And with a resounding "whack" of his gavel, it was over. We rose for the Justices as they filed out as one rippling midnight storm cloud. I silently prayed that they would make the right decision for the poor souls unduly suffering in Whispering Pines.

Once the door closed behind them, the marshal announced that we all were dismissed. As I began to turn to follow Annie out, Sullie grabbed my arm and held it tightly so that I could not move. I looked up at him in confusion to see him staring above my head. It was then that I caught a glimpse of Littman and Appleton over Annie's shoulder as they walked out the short gate in the partition.

"Thank you, Sullie," was all I could get to come out of my mouth, which was suddenly filled with hot acidic saliva. I swallowed quickly.

When the back door thudded closed behind the two men, Sullie relinquished his grip, and we joined Annie and Maxwell in the aisle. They were chattering about the possibility of this being a more widespread problem than we originally thought.

Annie turned, touched my cheek, and said, "You did so good, Clara. I'm proud of you."

Sullie's face was tight and his eyes snapped as he said, "Lass, you did fine, just fine. I'm proud of you, too. Although hearing all of it aloud like that makes me furious. And to think women from other counties might be unduly sufferin' as well!"

"Yes, it makes me angry, too," I said. "But I'm thankful that we are here to do something to right this wrong. And it's not just me. I couldn't have done any of this without all three of you. Oh, and Joshua, too! Where is he, anyway?" I looked about for the thin cowboy but could see him nowhere.

"He left before anyone else, Clara. I am sure he was anxious to get out of here after telling his story," Maxwell said.

My heart fell. "What about Doctor Mitchell? Is he still here?" I looked around but did not see the tall doctor.

"I am sorry, Clara, but he left right away, too," Maxwell responded.

"Oh, I wanted to thank them both. I'll do that later, I guess. It's probably not a good idea to talk with them until after Valsted's hearing anyway." I turned to my friends and clapped my hands saying, "I know I've said it before, but I'm very lucky to have you in my court. No pun intended!" Our laughter bounced from wall to wall of this great, beautiful room where justice is dealt out, and I felt a peace like I have never felt before. I had done what I could do. Now, it was in the Justices' hands, and I had a feeling that they would do the right thing.

As we left the room, several news reporters asked us for our comments. Maxwell was commanding as he pushed us along, telling them, "No comment." This time, I was glad that the case was important enough to warrant widespread news reports. The more attention it drew, the better.

In the following weeks we remained in seclusion, knowing the threat of danger increased as the day of Valsted's hearing neared. We did keep up with the investigation into the other women incarcerated, perhaps unlawfully, at Whispering Pines. Once again, the wheels of justice turned painfully slow. It was disheartening, yet not surprising. I was delighted, though, to see how close Annie and Maxwell became during that time, their eyes twinkling like midnight stars over their flushed cheeks whenever they were together.

One afternoon, while Sullie was at his weekly visit to Maxwell's office, Annie looked up from the book she was reading and stated matter-of-factly, "I'm deeply in love with Maxwell." And with a loud sigh, she commenced reading. I started at her sudden proclamation, my eyes shooting from my book to study my friend. She was reclined and oozing off of a settee that had golden threads running through it. One pudgy finger toyed with her upper lip, which was upturned into a bit of a smile. She looked like a cat lying in the sun cleaning its whiskers after consuming a huge bowl of milk. She turned her blue eyes to me before lowering her lashes to her cheeks and her finger to the page.

"So, what do you think of that, my friend?" and she chuckled, chins jiggling on her chest.

"Well, I'm not surprised, if that's what you're asking."

"I am - surprised, I mean."

"Why? You and Maxwell are so well-matched, Annie. You've spent some really nice times together, and you both are so happy."

"I'm surprised that I'm able to love anyone at this stage of my life, I guess. It's just that this sort of happiness feels damned uncomfortable after living for so long without it. You know, it's kind of like a too-tight jacket on a cold day. It feels good because of its warmth, but the snugness of it is almost suffocating in a way."

"Please, don't feel like that, Annie. Just enjoy it for what it is. It's so good to see you happy."

"I don't have a choice, the way I see it. My heart is winning this one, I'm afraid. I mean, I'm not afraid, just a little apprehensive. I've been alone so long, and you know as well as I do that letting someone in like I've done with Max also allows that person to bring you pain."

My head bobbed and my reply was barely audible, "Yep. That I do know all about. I so loved Bob and look at the pain that he's caused me."

"I'm so sorry, Clara! What in the hell is the matter with me, bringing up a subject like that?" Annie's eyes rose to the ceiling as she huffed into an upright position.

"It's all right."

"No, it isn't, but I appreciate your being so understanding. Now, let's order supper, shall we? The love of my life and the lo-- and Sullie will be here any minute to eat."

I tried unsuccessfully to put her slip of the tongue out of my mind. A smile played at the edges of my heart, though.

CHAPTER 20

The morning of July second dawned sunny and warm, but as the day progressed, a heaviness came to the air, the temperature dropped dramatically, and clouds the color of weathered headstones lumbered in over the mountains on a strong western wind. Although it was a weekday, Maxwell took a rare day off and invited us to his place. Because of the storm coming in, he gave the guards the day off, telling them their families needed them more than we did. By late afternoon, we were tucked inside the parlor at Maxwell's house, the fireplace snapping while we sipped hot chocolate and nibbled gingersnaps. We were visiting, our voices fighting to be heard over the roaring wind and the echoing thunder. Our gazes were fixed on the rain that was not so much coming down as shooting across outside the glass door. Occasionally, we saw a thin tree branch wing by, illuminated by flashes of lightning, and once we all gasped as a small bird fought and lost its battle against the wind, sailing off to who knew where. Despite the gloom, we were in good spirits.

We started a bit, though, when William, Maxwell's butler, appeared seemingly from nowhere and cleared his throat from the doorway. "Mr. Heinz, excuse me for interrupting, but you have a visitor. A Mr. Robert Terrell is at the front door. Will you see him?"

My blood froze at Bob's name, and I went numb. He was here? Now? Oh, Lord! This will not be good. My mind raced, but my body was frozen. The cookie I held fell onto my lap. I stared, mouth agape at William.

Annie gasped and looked from Maxwell to Sullie to William. "Maxwell, do not allow that drunken hooligan into your house! The guards aren't even here! Why, the nerve of that man to come here--" Her voice came to me muddled in with Sullie's. A hammer slammed into the side of my head.

"Max, this chap's dangerous, especially when he's drunk. It's your call, though, since it's your house," Sullie said.

Maxwell was the only one of us that seemed calm. He glanced around the room before fixing his eyes on William. "Does the man appear inebriated?"

"No, sir, he does not appear to have been drinking."

Maxwell rose to his feet and looked at each of us, saying, "This is actually no surprise to me. I have had a feeling ever since the news broke that Mr. Terrell would come to confront us. I do not know the man, but from what I have heard you tell of him, he does not seem the type to run from conflict."

"You're right. He's not," I said, wringing my hands.

Maxwell continued, "Nor does he seem the type to sit idly by while his wife causes upheaval among his newly found upper crust friends.

"Again, you're right," I said.

"I really see no reason to send him away. He cannot harm us with this many men in the house, guards or no guards, and he probably just wants an argument. Actually, I think it would be best to get this conversation over with. He is sober right now. If I send him away, chances are he will get drunk, and then he will be dangerous, and I cannot stand for that. What do you all think?"

Sullie and Annie were silent.

"I'd just as soon get this over with now as have to worry about him coming to us without warning later. It's bad enough that we have to worry about Valsted," I said and Annie and Sullie finally nodded.

"Okay. William, see Mr. Terrell in. And then remain near the parlor door, please, in case you are needed."

As William showed Bob into the room, we all stood. Somehow, my quaking legs lifted me, the gingersnap shattering at my feet. I took deep, ragged breaths until I felt the warmth of Annie's arm around my waist. Then, I was able to look at Bob. His clothes were clean, yet dripping, his white shirt plastered against his chest and rumpled where black suspenders pressed into it. I did not recognize the brown pants and wondered how he had afforded a new pair. He wore these new pants on the outside of his worn, mud-smeared boots, which I thought was odd since he always wore his pants tucked inside his boots. He had left a trail of wet from the door to where he stood.

Finally, he removed his sweat-ringed hat and handed it, dripping, to William who held it as though it were a flea-ridden kitten and left. Bob appeared calm yet tense, as a snake does right before it strikes. My stomach churned and my breath caught in my chest. I turned my face into Annie who held me tightly.

216

Bob's voice was far too loud, echoing off the walls. "Clara, Sweet Pea. I've come all this way, and you won't even look at me. Please, my Sweet, look at me." And so I did, surprised at the softness in his voice and at the endearment that he had not used for years. That is when I noticed that despite his soft words, his eyes were dark pits of soul-less nothing. A quiver went through me and every hair on my body stood on end. For some reason, the vision of Sullie placing his gun in the desk drawer in our suite came to mind. He did not bring it with him today for some reason. Hopefully, we would have no need of it anyway.

"Please, Bob..." my voice mirrored the helpless fright that possessed me.

"Are you all right?" It was Sullie's strong, deep voice that snatched the childlike fear from me.

"N-no. I'm not all right," I said, still staring into this stranger's eyes.

"Would you like to leave?" Sullie asked.

Bob's eyes flicked from me to Sullie, who stood a little to my left, and then back to me, and I saw the red anger begin in their depths.

"Yeah, Clara. Would you like to leave? And I mean with *me*, or have you all forgotten that this here's *my wife?*" Bob was pacing around the room in front of us now, waving his arms and keeping his fiery eyes only on me.

"No. I don't want to leave. Let's get this over and done with right now. And Bob," I said, unable to believe the strength that suddenly came over me, "I am absolutely not going anywhere with you. You betrayed me. You showed me just how much you hate me the night you beat me nearly to de--"

Bob's loud laughter cut off my words. "I betrayed you? Really? Oh my God, woman! How stupid of a bitch are you anyways? I betrayed you! How funny is that! Coming from you, a whore who ran away from home to come here to be with, with---" He stopped his pacing only a foot from me and waved his hand at Sullie and then at Maxwell. "Well, just take your pick! I suppose either of these assholes will do for you, since you're nothin' but a whore anyway!" His eyes bulged out from his now-purple face, lips curled back from yellow teeth. His hot breath rained down on me, the odor of stale booze and yesterday's onions making my stomach lurch.

Sullie took a step toward Bob, his right arm outstretched in front of Annie and me. "That's no way to speak to a lady."

Bob whirled at Sullie and shrieked, "A lady? Why, you are a dumb one, ain't ya? A lady! Ha! You have no idea what this whore is capable of!" Sullie tensed and his fingers curled into a fist. I feared a fight would ensue, but with amazing self-restraint Sullie loosened his shoulders and allowed his fists to fall to his sides.

Then, Bob's attention was on me again. Annie's arm tightened around me, and my senses were heightened. From over Bob's shoulder, I noticed Maxwell had moved almost imperceptibly to a desk that sat near the fireplace that was behind Bob. It appeared he was taking something from an open drawer. My attention, though, was on Bob, who had now moved away from me and was pacing and waving his arms like a duck trying to take flight as he screamed at us.

"And you!" Bob ranted, stomping toward Sullie and pointing his finger in his face. "You must be Sullie," sarcasm dripped from his snarling lips. "How dare you take my wife from me! I'll see you rot in hell before I let you have her, I'm tellin' you all right now! There's no damned way any of you are gonna have her! I'd rather kill you all right now than let either one of you go pokin' around on my wife!" I spared Sullie a quick glance, noticing the clenched fists were back and a knot of muscle jumped in his jaw. His eyes stared darkly at the lunatic in front of him.

Then, in one quick movement, Bob stooped down, raised his pant leg, and pulled a pistol out of his boot. I grabbed for Annie's arm as Bob raised the gun, pointing it right at my chest. The shot deafened me, and everything came to me slowly, as though I was under water. People weren't supposed to hear anything when they were shot. Were they? But, I heard it. How odd. Why was I still standing? Maybe Annie was holding my body up all on her own. A strong smell, like a chemical of some sort, filled my nose. My body. I held out my hands and looked down, searching for the blood that certainly would be on my chest. There was none. I pulled away from Annie and looked at her. Same thing. No blood. Sullie appeared to be moving through sand toward Annie and me, his arms outstretched and his lips saying something I could not hear. The cords in his neck created long bulging lines from his collar to his chin. Fear filled his eyes as they met mine and then moved to Bob.

My eyes followed Sullie's, and that was when I saw it. A deep red stain seeping through Bob's pristine white shirt. How strange. Then, reality came bursting in as though someone had opened the parlor door to let in the storm. Everything sped up. William rushed toward Maxwell. Sullie ran toward Annie and me. Thomas, Maxwell's other houseman, slid to a stop just inside the door, his face registering panic. Still, I could hear nothing.

Bob's gun bounced and slid a ways when it hit the floor. My eyes flew to Bob just as he looked up from his wound. He grabbed his chest and his side and fell to the floor on his back. His head turned and his eyes met mine. His lips formed "Sweet Pea."

A silent scream scraped from my throat, and in one strong motion, I ran to my husband, falling to my knees and cradling his head in my lap. My hands caressed his face and then moved to his side and chest, attempting to stop the blood flowing from him. Hot tears covered my face and neck, and I felt Bob's life hot on my legs as it seeped through my skirt. His fading eyes were on me, and I saw then the love in them, the deeply felt intimate love that I had not seen for years. I yanked my handkerchief out of my sleeve and wiped furiously at the pink foam coming from his mouth, which only managed to smear it grotesquely across his cheek, so I dropped it on his chest and touched his face as the pink turned a deep crimson. A thick liquid.

My hearing came back suddenly and I heard myself say, "I loved you so much, Bob." Gurgling was the only reply. Then, a large red bubble came from his mouth, and the dim loss of life crept into his eyes. I pulled his head to my chest and heard animalistic wails coming from me.

Suddenly, Sullie was beside me, pulling me gently away from Bob, his soft coos and whispers coming through the fog, "Shh, lassie, shh. It's okay now. It'll be all right. Come back to me. Here, put your arms about me. He's gone now. Shh. That's it, that's it." He brought me to his chest, arranging my limp arms and hands around his hips as he sat on the floor gently rocking me, Bob's blood transferring onto his clothes.

Annie's voice came to me as though from far away, "William, go telephone the police. Get them out here right away. Thomas, get over here and help me tend Maxwell!" She knelt next to Maxwell who had sunk to the floor beside the desk. He was nearly translucent, whitish-gray, and trembling like a newborn foal. His vacant eyes stared at Bob. A very large pistol lay next to his limp right hand, and one thought came to me with a rush that made my breath stop for a moment. It settled in my head and all of my frazzled thoughts lined themselves up around it: Maxwell killed Bob.

My head shot up from Sullie's chest, and I struggled to pull myself upright and out of his grip, but he held me tightly to him, saying, "No, Clara. Just stay right here. Right here where it's safe."

"No! Let me go!" I struggled against him, pummeling him with my fists until he stilled them in one of his huge hands. The other pulled my head back to his chest.

Thomas and Annie got Maxwell to his feet and over to the sofa. Annie tried to comfort him, telling him that everything would be okay. That he had done the only thing he could do. That he had saved all of us. That it was in self-defense. That he had done nothing wrong. Maxwell just stared vacantly at Bob.

William came into the room with a rush saying the police would be here at any moment. Always efficient and attentive to his boss, he took a blanket from the back of a chair and gently placed it over Maxwell, vigorously rubbing life back into his arms. Annie began caressing Maxwell's cheeks and she said softly, "Honey, Max, I'm here. I'm here. Hey, look at me. Look here at me. Please…." She choked on the words, tears streaming down her round cheeks. These were the things that brought Maxwell back to us. His eyes flickered away from Bob for an instant and settled on Annie, slowly focusing on her. He slowly raised one hand and brushed it against her wet cheek. She grabbed it and pulled it against her bosom, saying, "Oh, yes! That's it, my Max. That's it! You're okay now. Just breathe. Take a deep breath. That's it." Her cooing to him and Sullie's caressing my head and shoulder continued until the police arrived.

There were two of them. They came in the parlor with a rush of cold air, their knee-length wool uniform coats dripping water. When I noticed their drawn pistols, I screamed and pushed my face into Sullie's chest.

"Put those damned things away, you idiots!" Sullie exclaimed. "Can't you see you're frightenin' these people?" His entire body tensed as he pulled us both to our feet. My legs, though, were too limp to hold me, so his strong arms swept me up and placed me into a nearby chair. Somehow, I managed to hold myself upright. I stared silently at the activity unfolding like some macabre play on a stage in front of me.

Sullie directed the show, standing with the policemen explaining what had transpired, gesturing to Bob and then to Maxwell and then to me and then to the two guns lying on the floor, one in a pool of blood that was congealing around the edges of an egg shape that was broken only by my husband's lifeless body. I sucked in my breath and tore my eyes from it. Every few seconds, Sullie pulled his fingers through his hair and swiped his hands down his face. He shifted uncomfortably from one foot to the other, and I knew he wanted to pace yet was unable to do so. Both policemen nodded and muttered softly to each other and to Sullie, who nodded his head occasionally.

Finally, they spoke loudly enough that I could hear them.

The older of the two officers wrung his hands and said, "Okay, first of all, we need to get the room cleared so we can investigate and verify what you've told us, Mr. Sullivan. William, Thomas, will you please escort the ladies from the room? Make them comfortable somewhere else."

Thomas came and helped me from my seat and led me out of the room. In the foyer, the front door burst open with a wet cold gust and blew in a frail little man wearing a wool coat that hung nearly to the floor. He also wore a frown that creased his entire face with worry. His eyes shifted around the foyer. Behind him was a very tall young man carrying a folded up stretcher.

Thomas pointed to the parlor door and said briskly, "In there." He then guided me gently into the kitchen which was warm and filled with the scent of freshly baked bread and seated me at the table. William did the same for Annie. William brought a basin of warm, soapy water and gently wiped my husband's dried blood and my wet tears from my face before he submerged my hands in the basin, caressing them and turning the water deep red. Thomas prepared fragrant cups of tea, and when he placed them in front of us, his hands shook so badly that I feared the cups would shatter on their saucers. I could do nothing but stare into mine. Annie, too, was uncharacteristically silent.

Finally, I found my voice. "Who were those two men we just met?"

"I'm sorry, ma'am. That was the coroner and his assistant. They've come to take your, err-, Mr. Terrell's body away to the morgue." Thomas's voice trailed off and I felt dark, thick silence fall like a woolen cape over me. The three of us sat in silent reverie, listening to hushed voices and distant footsteps as people moved in and out of the parlor.

CHAPTER 21

The storm had blown itself out and night had fallen into a cloudy disarray by the time the older policeman came to us in the kitchen and asked each of us to describe what happened in the parlor. Thankfully, he began with Annie, who was capable of forming complete sentences and managed to tell in great detail all that she had seen. The officer scribbled her statement on his notepad, looking up periodically to ask her a clarifying question.

When Annie finished, he turned to me with a grim face, expressed his condolences, and asked if I had anything to add. I managed to shake my head no.

"I appreciate your help in this, and again, my condolences to you. I feel terrible that you had to bear witness to such a tragedy. I really do." And with that, he closed his notebook, put his pen in his front shirt pocket, and stood to leave. Thomas stood as well and showed the man out before he returned, his hand on Maxwell's back. Maxwell was a pale gray shadow, his eyes on the floor. Sullie came in behind them.

Annie ran to Maxwell's side, brushed Thomas's hand away, and asked, "How are you, my dearest? Please, speak to me."

Maxwell finally looked up at Annie and said, "I will be all right. Do not worry. Okay?"

"Ha! Fat chance of that happening!" Annie said, guiding Maxwell into a chair and sitting in the one next to him that Sullie had pulled out for her. "What's happening, Sullie? What's going to happen to Max?"

Sullie sat next to me and said, "As you know already," his blue eyes dark with concern bored into mine, "Bob is gone. Passed away."

I bit my lower lip hard as I tried to quell my tears. When that did not help, I tipped my head back and stared at the ceiling. The tears ran down the sides of my face anyway, soaking the collar of my blood-stained blouse.

"Yeah, we know that. Now, what's going to happen to Max?" Annie's voice shook with emotion.

Sullie drew in a deep, ragged breath and answered, "The officers telephoned the chief of police, and he told them that because their investigation showed that Max acted in self-defense, well, in the defense of himself and others in his home, probably nothing will happen to Max."

"Oh, thank God! That's the best –" Annie exclaimed, patting Maxwell's arm.

"Don't get ahead of me, lass. I said 'probably.' He still could be charged with, well...with murder." Annie gasped and my eyes flew to Sullie. He appeared surprisingly calm, only raking his fingers through his hair every now and then. "But," he continued, "That's highly unlikely. The police chief just needs to explain what happened to the district attorney to make sure no charges need to be filed."

"I see." Annie shrank back in her chair.

"We'll know tomorrow for sure. There's nothin' to do now but try to rest some before mornin'."

"You will stay here, won't you?" Thomas's voice was quiet and strong.

Annie answered, "Yes. Thank you. Sullie, you and Clara can go if you want, but I'm staying. I won't leave Max right now."

"Clara, what would you like to do? Stay or go? It's completely up to you, lass."

Somehow I found my voice. "We can stay, Sullie. If it's okay with Maxwell, that is." I looked over at the rumpled little man who had killed my husband and something stirred in me when his bulging eyes found mine, and I saw my sorrow reflected in them.

"You are all most welcome to stay here, and Thomas, please get Mrs. Terrell clean sleeping attire and have her clothing cleaned before morning," Maxwell said quietly.

When I looked at Bob's blood caked on the front of my clothes, I was overcome with the need to get the clothing off, so I was grateful that William and Thomas showed Sullie and me quickly to our rooms upstairs. We left Annie and Maxwell quietly talking in the kitchen, and I knew that is where they would be all night.

I allowed my feelings free rein as I lay on the bed in the clean nightshirt Thomas brought me, and images tumbled around in my mind. I closed my eyes as I went through the years of my marriage, and somehow the good times came clearest to me. The high-pitched giggles of my boys swirling with Bob's low chuckle as he led them around the yard on our old horse...more laughter, this time from the kitchen as I lay in bed, pretending to sleep as they all made me breakfast in bed one Mothers' Day -- all of which was charred by the time they were finished -- which made it all the funnier...Bob's sinewy arms and strong, calloused hands holding baby Julia, rocking her in that old chair, his face etched with concern as she gasped in her sleep...Bob's face relaxed and tender above me as I lay beneath him, loving him with all I had.

The negative events came at me then, thick with emotion: the fear when Bob was raging at me, his face purple and his eyes bulging; the physical pain of Bob's hand striking me and even worse, the emotional pain of knowing he couldn't love me and beat me like that; the emptiness of losing Julia; the longing that remained after each of my sons had ridden away to begin their lives elsewhere.

Hot anger rode on the shoulders of these events and pounced on me. Anger at Bob for being, as Annie would say, a "stinking bastard." Anger at God for taking my world away from me. Anger at Valsted. Anger at Littman. Anger at myself for being so stupid as to love and trust Bob when I should have known better. Anger, too, at Maxwell for allowing Bob into his house. Anger, anger, anger.

I tried to keep it at bay by concentrating on more practical concerns such as now that neither Bob nor I was at home, there was no one to care for Champ and the other animals. My heart was heavy with concern for them. Suddenly, my eyes flew open as a new problem presented itself. Somehow, I had to tell my boys about their dad's death. I lay through much of the night sorting out these feelings and problems. Worry, worry, worry, and more anger. At one point I screamed so loudly and for so long into my pillow that I thought I was going to pass out.

That is when I began to pray. I prayed for strength, and my favorite Bible verse came to me,

"I can do all things through Christ who strengthens me" - Philippians 4:13. I felt His arms around me as He quieted my mind enough to allow me to sleep.

The next morning, Annie was coming up the stairs as I came out of my room, and her cheeks flushed as she rushed to me, soft arms engulfing me. When she relaxed her hold, we pressed our foreheads together. The heavenly vanilla scent of her rushed through me as she asked, "Tell me. How are you?"

Taking a deep breath, I said, "I'm okay, I think. I felt so angry last night but now I am just confused and worried. My heart is aching some at the loss of Bob, too. It's odd that I'd feel this way, seeing as how he was not a good man at the end."

"You feel whatever it is that you need to and don't ever feel bad about those feelings. Really, we have no control over them, and you had a lot of good years with that man, too. Those can't be ignored." Annie pulled back and I saw concern darken her eyes. "But, if I may say so, he was certainly no prize as a husband to you. I do understand, though, and will be right here for you. You can talk about anything with me. You know that, don't you? The good or the bad."

I could only give a short nod as my throat tightened around a big knot.

"Now, let's go downstairs."

The storm left a mess of branches and debris on Maxwell's grounds. Men were there cleaning it up by the time Annie and I came into the kitchen. I was pleased to see that some color had returned to Maxwell and surprised when he asked me to join him in the dining room.

"Clara, I just want you to know how sorry I am about Bob. I hope you can understand –" Maxwell's cheeks flushed and he wrung his hands together.

"You don't have to –" I interrupted.

"Yes. I feel I do have to explain." He said, taking a deep breath before he looked into my eyes. "I hope you know that I did what I had to do in order to protect all of us. I regret even allowing Bob into the house, but I felt it best to let the man say his piece while Sullie and I were with you and Annie. You know, to make sure you were safe. I had no idea that he would go so far…." Maxwell's eyes became glossy with the remembering.

"I know. And I understand, Maxwell. I thought long and hard about it last night and know that it was Bob's fault, not yours. Let's just let it be what it is." I patted his arm and his eyes returned to mine. "And thank you for saving us. I wish it had never happened, too, but it did. We must accept it. Okay?"

"You are right. And thank you for understanding. There is one more thing, though," he said.

"What is it?" I asked.

"Well, your sons need to be told about what happened, and I hope I am not overstepping boundaries here, but feel free to use my telephone to call them. I know the calls will not be easy, and it might be best if we all are with you when you make them." My admiration of this little man grew even more.

"Thank you," I said, staring at the lace tablecloth. "I've been worried about telling them. You know that they're not too fond of me right now anyway, and I'm sure this will upset them even more."

"I think it best to get those calls done right away then," Maxwell said.

I rose, too, and we joined Annie and Sullie in the kitchen where shortly after, I made the call to Robby. I told him what happened and informed him that I would arrange to have Bob taken back to Bergen for burial. He was furious. At me. At Maxwell. At the world, I think. Even though I tried to explain, he was not accepting anything I had to say, so I took as much of his verbal abuse as I could handle before hanging up. Lucas and Peter did not have telephones, so I called my contacts for them: the general store in town for Luke and Pete's neighbor. These calls were a bit easier for me; however, my heart ached knowing how difficult the news would be for my sons. I left the hotel's number in case the boys wanted to contact me, but in my mind I knew that was unlikely. They would turn to each other in their grief. I would be the cause of the grief and thus the target of their anger, just as I was for Robby.

Once I finished the calls, Sullie rubbed my arm and Annie cooed to me as hot tears plopped into my lap, creating perfectly round spots on my skirt. Finally, I recovered as best I could and wiped my face.

A short while later, the telephone rang, and I nearly jumped up to answer it thinking it was one of my sons. It was not. Instead, Maxwell took the call that told him his fate. Silence filled the room and we stared at him until he hung up the receiver.

Annie went quickly to Maxwell's side, asking for the news.

Maxwell looked at all of us and sank heavily into the chair next to Sullie. "Well, it is good news."

"Oh, thank God!" Annie exclaimed as she perched on the edge of a chair. "Go on, dear. Tell us what he said."

"The District Attorney looked over our statements and the statements made by the officers, and he decided no charges are to be brought against me. I acted in self-defense and in defense of you all." He blew out a long breath.

Sullie pulled a hand through his hair and rubbed his face. "That's just great, Max. I'm happy and relieved about it." And so was I.

Shortly after the barrage of telephone calls, Annie, Sullie, and I went back to town. Helena was readying itself for a huge Independence Day celebration. Buildings were draped in red, white, and blue bunting. White canvas tents of all sizes had taken up residence in the parks and on the capitol grounds and waited to be filled with vendors and their wares. Flags were everywhere. People scurried about buying groceries and decorations for their houses since all of the stores would be closed the next day.

We picked up our guard for the day at his house and drove to the hotel which had been transformed into a display of patriotism. As we entered the front door, it was obvious that the hotel personnel knew what had transpired as they all avoided eye contact with us when we came in. Not even Mr. Kershaw, the porter, looked directly at us. News like a murder spreads quickly in a town the size of Helena.

The Fourth of July festivities went on without us. It was the first I could remember not having celebrated. I was uncomfortable just sitting in our suite listening as waves of laughter, conversation, and music came to me from the open windows, but none of us wanted to join in.

The next day I asked Sullie for advice about how to get care for the animals back home. His blue eyes darkened and his thick eyebrows created two vertical creases between them before he said with a low, soft voice, "Now, sweetheart," I started a little at the endearing term he used. "To calm your nerves, I'll tell you somethin' but you have to promise not to be mad at me. Okay?" I nodded and stared at him, his face so strong and comforting. "You see, well, I took the liberty of taking care of all that for you. At least while we're gone. My assistant, Patrick, always had a wee bit of the farmer in him, so I telephoned him the day before yesterday, and he agreed to go out to your home place every day until you get back and take good care of everything for you, so no worries."

My eyes widened. "But –," I said.

"No 'buts.' He's agreed to do it, and gladly, too."

I took a deep breath and nodded. Sullie took my hands and looked into my eyes. "There's somethin' else, too." He squeezed my hands. "I arranged for Bob to be taken back to Bergen."

A spark of anger flared in my belly. I tensed and pulled away, but Sullie gripped my hands tighter. "You had no—" Quickly, I suppressed my anger. This kind, generous man was doing me favors, taking care of me, and I was going to rebuke him for it? Now, that would be nearing insanity.

"Please, don't be angry. I just wanted – " Sullie said. I relaxed and smiled up at him.

"Don't be silly. How could I be angry at such kindness, Sullie?"

"Good. So Patrick will handle everything in Bergen for you and your sons, you know, with Bob." He squeezed my hands again. "Is that okay?"

"Yes, it's fine. I just hope all this doesn't inconvenience Patrick too much."

"I talked to him yesterday, and he's having a great time, especially with Champ. He's bonded a bit with that pup, I'm afraid. And he never passes up a chance to do a kindness for someone. He's happy to do it."

"Thank you, Sullie, and please tell Patrick how grateful I am to him, too, the next time you visit with him."

"I'll do that," Sullie smiled and patted my hand.

My heart lightened with the knowledge that this kind, dear man cared enough for me to take care of my worries before I even expressed them. It was a strange and yet welcome feeling. Warm and comforting.

CHAPTER 22

Again, we settled into our seclusion, a guard ever-present at our door. We were safe, yet I felt like a prisoner. Time passed so slowly.

Then, on July twenty-fifth, Maxwell and Sullie burst into our suite, breathless and flushed. Annie dropped her book, and I sloshed a little tea from my cup. I blotted it with my handkerchief as Sullie shouted, "Lassies! You'll never guess what we've just heard!"

"Yes, guess what?" Maxwell said around a smile.

"Well, out with it, you two. We certainly have no idea what you're so excited about," Annie said.

"It is a day early, but we just heard that the Supreme Court Justices filed their opinion today. A day early, can you believe that?" Maxwell was fairly shouting, and I set my teacup down so roughly it is surprising it did not break. My heart was in my throat as I sprang to my feet.

"What did they say?" I asked excitedly.

"The opinion states that Littman is disbarred! He can no longer practice law in this state!" Sullie said. "And, Joshua Miller isn't culpable in any way for sendin' Rebecca away since he was unduly influenced by Valsted. You did it, Clara lass, you did it!" Sullie pulled me into his strong arms, crushing my arms to my sides and my face to the side. His deep laugh vibrated against my cheek, and suddenly I was freed only to have Maxwell's and Annie's arms come tightly around me. We were all jumping up and down, grinning like a bunch of schoolchildren during recess. Our exuberance lasted only three days.

It was about noon. I was so tired of being locked up in our suite that when Annie suggested we go out to lunch and then to the laundry to pick up our clothes rather than having them delivered, my heart jumped in excitement. I begged Sullie to let us go. Finally, he agreed, against his better judgment and only if he went with us. So off we went, our guard following close behind.

We ate a delightful lunch at a café two blocks from the hotel and chatted happily as we left. Annie's hands flapped as she talked nearly nonstop, Sullie's face creased deeply as he smiled, and my spirit was lightened. We had walked about half a block when suddenly Sullie stopped, halting Annie and me with his arm.

"What the —" Annie said as she dropped her hands.

"Look, just look over there," Sullie said. His brow furrowed as he nodded his head in the direction he stared.

"Oh, my God!" Annie exclaimed with wide eyes.

"It's Valsted and Belzer," Sullie said in a low voice.

Then, I saw them. My hands flew to my mouth and my eyes widened. Across the street, two huge men in dark suits stood facing us. Judge Valsted sneered. I could not make out Doctor Belzer's expression since his hat was pulled low over his face.

"Lasses, don't be alarmed. Of course they're here since Valsted's hearing is less than a week away. I'm sure Belzer is here to support his good buddy."

Annie glared across the street and said, "Well, I don't like it one bit."

"Maybe Doctor Belzer is here because Doctor Mitchell started the proceedings against him. You know, with the state medical board. Maybe he's here to defend himself. Oh, I hope that's it," I speculated.

"I hope so, too, lassie. At any rate, they have every right to be here on the street."

"Sullie, don't be so damned naive. It's no coincidence that they're over there just as we're coming out of the café," Annie said. "Brutes!" She shouted and shook her fist at them. The people around us gaped at her and moved quickly on their way.

"Annie! Don't provoke them!" I pulled her fist down as Sullie called for our guard. The man was nowhere in sight.

"Where is that guard?" Sullie said as he pulled us back toward the café.

"Yoo-hoo! Mrs. Terrell – oh, Clara! Look what I have for you!" Valsted cupped his left hand over his mouth as he called across the street in a falsetto voice at me. I stopped, pulled my arm from Sullie's grip, and looked at the two men again. As I did, Valsted pulled his suit jacket to the side and revealed a pistol. He gestured with his left hand making his threat clear. A woman walking near Valsted screamed at the sight of the gun, and all of the pedestrians scampered away, disappearing into shops and restaurants.

Lightning quick, Sullie leapt between us and the street, shielding Annie and me from the two men.

"Come on!" He cried, pushing us toward the café and calling for the guard who finally appeared in the doorway, laughing at something someone inside had said. His face fell and grew taut at the sight of us.

"What is it, Mr. Sullivan?" He asked, drawing his pistol and looking wildly around us.

"There –" Sullie pointed across the street. At no one. Valsted and Belzer had disappeared. "They were just there!" Sullie panted.

"Who?" The guard asked, scanning the street with trained eyes.

"Valsted and Belzer. They were just there. Now, they're gone. We've got to get these lasses back to the hotel. Quickly! You, though, keep your eyes open for two large men in dark suits. One of them is armed and threatened Clara!" Sullie's long strides forced Annie and me to run back to the hotel, our skirts flying. Our heads twisted from side to side as we looked for the two men. Mr. Kershaw saw us coming and rushed out to help.

"What is it, Mrs. Hazelton?" He asked, taking Annie from Sullie and leading her into the hotel lobby. The guard, Sullie, and I were right behind them.

"Thank goodness we made it back here, Mr. Kershaw. Why, the most terrible thing just happened!" Annie then told the porter about Valsted and his weapon.

"You have nothing to fear in here, though. Not while I'm on watch," Mr. Kershaw said, his mouth a tense line and his face flushed.

Sullie paced and pulled his hand through his hair. "What the hell were you doing, man?" he said to the guard.

"I was –" The man was pale and pulling on his jacket as he looked at us. "Well, I was visiting with a friend in the café."

"Visiting! That's unacceptable! You were hired to –" Sullie towered over him with a finger in his chest.

"I know, and I'm terribly sorry, sir. I really am!" The man backed up and was nearly in tears.

Sullie began shouting orders, his accent thick. "Mr. Kershaw, you and this fella," he pointed at the guard, "get these lasses up to the suite. I'm callin' Max to tell him what's happened. I'll be up there straightaway, lasses." He stalked to the lobby desk and demanded the clerk dial Maxwell's office as Annie and I were briskly escorted up to the suite.

The guard stayed beside the door, and Mr. Kershaw stayed with Annie and me. As adrenalin fought to loosen itself, I began shaking and my head pounded. Darkness played with bright spots of light at the edges of my vision, but I could not stop pacing and wringing my hands. Annie sat heavily on the settee and wiped at the sheen of sweat on her face.

"Are you all right?" she asked.

I shook my head. Honestly, how could I be all right?

"Of course you're not. Silly me," she said, popping to her feet and grabbing my arms to still me.

"My head…" I reached for my temple and Annie released me, running for my medicine. Mr. Kershaw took my arm and gently placed me in a chair where I gratefully took some of the medication from Annie who was nervously babbling. I could not make out her words.

239

Finally, Sullie arrived, released Mr. Kershaw, and sat in a chair opposite me with his hands clenched between his knees. The medicine dulled the hammers some and I was grateful. "Max is calling the police to see what can be done about those two and then he will come right over."

"Will he be safe, Sullie?" Annie asked frantically.

"Yes, lass." Sullie said, reaching over to pat her hand. "He'll be extra cautious, and he has his bodyguard with him. A more capable fella than that imbecile we've got out there!" Sullie's head jerked toward the door.

Awhile later, we all stood as Maxwell's loud voice came from the hallway. He shouted at the guard, threatening to fire him. Every so often, the guard murmured what I assumed was an apology. Sullie frowned, ran a hand through his hair, and went to join them. Maxwell must have turned on Sullie.

"Damn it, Sullie!" he screamed. "I trusted you to keep her safe and look what has happened!" My eyes flew to Annie who was frozen, staring at the door with her mouth open.

"I had no way of knowin' they were in town, Max. I know I should've been more cautious and I'm sorry."

"Sorry? You are sorry? She could have been killed! Clara, too!" Annie started for the door, but I stopped her with a short shake of my head. "And I suppose you did not even have your gun with you," Maxwell accused.

"Now, just you hold on there. I did the best I could and yes, I did have my gun, but I didn't draw it for fear it would've provoked Valsted into actually drawing. Not to –"

"A gun is only good if you are willing to take it out when it is needed, Sullie."

"--Not to mention the fact that there were quite a few people around that could've been hurt or killed if we started firing. You would've done the same thing I did. And what I did got the lasses back here safe and sound." It was silent for a moment except for the thudding in my head. I drew a deep breath and let it out.

Maxwell's voice was calmer and softer. "I lost my head there, Sullie, and I am sorry. I did not mean to chastise you so."

"I understand. The tension's got us all on edge lately. That's why we went out today in the first place. We just needed some relief. I hope you can understand that."

"I do. I do not like it, but it happened and thankfully no one was harmed. Now, you stay right here and actually *guard* this hallway. Do you understand?" There was a mumble as the door opened, and Sullie and Maxwell entered. Rumpled and red-faced, Maxwell stalked to Annie and held her at arm's length looking her up and down.

"Are you all right, my dear?" he asked.

"I think so. Just scared half to death is all," she said and broke down. Maxwell took her in his arms as best he could, cooing to her and rubbing her back. Her tears made wet circles on the shoulder of his suit coat.

Sullie stood beside me, his hands in his trouser pockets, his face grim.

Once Annie was calm, Maxwell told us that he had telephoned the police. A few other people had called before Maxwell did, so they took the complaint seriously. They promised to send officers to warn Valsted to stay away from us and the hotel and to have officers make regular passes by the hotel, but other than that, there was nothing they could do since no one was harmed. Valsted had just threatened me. Our voices created a cacophony at the injustice of it, but in the end, there was nothing we could do but be extra cautious from now on. Annie and I would go nowhere until Valsted's hearing. Sullie would no longer go to Maxwell's office. Instead, he would remain with us in the guarded suite at all times. The two men decided not to fire the guard. He just had a lapse in judgment and now that he realized just how serious our situation was, he more than likely would be even more alert.

Although Valsted's hearing was less than a week away, it seemed like forever. Each day stretched out before me and was the same as the last. Tension and boredom frayed my nerves. It was a long few days.

CHAPTER 23

Finally, the day arrived. That morning, the morning of Valsted's hearing with the Judicial Standards Commission, I rose early having slept little the night before. My trepidation dissipated once I had prayed and readied myself for the day, taking deep breaths. Annie had ordered a stunning summer-weight suit in a creamy yellow delivered for me to wear to the hearing, and as I looked at myself in the mirror, I could not believe my own reflection. Was that slender woman with such strength emanating from her body and eyes really me? Could I have transformed into such a woman in so short a time?

My shoulders straight and my head light, I walked into the living area of our suite where Annie, Maxwell, and Sullie waited. The two men gaped at me, and Annie's eyes shone with unshed tears. "Oh, my goodness, you look absolutely wonderful!" She exclaimed, clasping her hands and giving me a quick embrace.

"Power, absolute confidence!" Sullie nodded and I blushed as he swept his blue eyes over me, their intensity glittering with approval.

"Okay," Maxwell said, "we had better get going, or we will surely be late, and we certainly do not want to miss a minute of this hearing. It is the last one, after all." He gently led a chattering Annie out of the room while Sullie took my arm, and we followed them downstairs and into a waiting car. The bright sun in

243

the cloudless blue sky felt like caresses from Heaven on my face as we sped to the capitol building. What a glorious day!

Our heels clacked as we walked down the broad hall and into the chambers where the hearing would take place. Our guards flanked the door, and Maxwell whispered what I assumed were instructions to them. I stopped suddenly as my eyes took in the nearly filled spectator seats. My heart thudded and I was thankful I did not have to testify in front of all of them. Sullie tugged my arm and led me to our seats. Annie sat next to me quivering with excitement.

"Well, like it or not, here we go," she said, bobbing her head and flapping her hands. "Have you ever seen such a crowd? Now, this is exciting!"

This was the same room in which I had testified in front of the senators, and so it was familiar with its long row of dark wooden tables behind which padded chairs loomed like ghostly fellows waiting for their occupants to give them life. The same raven-haired man, pencil and paper in front of him, sat just to the right of the polished podium at which I gave my testimony.

I clutched Sullie's hand and drew in a deep breath as Valsted walked to the front, his tiny, well-dressed attorney following close behind. They sat at a table on the other side of the podium, too close to Maxwell for my comfort. The door to the right of the tables opened, and the man who had sworn me in during my first visit here came in and stood to the right of the doorway, asking us all to rise. Chairman Brink strode in first, his blue denim jeans once again peeking out from the hem of his black robe. I smiled when a chunk of what I assumed was manure fell off his boot and was squashed onto the bottom of Senator Dandridge's shiny black shoe when he came in on the heels of him. Oblivious to the manure, Dandridge stood with snappy eyes darting around the room as the other three men came in and stood behind their chairs.

After the recitation of the Pledge, Chairman Brink's voice boomed throughout the room, "The Montana State Supreme Court created this special Judicial Standards Commission due to allegations of misconduct by District Court Judge Edward Valsted in Beaver County, State of Montana. The claim of misconduct originated from Mrs. Robert Terrell, who is present here in this chamber today but who does not have to testify since she did so at an earlier hearing at which we all were present. Copies of her testimony at that hearing were given to each of us and to Judge Valsted for perusal as well. The fates of thirteen women now incarcerated in the Montana State Insane Asylum, Whispering Pines, lie partially in the hands of this commission, and the Justices felt it would be best if the same five men who heard Mrs. Terrell's accusations also heard the testimonies of the three men today."

He paused briefly and his twinkling light blue eyes met mine before he continued, "In essence, Mrs. Terrell claims that fourteen women in Beaver County were falsely arrested and then sentenced by Judge Valsted to spend the remainder of their lives in Whispering Pines. Today, we will hear testimony from Judge Edward Valsted, from Doctor Edward Mitchell, and from Mr. Joshua Miller. The task before us is to determine if Judge Valsted acted in any way outside of the boundaries of his position as district judge. If, and

245

I stress the word 'if,' Judge Valsted is determined guilty of misconduct, then we must decide what his punishment will be. Also, we will hear testimony about the health, both mental and physical, of the Beaver County women who are incarcerated at Whispering Pines. And finally, I must advise everyone here that the names of the incarcerated women will be kept confidential."

I took a moment to look around for Doctor Belzer, who would naturally be present, and located him behind and to the right of us. My fingers bit into Sullie's forearm at the sight of him, and Sullie squeezed my hand.

"It's okay, lass," he whispered. "The guard's watchin' him. We're safe." I relaxed a little.

Chairman Brink rustled his papers as he looked at his fellow senators and said, "Gentlemen, please hold your questions until each man has given his testimony in full. Agreed?"

Simple responses of nods and "yes, sir" came after which Brink undid his robe, pushing it aside to reveal a wrinkled white shirt with a cigar sticking out of a front pocket. He then called for Valsted to come forward and be sworn in. The puffy-cheeked man rose and straightened his suit jacket which somehow fit perfectly over his rotund figure. The image of him pulling it aside to reveal a gun came vividly to me. I shuddered. His attorney rose with him. As they walked to the podium, I noticed Valsted did not appear nervous in the least; in fact, he looked bored. His smooth, chubby face was relaxed and his eyes were hooded. Until he looked at me with pure hatred burning in his eyes. There was no soul behind them, just a dark emptiness. The moment was fleeting but effective. I began to tremble. Valsted veiled the hatred with boredom and looked forward at the senators. Sullie leaned into me and caressed my arm, stilling the quaking in me.

Once Valsted was sworn in, Chairman Brink asked if he had received and read the testimony that had been sent to him. Valsted answered that yes, he had. Then, Brink asked him to tell the commission his side of the story. Chairman Brink leaned back in his chair, crossed his dirty boots in front of him, and pulled out the cigar. This was all a familiar sight, but remembering my disbelief at first seeing the informality of the man in charge, I wondered what the reporters would write about him.

"Senators, thank you for asking me to come and for giving me the opportunity to speak against the allegations made against me. I humbly ask that you all keep an open mind when you hear my answer to them and also when you hear the testimonies of the other two men who will speak today." Valsted's deep voice dripped with syrupy sweetness.

"Let me begin by stating the obvious, which is that Mrs. Terrell was quite distressed about what she overheard in her husband's barn on April twenty-fifth of this year. And in her state of mind, I can understand how she misconstrued what she heard." My state of mind? Misconstrued? He's going to say I am insane, isn't he? "Bear in mind, gentlemen, that I was there by invitation of her husband, Mr. Robert Terrell, who I might mention cannot testify on my behalf here today because he was shot and killed last month at the hand of one of Mrs. Terrell's newfound friends and cohorts in this travesty of justice that is brought before you today."

All the senators except Chairman Brink squirmed in their seats, and there was an audible gasp from the spectators as they waited for the chairman to respond to Valsted's accusation. Brink replied with a scowl at Valsted and a "Thwuck!" as he spit a chunk of the cigar into the spittoon. The tension in the room was palpable, and the rasp of pencil lead on paper was loud as the reporters scribbled furiously in the silence.

"Go on, Judge Valsted," was all the chairman said, remaining in his relaxed repose.

Valsted sighed deeply and continued, "I was conversing with Mr. Terrell in the barn that day about the possibility that Clara might be a danger to herself or others due to her hysteria which had become increasingly violent. Mr. Terrell was concerned for himself and for Clara and was asking me for advice about what he could do for her. I was merely there with a few friends of mine who had gone through the same sort of thing with their wives in order to give Mr. Terrell the option of having his wife committed to the State Insane Asylum so that she could get the help she so clearly needs."

I looked at the line of senators. Mills and Palmetto were once again scribbling in their notebooks, apparently not paying much attention to Judge Valsted. Had they already made their decision? Probably not in our favor, either. My eyes fell on Dandridge, the deciding vote if that happened. He sat erect, fiddling with his pencil, his head swaying slowly back and forth as his tiny black eyes glared at Valsted. Did he make

Valsted as nervous as he had made me? Did Valsted even notice the man at all?

"As you all are aware, at times in the service of our communities, we must do unpleasant tasks," Valsted continued. "And one of the worst duties I performed in Beaver County was committing those women to Whispering Pines; however, I do not regret doing so. I believe that I made the only right and just decision regarding those women in order to prevent violence against themselves or others. I swore to uphold peace and to counter violence in my district and that is exactly what I did. I have no regrets and I feel that you will see that I did indeed uphold the law and conducted myself as any judge would have, given the circumstances I faced." Judge Valsted stepped back from the podium, looked at his lawyer who nodded at him, turned back to the senators, and said, "That is all I have, gentlemen." He began to walk back to his seat, but his lawyer grabbed his sleeve at which Valsted yanked his arm back and raised it as though to strike the tiny man. The lawyer cowered and backed away. The air shifted as all of the senators came to attention.

Chairman Brink swiftly brought himself into an upright position and shouted, "Judge Valsted! You will conduct yourself appropriately in this room. Do you hear me, sir?" The man beside the door had a wooden baton in his hand and moved toward Valsted, but he stopped when Valsted lowered his arm and calmly faced the senators.

"My apologies, sirs."

Annie's fingernails bit into the skin of my arm, creating little half-moon shaped marks on it. My breath rushed out all at once. Over the sound of

249

rushing water in my head, I heard scuffling of feet and paper as the crowd settled down again. Mills and Palmetto resumed their scribbling.

"Let's proceed, shall we? Do any of you senators have questions for Mr..., I mean Judge Valsted?" Chairman Brink actually smirked at his sarcasm around his cigar.

"Yes, I do have a question." This from Senator Gable. "How many women did you have sent to Whispering Pines?"

"To my knowledge, there were fourteen of them."

"Fourteen. And did you find any woman brought before you on these charges to be innocent? In other words, did you ever decide in favor of a woman brought before you due to her supposed insanity?"

"Well...no. I did not." There was a shifting in the room as the crowd reacted. "They all were clearly insane. Otherwise, their husbands would not have needed for the law to intervene."

"Okay. I would like to hear how it was that you came to believe that these women were indeed insane and as you put it, 'a danger to themselves or others'."

"Well, it was obvious by the testimony presented to me during their trials that they were insane. They were clearly a danger to themselves or to other people. Otherwise, I would not have had them committed to Whispering Pines."

"Okay. Then, I have another question," Senator Gable said. "You say you heard testimony that they were insane. Who gave that testimony? Did the women themselves ever testify on their own behalf?

Keep in mind, sir, that we have read the trial transcripts. I just want it clearly on the record for the public."

"Well..." Valsted's voice trailed off and he sighed deeply, obviously trying to collect his thoughts. "Let's see...once a woman was brought before me with these charges against her, the husband of the woman and I remember a son of one of the women also testified about her behavior. Mostly, though, it was the husbands who did the testifying." Valsted ran a hand down his fat cheek and turned slightly to his lawyer who just nodded at him.

Senator Dandridge suddenly came to life, sitting forward in his chair with his hands folded neatly in front of him. "I do believe, sir, that you failed to answer the other part of Senator Gable's question."

"Huh?" was Valsted's unsophisticated reply.

"The second part of Senator Gable's question, sir. He also asked you whether the women ever testified on their own behalf. You must answer that question as well. I am terribly excited to hear your response." Dandridge pulled his thick red lips back and glared at Valsted. I knew then that Dandridge was on our side and had not been influenced by Mills and Palmetto. I figured the best they could get would be a tie, and hopefully, Brink would vote our way like he did at the first hearing. A lightness flooded my spirit.

Valsted drew in a ragged breath before he continued. "Oh, yes, that. My apologies. Well, actually, no, the women never did testify in front of me." A collective gasp came from the spectators, and Mills and Palmetto stopped their incessant scribbling to stare at Valsted. "I figured that in their precarious mental state they did not need the added stress of testifying in a courtroom, so I just allowed them not to have to do so."

"Excuse me?" This from Dandridge again. "You honestly want us to think that you were upholding the law and not only that, but that you were doing these women a favor by not having them testify on their own behalf? You really think that we are so stupid as to believe that these women had no right to defend themselves just because their husbands thought they were insane, or better yet that their husbands wanted to get rid of them because they had grown tired of them? Isn't that really at the heart of this matter, Judge? This was just a convenient way for the men of Beaver County to get rid of their older wives so that they could replace them with younger ones. Wasn't it?" Dandridge was nearly standing by now, so Brink asked him to calm down and to sit down, which he did, never once taking his narrow black eyes from Valsted. Palmetto leaned over and whispered something to Mills who nodded his head.

Valsted wiped his brow with a handkerchief his lawyer passed to him and said, "In my own defense, I thought it best that these women get the help they needed from trained professionals at Whispering Pines. I have nothing else to say in the matter."

Gable leaned forward and said, "Please, Judge Valsted, just answer a question for me. Where were the women during their trials?"

"Umm...uhh...." Valsted wiped his brow again and looked at his lawyer, whose only job it seemed to me was to nod his head. "Well, in the interest of public safety, they were kept in their cells during their trials."

"In their cells? *During* their trials? You mean to say that these women were arrested, brought to the jail, and then *left in a cell* while their fate was decided by you? Is that what happened, Judge?" Gable asked.

"Well, yes. That is correct."

"Were any of these women represented by an attorney?"

"No, they were not."

The tension in the room rose as did the corners of my lips just thinking about the news stories that were sure to follow.

Mills pushed up his black glasses and asked, "So you committed fourteen women to Whispering Pines in the course of how many years?"

"Well, I guess it was around four years' time."

"That's all I have, Chairman Brink." Mills turned toward Palmetto and rolled his eyes. My heart fluttered.

Dandridge again, more calmly asked, "Was your wife treated in the same manner as the rest of the women, Judge?"

Silence filled the room as we all waited for the response.

Valsted turned halfway toward the spectators, and I noticed a slick sheen on his face. He turned back to the senators and said, "My wife was insane, and so yes. She was treated just as the other women were." His suit coat pulled tightly over his back as his shoulders drooped.

"Thwuck!" another wad of Brink's cigar landed in the spittoon.

Dandridge continued, "So, you had a sheriff come to your home, arrest your wife, handcuff her, and take her to a cell at the jail. Then, you and District Attorney Littman discussed the matter, deemed her insane, and sent her away to Whispering Pines. Is that about it?"

"Yes. It is. Doctor Belzer, a physician in Bergen, also was present at the trial and heard my testimony and diagnosed her as insane. The only thing I could do was to have her committed to the asylum."

I stole a glance at Doctor Belzer. His face was red and he was staring at the floor.

"Was Doctor Belzer present at all of these trials?"

"Yes."

"And did Doctor Belzer diagnose all of the women as insane?"

"Yes."

"Does Doctor Belzer have any background training in mental health?

"Not to my knowledge, but you would have to ask him."

"And yet you used him as an expert in these trials?"

"Yes. He was the only doctor available."

Dandridge's pale face pinkened. "How convenient for you and the other husbands. I just have one more line of questions for you, Judge. Were you present when your wife was handcuffed and led kicking and screaming to a jail cell? Or better yet, did you deliver her sentence to her in person and see first-hand her reaction to your sending her to an insane asylum for the rest of her life? Did you witness her cries and her screams as she was led off to that place?"

"Well, no. Actually, I was not present for all of that drama, if indeed it occurred. I hope she would have acted in a more dignified manner than you described, though."

"Really? You expected her to act dignified even though she was insane?" Dandridge shook his head disgustedly, his eyebrows pulled low and his lips pursed. "You do not have to answer that, Judge. Chairman Brink, that is all that I wanted to ask."

Brink pulled what was left of his chewed up cigar from his mouth and put it back in his pocket, pulled his boots under his chair, and sat upright again. He ran a hand through his thick white hair and asked if any of the other senators had any questions for Judge Valsted. When there was no reply, he dismissed Valsted and his attorney, thanking the man for his testimony. Valsted, clearly shaken, walked unsteadily to his seat and sat down with a heaving sigh. His lawyer only nodded. I glanced at Annie. She was grinning.

CHAPTER 24

"All right, gentlemen. Now, let's see who we have up next." It was Chairman Brink, shuffling through his papers. "Oh, yes. Now, we will hear testimony from Mr. Joshua Miller. Mr. Miller, please rise and come to the podium."

There was shuffling from the back of the room as Joshua came forward. He looked terrible. His bony shoulders showed through his wrinkled jacket, and he held his weathered hat in his hands. He managed to look up every once in a while, shaking his head with a horselike jerk to get his hair out of his eyes. Mainly, though, he looked at the floor in front of him as though his head weighed far more than his neck could hold up.

Once Joshua was sworn in, Chairman Brink thanked him for coming and asked him to state his testimony for the senators. I listened with only half an ear, having already heard the dreadful story about his dear wife Rebecca and how she killed herself in that awful place after he had her committed. My heart, feeling pity for the poor man, warred with my head which blamed Joshua for it all. I tuned him out after a while, allowing God to take that one over for me.

Finally, Joshua was dismissed after answering a few questions from the senators. Valsted and his lawyer had none. Joshua glanced at us and nodded curtly before shuffling down the aisle, chin down, his hair hanging over his face. I heard the door open and close as he left the room.

Chairman Brink then called Doctor Mitchell to testify. When Doctor Mitchell went by, the comforting scent of sawdust and pipe tobacco came to me. My visit with him shot through my mind, relaxing me.

Doctor Mitchell told about the physical and mental state of the women incarcerated at Whispering Pines and about the conditions at the asylum much the same as he did at Littman's trial, so I used the time to assess our chances of getting Valsted impeached. Gable, I knew, would vote in our favor, and I felt that Brink would do the same. They had been partial to our side the entire time, and now that they had Joshua's and Doctor Mitchell's testimonies to corroborate mine, I felt confident they would do the right thing. Upon hearing Dandridge's line of questioning today, I was fairly certain he would vote with Gable, which would mean another tie if Mills and Palmetto voted in favor of Valsted. As I watched the two, though, I became hopeful that we would get a unanimous vote in our favor. They listened intently to Joshua's and now Doctor Mitchell's testimonies and did not write in their notebooks or pass covert looks to one another the entire time. The tension in my shoulders and back eased even though I knew that this proceeding was far from over and that the vote could go either way.

When Doctor Mitchell was finished, Brink leaned over and spit into the spittoon again before he sat upright in his chair, folded his hands over his papers, glanced at his fellow senators, and said, "Thank you, Doctor. Now, then," and he looked over at

257

Valsted, "Do you have any questions for Doctor Mitchell?"

The lawyer leaned over as Valsted whispered to him. The tiny man nodded and stood next to his chair. The look on his face was like a puckered seam. Sullie's thumb caressed the back of my hand, and his fingers tightened against mine.

The lawyer straightened his tie and said, "Okay, Doctor Mitchell, exactly what is it that makes you think that you are more qualified than Doctor Belzer to diagnose these women's mental states?" A good question, I thought, and my fingers clenched against Sullie's so tightly I feared hurting him.

Doctor Mitchell turned toward Valsted's table and began, "Well, sir, I along with my colleague, actually *examined* the women. We did not do as Doctor Belzer did and just take the word of some other person, namely their husbands, about their state of mind. Also, I have studied extensively about menopause, I know the symptoms and how they differ from true insanity, and I feel I am quite qualified to see the differences between the two. I might add, as long as we are on this subject, that Doctor Belzer actually came to visit his wife at Whispering Pines shortly after her incarceration. He must have witnessed the deplorable conditions at the asylum, and he had to have seen how his wife was living in filth, medicated into near unconsciousness, and yet he made her stay there. Not only that, but the man helped to send even more women there. All for what purpose, I wonder?" His voice trailed off.

I looked at Belzer again. He stared at Mitchell and I read hatred in his eyes.

"Doctor Mitchell?" At his name, the doctor came back around.

"Yes?"

"If Doctor Belzer is so terrible a doctor, then why is he still practicing in Beaver County?"

"Good question. Hopefully, he will not be for too much longer. A physician is sworn to do no harm, and I feel that Doctor Belzer did indeed do much harm to these women. He needs to be held accountable, and he will be as I have already begun proceedings with the state medical board to have his license revoked in our state." Audible gasps and shuffling of papers commenced at his announcement. I glanced at Belzer again. He was still glaring at Doctor Mitchell.

Once the room quieted, Chairman Brink leaned forward and asked the lawyer if he had any more questions. The little man looked down at Valsted who shook his head and scowled. The lawyer nodded but his mouth said, "No, sir. No more questions."

"I will ask that my fellow commissioners ask any questions they have for Doctor Mitchell," Brink said once again reclining in his chair. "Go one at a time, men."

I had watched Senator Dandridge long enough to know that he was itching to ask his questions; however, he held himself in check while Gable went first. "Doctor, please tell us how you came to be involved in this case."

Doctor Mitchell leaned forward, his hands relaxed on the podium, and said, "I had no idea that anything like this was happening to women anywhere, let alone in our fine state, until Mr. Heinz told me what Mrs. Terrell overheard the men discussing in her barn.

259

He and I arranged for Mrs. Terrell to come to my office for a checkup and to discuss her symptoms, which she did once she arrived in Helena. She was quite concerned that her husband was correct and that she was indeed insane, which I assured her was not the case. She is merely menopausal." Doctor Mitchell turned to me, his chocolate eyes meeting mine.

"It was during the course of Mrs. Terrell's examination," he continued, "that I had her tell me about what had happened in Beaver County. Needless to say, I was appalled and yet intrigued. I told Mrs. Terrell that I would help in any way I could, and when I was later asked to help her and her friends get the other women freed, I was happy to do so. I hope that answers your question, senator."

"It does. Thank you. I have nothing further."

Dandridge leaned forward, his head finally still, and said, "I just have one question." Doctor Mitchell's head swung to the left to look at Dandridge. "Why did the doctors at Whispering Pines not work to free these women, if they knew they were only menopausal?"

"That is a good question and one that I asked the doctors themselves. I can only relay to you what they told me. According to the doctors, they are basically overworked and underpaid. The asylum is terribly overcrowded and understaffed." Doctor Mitchell's shoulders and back seemed to grow more tense with each word he spoke. "The doctors there have too many cases, and although they would like to discharge the menopausal women sent there, they cannot without going through the proper channels, such as these hearings and trials, and they simply don't have the time. Also, since the women are sent there as prisoners, there are added problems with getting them released. The doctors said they cannot simply say that the women are sane and then send them back home again since there are judges like Judge Valsted out there who sentence them to the asylum. Simply put, there is too much red tape and not enough time in their days to help these women. Another thing about the staff at the asylum is that they generally are not there long-term. The doctors who work there have no desire to stay for longer than a year or two. They get some experience working with the mentally unstable and then they move into private practice for the most part." Doctor Mitchell's back finally relaxed as he drew a deep, audible breath.

"Why do they go to work at the asylum if they do not wish to stay long-term, do you think, Doctor?" Dandridge asked.

"Well, I think that they are good people, but a bit idealistic in that they want to save these patients, cure them if you will, and that just is not possible in most of the cases. The doctors quickly lose their optimism in such conditions, and then they move on. Also, it is not a nice place to work. The facility is dirty and the patients, as well as the staff, are not happy."

"Why do you think that is the case?"

"As I said before, the state is not giving the asylum enough money to buy the proper cleaning supplies and to pay for enough custodial help. There are far too many patients in the facility, too. The rooms I observed were designed to hold one or two patients in each, and they each held three or four."

Again, the room gasped. Even the senators shifted in their seats. Doctor Mitchell waited for quiet and then continued, his soft voice edgy. "It is terrible that mentally unstable people should have to share rooms with each other at all, let alone with two or three others, all equally ill."

"Yes. Thank you, Doctor, for your candor. I have no further questions." Dandridge sat back.

"Any other questions, senators?" Brink asked after a few seconds of silence. I found myself holding my breath. "No? Okay, Doctor Mitchell, thank you for your testimony here today. It was quite informative. You may sit down now."

Doctor Mitchell turned and I could see the stress etched on his face as he walked to his seat. Chairman Brink stuck the cigar in his pocket and leafed through the papers in front of him. I wondered what was next. Sullie released my hand and the sudden emptiness of it felt uncomfortable.

After what seemed a long time, Brink cleared his throat, looked up, and said, "Well, here's what we're going to do. We are all going to take a break and go have a nice long lunch. Then, the five of us will meet back in the conference room at two o'clock to take a vote and to discuss the guilt or innocence of Judge Valsted. Once we have come to a consensus, a majority agreement, which is what we need to decide this case, we will make our ruling public. Let's all reconvene here at four thirty this afternoon. Hopefully, we will have a decision by then, but if not, the five of us will keep meeting until we do." He and the other four senators stood, and they floated out, their black robes waving.

I sucked in a huge ragged breath, making myself lightheaded, and blew it out. Shuffling papers and the murmuring voices of the spectators filled my ears as everyone stood and departed the room, one row at a time as if we were all leaving church. Thankfully, Valsted and Belzer stalked out before us.

Once we were out in the hallway, our guards nearby, Annie grabbed my hand and said loudly, "I think that went great! They will vote against Valsted, I just know –"

"Shh! Be quiet! We cannot make predictions like that, Annie, at least not here," Maxwell admonished, frowning at Annie, whose grip tightened around my fingers at his scolding.

"Well, I never! Maxwell Heinz I can say –"

"He's right, lass. We need to be discreet right now. There's ears and eyes everywhere here," Sullie said to Annie. "Now, we'd better go have some lunch and then decide what to do from there. There's a nice quiet restaurant just down the block from here. We can talk more openly there."

"That sounds just fine, Sullie," Annie said quietly, giving Sullie a slight smile. She huffed and glared at Maxwell, though, as she turned toward the door.

I spotted Doctor Mitchell's head poking up from the crowd and without thinking, headed straight for him, weaving in and around other people to get to him. I heard Sullie call my name, but I just had to speak with the doctor. Finally, I reached him and tugged on his sleeve, making him pull back, but when he saw it was me, his huge hand clamped over mine and he said, "Why, Clara, just the person I wanted to see."

The crowd's momentum pulled us toward the doors as though we were sticks caught in a current, so Doctor Mitchell maneuvered us far to the side where there was an empty bench.

Sawdust and pipe tobacco filled my nose and created the sense of comfort that I now associated with this special man. He sighed as though a huge burden was leaving him and I said, "Doctor Mitchell, please forgive me for interrupting you, but I just wanted to tell you how much I appreciate what you've done for me and for the women locked up at Whispering Pines."

"You're not interrupting me at all. I was just thinking that I wanted to speak with you and your friends. To tell you all that I admire your determination and your attention to this situation."

Sullie was suddenly in front of us. "Lassie, what - - ? Oh." His voice rose when he saw I was with the doctor. "Why, it's the good doctor!" Sullie stuck his hand out and Doctor Mitchell rose to grasp it. "I was just worryin' where Clara was off to, and here she is. Lassie, remember it's not safe yet—"

"What's that?" Doctor Mitchell asked.

Before Sullie could answer, Annie and Maxwell were beside us, and Annie suggested that Doctor Mitchell accompany us to lunch, which he readily agreed to. As we walked, Sullie pointed out our guards and explained the danger we had been in. Doctor Mitchell was startled and concerned, but Sullie assured him we were safe as long as the guards were nearby but that Mitchell needed to be on alert now that he had testified and had started proceedings against Belzer. The doctor explained that he had already been vigilant since the proceedings against Belzer had begun back in

264

May. He had not experienced any threats nor had he sensed any danger, thankfully.

We had a nice but tense lunch during which we discussed the case against Valsted. We all were hopeful, but Annie was the most certain of us all that Valsted would be found guilty.

Free to speak her mind aloud, she voiced her opinion loudly. "I think the senators should just send that lowdown son-of-a-bitch, excuse my language, to Whispering Pines for the rest of his life! Ha! Wouldn't that be something?" Heads turned toward our table, and a few of the other patrons whispered behind their hands. Annie did not seem to notice.

"Yes, my dear, that would be a just punishment," Maxwell said in a tone that calmed her. "However, that is not how the system works."

"Well, to hell with the system then," Annie said flapping a hand at him.

"Now, now," Maxwell continued, "the senators cannot give out a punishment such as that. They can only decide whether or not to impeach him."

"If I may say so, knowin' the kind of man he is, if he has his most valued treasure, his position as judge, taken from him, that will be punishment enough. He'll lose his income and his status in the county, and he'll suffer from that, I can assure you," Sullie said.

"If you say so, Sullie," Annie said. "At any rate, it's out of our hands, and we just need to wait and see what happens." We all nodded.

Doctor Mitchell relayed what he knew about the investigation into the other women at Whispering Pines. He told us that no order had come his way yet, but he was confident the Justices would get it to him as soon as Valsted's trial was concluded. He then told us even more details about the deplorable conditions at Whispering Pines, his brown eyes flashing as he did so. His main wish was that more money would be allocated to the asylum so that it could be staffed and maintained properly, giving the patients the dignity they so deserved. He also explained the process of getting Doctor Belzer's medical license revoked, telling us that he was quite sure the state medical board would do just that, especially if Valsted was found guilty. Just being in the presence of the power and conviction of this man instilled strength and confidence in me.

The four of us lingered long after Doctor Mitchell left us to go back to his office, explaining that Nurse Compton would have his hide if he did not return soon. Since he had patients to tend to this afternoon, he would not be able to return for the possible verdict, so we assured him that one of us would call him and update him as soon as we could.

Finally, it was time for us to go back for the possible verdict. My nerves prickled, making me jumpy and unfocused. Somehow in the already crowded room, we found four seats together and settled in for the news. As I looked around, I noticed more reporters than there were in the morning. Either word had spread of the case, or the verdict was more important than the hearing. Either way, I was thankful for these men who would get the word out about the plight of these women and the conditions at Whispering Pines. My prayer was that they would represent it all fairly and honestly. My mind wandered to Joshua Miller, and a desire to thank him filled my heart. As I perused the room, though, he was nowhere in sight. I wondered if I would have to wait until I got back to Bergen to talk with him.

As my thoughts fell on my hometown, a tightness came to my throat. What would my life be like now that Bob was gone? How would I manage? I could not run the farm by myself, that I knew. Would I have to sell it and move? I hoped not.

A palpable silence pulled me back to the present, and I noticed the court reporter was back at his table, coal-black hair slicked back from his face, his back ram-rod straight. The man in the gray suit stood sentry at the door to our right. I stiffened as I saw Valsted and his nodding attorney sitting at the same table where they were that morning. My palms became damp and I felt a flush rise from my chest to my cheeks. Sullie, sensing my discomfort, wrapped my hand in both of his and gave me a quick smile.

"All rise!" Everyone obeyed the sentry, causing quite a cacophony to echo off the walls of the huge room. Then, all we could hear were the quick footsteps of the senators as they entered, their robes like prairie thunderclouds on a summer day. I hoped that was not an omen of things to come.

Brink perused the crowd, nodded, and gestured for his fellow senators to take their seats. All five of them floated into their chairs. I tried so hard to read the verdict on their faces, but to no avail. They were completely stoic.

"You may be seated." Brink's demeanor seemed rigid. A rivulet of sweat ran down my chest, and my back tickled where the fabric stuck to it. Annie grabbed my hand and with my hands engulfed in my friends' I felt a little relief. However, a ringing had set

267

up in my ears so that I had to concentrate extra hard on what was being said. As Chairman Brink seemed to be repeating what he had said in the morning, I forced myself to take a few deep breaths as I looked around at the reporters and other spectators, noticing for the first time that several women were in attendance, too. Had curiosity brought them here? Or was there a more personal reason for their presence? Perhaps they knew some of the incarcerated women or perhaps there were more women. I shook my head back into focus as those thoughts would do me no good at all.

"...and so we do indeed have a ruling in this case at this time." Annie's grip was painful. "If the defendant would rise, I will read the verdict." All eyes fell on Valsted as he pushed his chair back and stood next to his attorney who was dwarfed by him.

"Edward Valsted, we find you guilty of corruption and making unlawful rulings as a district court judge of this state." Guilty! Tears shot out my eyes and a tingling went from my feet to the top of my head. Sullie glanced at me and let go of my hand to put his arm around my shoulders, cupping me to him. The ringing in my head ceased as I listened to the rest of Chairman Brink's words, my chin resting on my damp chest as my head was suddenly very heavy.

"We hereby sentence you to be removed from your office as District Court Judge of the county of Beaver in the state of Montana. In addition, you must never hold any public office in this state." Brink cleared his throat as he waited for the noise in the room to die down before he continued, his deep voice soothing me. "I would like to say something to you, sir, and let this be on the record for all the public to read. I personally think you are a despicable human being, without conscience and without morals." The power in Chairman Brink's voice gave me the strength to lift my head. "I pity any woman who might be bluffed by your facade of prestige, any woman who might be blinded into a relationship with you out of desire for wealth and privilege. You are a wolf in sheep's clothing, removing anyone in your life that you get tired of or bored with, including your wife of twenty-odd years. It is incomprehensible to me that you were allowed to stay in your office for as long as you were, perpetrating this travesty of justice on fourteen women who you were sworn to protect and serve.

"Only the courage of one woman, Clara Terrell, with the help of her friends, put a halt to this horror." My cheeks burned scarlet at the accolades, and I squeezed Annie's hand and glanced at her. She was beaming straight ahead. "I commend them for their actions, but you, Valsted, I have nothing but contempt for. I wish above all else, that we could have sentenced you to prison time so that you could get a small taste of what the women you unjustly sent away have felt all these years. However, this commission doesn't have the power to do that, and for that, you should be eternally grateful. If it was up to me, I would send you to prison and give you no chance to ever see the light of day again. Now, sit down!" Valsted wiped his face, his attorney nodded, and they sat.

Brink shuffled papers, allowing time for the spectators to quiet themselves, before he continued. "This same commission is set to meet with the Supreme Court Justices tomorrow to determine the fate of the incarcerated women from Beaver County. We will treat each woman's case individually, and within two days we hope to determine those rulings and then make a public announcement. Thank you, that is all." And with that, the sentry asked us to rise, the senators floated out, their robes looking like the somber foundations of justice that they really are. My heart was light; my head was clear.

As I lay in bed that night, after praying my gratitude until my knees cramped up, I reflected back on the rest of that evening. Reporters flocked around the four of us as we attempted to leave the building. Thankfully, Sullie took command and gave a short statement about how I decided to start these proceedings and how overjoyed we all were about the verdict not only against Valsted but also against Littman. He deferred the questions about Doctor Belzer, telling the reporters they needed to talk with Doctor Mitchell about his case, explaining only that Doctor Mitchell was having his conduct reviewed by the state medical board. Sullie then ended by thanking them for their attention to the case and asking that they keep all of the unlawfully incarcerated women in their prayers and that we were hopeful that the Beaver County women would be released as soon as possible and that the new investigation into the possibility that other Montana women suffered the same fate begin soon. But we would have to wait, as they would, for those decisions.

We had a celebratory supper at a fabulous restaurant that Maxwell chose for us, the ever-present guards watching over us. As we often did, we speculated about the identities of the women. Our list of possibilities had climbed to all fourteen at this point. By now, though, the women's names were not as important to me as getting justice for them and getting them home.

Lying in bed that night, I still could taste the rich tangy spices and feel the comfort of my friends. I smiled as I drifted off, our rushed conversations and our hopeful predictions about the fate of the women playing in my mind.

CHAPTER 25

The next day was bright blue, sunny, and warm. Maxwell was at his office catching up on the work he had neglected during the hearing, but mid-morning he came to our suite, rumpled, flushed, and breathing hard. "I came as quickly as I could," he panted. We all stood and my stomach flipped. Now what? "I just got word that Valsted and Belzer were on this morning's train. We are safe again. Well, at least here in Helena."

"I'm glad they're gone," Annie said, "but they will be in Bergen when we return, and that scares me half to death, what with the incompetent police there and Littman and Valsted no doubt angry and blaming us for their punishments. It's frightening, Max." Annie reached her hand for Maxwell, and he clutched it to his chest.

"You are right, Annie, but I will make certain there is no danger in Bergen before I allow you to leave here. Make no --"

"*Allow* me? Please tell me you didn't just say 'allow,' Maxwell Heinz!" Annie exclaimed, attempting to pull from the small man who stood with his mouth gaping.

"Uh—Well, yes. I guess I did say that." Maxwell held Annie's hand tightly as Sullie and I watched, amazed and waiting for Annie's next eruption. "But you listen here, Annie," Maxwell boomed. "I will never tell you what you can and cannot do. *Unless,* you are about to do something unsafe. I simply must intervene when it comes to matters of your safety. And you, my dear, will just have to get used to that!" Maxwell humphed and dropped Annie's hand which she put to her lips.

"Why, Max, that's the sweetest thing anyone's said to me in a long time." Annie's eyes were moist as she gazed at Maxwell. I was stunned at the change in my friend.

Maxwell then dismissed our guard, and some of the tension left with him. We decided it would be best to remain in Helena until we came up with a solution to the question of our safety in Bergen. Sullie and Maxwell left for the office to conduct business, which left Annie and me sitting and half-heartedly reading.

I cleared my throat before I began, which caused Annie to look up from her book. "Annie," I began, "I'm in a quandary and can use some advice."

"Okay, then," she said, closing her book before placing it on the side table. "What's bothering you, dear?"

"I don't know what's to come of me now. That's what's bothering me," I spurted out, my eyes becoming damp as my swirling thoughts became words.

"Whatever do you mean?" Annie leaned as forward as her ample bosom would allow, her round face filled with concern.

"You know...once we go back home. Without Bob, how can I run the farm? How will I be able to live?" I swiped the tears away and took a deep breath before looking into Annie's serious eyes.

"Oh, my heavens! Is that what has you all worked up and nervous?"

"Yes, it is. Can you give me any advice about what to do? I just don't know what's in store for me..." I trailed off, looking out the window behind my friend.

"Well, I have no real proof or anything, but I'm thinking that one very dear Irishman might have an idea or two about your future back in Bergen."

My eyes flew to hers. They were twinkling round stars in her flushed face. "What?"

"Ho, ho!" she boomed. "I got you there, I did!" She leaned back laughing. Then, she became more serious as she saw my startled face. "Clara, think about it. You and Sullie are so comfortable with each other. And you are so happy when you're with him. Truly, I think that---"

"But--" I interrupted.

"No buts! Listen to me! I think that our Sullie is enamored with you, and if you'll admit it to yourself, you care for him, too. So, I see no reason for you to fret about your future. I'm almost certain that Sullie will see to that."

"What do you---" I stammered, my face bright crimson. I put one cool hand on my neck in a vain attempt to cool it. "Oh, never mind," I sank back in my chair and looked directly in my dear friend's eyes. And with a chuckle, all the embarrassment vanished.

"Well, like you told me, just allow God to do His work in your life." And with that, Annie picked her book up and began reading again. So did I, but the book could have been upside down for all I knew.

The next evening, a terribly fidgety Maxwell asked Annie to go to supper with him, just the two of them, so Sullie and I went downstairs to dine in the restaurant for the first time in ages. We discussed the danger in Bergen, and Sullie explained that we just needed to be brave and face it head-on…and that he would hire us private guards if need be.

At the thought of living under guard while at my own home, I shuddered, yet I agreed with Sullie. We simply could not cower in Helena forever hiding from Valsted, Littman, and Belzer. It would be as though they had won, not us.

Sullie explained that he had made arrangements for us to return to Bergen on the train in four days and that Maxwell would tell Annie about it. Although I was apprehensive about going home, I was also anxious to return.

Sullie and I also discussed the future of our two friends, agreeing that Maxwell was probably asking Annie for her hand in marriage and then speculating about where they would live and what the years ahead had in store for them.

Since Sullie no longer needed to stay in our suite overnight, I invited him to stay for coffee while we waited for Annie and Max to return with what we just knew would be wonderful news, and he did just that.

Sure enough, a flushed and breathless Annie rushed into the room ahead of Maxwell and announced, "I'm so happy that you're here, too, Sullie!" she said, reaching for Maxwell's hand and beaming at him. I had never seen either of them look as happy as they did right then. "Guess what? We're getting married! Can you believe it? Can you?" Laughter filled the room as Sullie and I soaked in their excitement. Sullie ordered champagne to celebrate and once it came, we toasted the two lovers' future.

The plan was for Annie to go back to Bergen with us in four days, and for Max to come in about two weeks. They decided to have a small ceremony at her house in Bergen at the end of the month. They simply could not wait any longer. The parlor was the perfect place for such an affair, she exclaimed. She would fill it with yellow roses, her favorite, and Sullie and I would be their witnesses, of course, and there would be sweet treats and punch and a cake, and...her words all tumbled together. Then, the newly wedded couple would put her house up for sale and Annie would move to Helena.

At this, my ears perked up. What would I ever do with my lifelong friend so far away? My heart thudded. I had come to rely so much on her. My wits returned, though, and I silently rebuked myself for my selfishness. Annie would be happy, and that was all that should matter; however, I still had to consciously remove the tension from my face.

"I'm excited for you both. And honored, too, to stand up for you on this special day. Thank you for including me," I managed.

"Aye, you two are just a perfect match as far as I'm concerned," and Sullie clapped Maxwell on the back, making the small man flop forward at the waist. Once he regained his balance, the grinning Maxwell shoved Sullie back. The two men shared a good chuckle. Tears welled in my eyes and a hot flush went from my chest to my cheeks as I tried to keep them from falling to my cheeks.

My wet eyes turned to meet Annie's voice, "I hope those are tears of joy, my Clara." I managed an unconvincing nod as Annie enveloped me in her soft arms, pressing my cheek into her hair. She whispered, "I know. I'll miss you, too, dear friend, and I'm sorry to hurt you."

"No. I'm very happy for you b-both," I stuttered. "It's just that I'll miss you living close by. It'll be different. We'll have to adjust is all."

"Of course you'll adjust, silly lassies!" Sullie boomed. "You've done it before, too, now. Haven't you? And, if your stories ring true, it'll all be just fine. Writin' to one another and now you can even call each other on the telephone and hear each other's voices when you get all lonesome and such. Right?"

We both nodded and wiped our faces. Maxwell was a little taken aback by our display of emotion, I think, as he fidgeted from one leg to the other, his hands pulling on his rumpled jacket.

"Okay, you two," Annie said and gestured to the men, "we've had a very busy day and must get some rest, so off you go." Maxwell gave Annie a quick kiss, blushing as he walked to the door, and Sullie just squeezed my arm, nodded to Annie, and followed Max out.

It took Annie and me awhile to settle into our own rooms. She was too excited to sleep and kept coming into my bedroom under one pretext or another before finally laughing at herself and vanishing into her room with the promise that she would not see me until the morning.

The next morning, Annie was already up, ready to face the day, and pacing the floor by the time I came out into the sitting room.

"Oh, good! You're finally up!" She fairly shouted before giving me a big hug. "I'm as nervous as a child on Christmas morning, I tell you!" Her round red cheeks jiggled as she chuckled deep in her chest.

"There's nothing to be nervous about, Annie. Everything will be just fine. Now, let's go get some breakfast and then start getting our things ready to be packed. Okay?"

"Great idea." She tugged me to the door. I could hardly keep up with her as she nearly ran down the stairs. I had never seen Annie like this, and warm tingles coursed through me at her happiness.

The day passed with organizing our things, and later that afternoon, there was a knock on our suite door. Annie answered it, and Mr. Kershaw handed her an envelope.

"It's got your name on it, Clara. Look here." She nearly ran it over to me from across the room. I was bent down putting some of my new clothes into a leather traveling chest that Annie had presented me with for my trip home. I put one hand on the small of my back as I straightened, and she slapped the envelope into my other one. She stood back, rubbing her hands together.

"What is it?"

I quickly scanned the tall, perfectly formed letters on the page.

"Who's it from, Clara?"

My eyes flew to the signature at the bottom. "It--It's from Chairman Brink!" Of its own accord, my left hand reached for Annie's, gripping her fingers tightly as I read aloud:

"Dear Mrs. Terrell:
      Before you read about it in the newspapers later

this evening, I wanted to personally inform you of the decision made about the fate of the women from Bergen who were sent to Whispering Pines. Our committee met with the Supreme Court Justices this morning, and a quick decision was made. We found that the women were all unlawfully incarcerated, and although our desire was to free all fourteen women, we could not." I let go of Annie's hand and covered my gasp.

"What the hell? Oh, I'm sorry, Clara!" she exclaimed. "Continue on."

My hands began to tremble so that I could barely read the print. "As you already know, Mrs. Rebecca Miller passed away while there. Then, as Doctor Mitchell expressed, one woman was incapacitated due to an overdose of medication. We ruled that she remain at Whispering Pines for her care until someone can be contacted who is willing to take over her care. A third woman actually was deemed mentally insane, probably due to her suffering the conditions at the asylum; and regrettably, we ruled that she remain there as well. The other eleven women are to be freed as soon as possible. As soon as their families are notified and come to get them.

"We are so grateful to you and to Mrs. Hazelton, Mr. Heinz, Mr. Sullivan, Doctor Mitchell, and Mr. Miller for speaking for these women who could not speak for themselves. Mrs. Terrell, if it were not for your fortitude and character, this matter would have gone unnoticed by us and by the state, and I apologize on behalf of the entire committee and the Justices, too, for our lack of awareness. We are beginning to investigate the cases of the other women

279

at Whispering Pines to determine if any of them suffered the same fate as the Beaver County women, and we promise to be more vigilant in the future. You are truly a heroine in our eyes." Tears blurred my vision so that I could not read any more, so Annie took the letter and continued.

"You are truly a heroine in our eyes. Thank you, dear lady, from the bottom of my humble heart, for having the courage to come forward and for putting yourself into such dangerous situations to do so, for the well-being of your fellow persons. You are the definition of a true hero.

Sincerely, Senator George Brink"

"Oh, Clara, don't cry. Please don't cry." Annie took me into her arms and my head fell onto her shoulder, and I did just that. I sobbed.

"I just have such mixed emotions. I'm happy that they're getting out. Well, most of them at least. But I'm so sorry that I didn't find out sooner so that we could have gotten to them years ago. You know, before Rebecca..." My voice failed me.

"I know," Annie patted me, the letter rustling against my back. "But we did what we could and on God's time, sweetie. Let's just be grateful that He led us here and that we were strong enough to do what needed to be done."

"You're right, of course," I said as I pulled away and dried my face. "I must look a mess."

"No, you're just as beautiful as always," Annie comforted me.

Once we sat for a while absorbing the news of the women's release, we finished our organizing and initial packing. As my hands moved, my mind occupied itself with visions of the women reuniting with loving family members and arriving back at their homes or the homes of their children and beginning their lives anew. In my naïveté, their husbands were conveniently missing from my revels.

Sullie came by just as we were finishing and was as emotional as we were at the letter and the good news it carried. He left to call Maxwell and the four of us got together later for supper at one of our favorite restaurants downtown. There we shared our thoughts about the journey we had been on for almost four months. How we did not know each other in May, and now look at us. How Annie and Maxwell found love. How one short overheard conversation had started the wheels of justice rolling. How those wheels would keep turning even after we went back home. How good it felt to know the women would finally be free and that more might follow. How much we all had changed through the process.

We retired to our rooms and Maxwell to his home after supper, and I went to bed straightaway, my sleep dreamless and deep.

The next morning we were up early, and sure enough, the news had made it into the papers. Even the *Billings Review*, the largest newspaper in the state, ran the story on the front page.

As Annie and I packed our things that day, my mind worked as much as my hands. I was thankful that justice had been restored and that the Lord had used me in the way He had; however, I was apprehensive about all of the changes that it had brought to my life.

Some of my tension eased the next afternoon, the day before we were to leave Helena, when Sullie burst into our suite, his hair messed and his face flushed. "Lasses, come quickly!" he shouted.

"What is it, Sullie?" I asked.

Sullie took our hands in his and looked at Annie and me. "I just talked with Patrick back in Bergen, and..." Sullie drew a deep breath and squeezed our hands. My heart thumped in my throat and my mouth went dry. What had happened?

"Come on, Sullie, tell us!" Annie exclaimed.

"Well, here 'tis, then. Patrick said that both Bergen and Glendive were buzzin' when ole Valsted and Belzer got back. News of the hearings had gotten around, so they weren't greeted with open arms, I guess."

"Good! I only wish they'd been run out of town!" Annie's voice boomed.

"That's the best part, lasses!" Sullie exclaimed. "They were, in a way. Yesterday, when the news reports came out, the townspeople were so angry that they demanded all three of them - Valsted, Littman, and Belzer – be asked to leave town, or else. I guess the police complied and told 'em to leave and they did just that!"

"You mean, they left their homes?" I managed to whisper. "They are gone?"

"Aye, Clara. That's exactly what I'm sayin'. They've left. Put their houses up fer sale and left sometime last night!"

"Oh, thank the good Lord. That's the best news ever!" I exclaimed as tears trailed down my cheeks.

Relief made me nearly faint. I would never again have to face those horrible men, and it sounded as though the townspeople were thankful for what we had done. That was good news indeed.

The four of us went out to dinner that night at the fanciest restaurant in Helena. We celebrated our hometown, our friendship, and our safety. The relief was juxtaposed with the sadness of Annie having to leave Maxwell, even for a brief time.

The next morning, there was a buzz in the lobby of the hotel as we checked out. The hotel personnel knew who we were, of course, and bustled around us like bees on clover, lighting here and there. Mr. Kershaw and Gretchen thanked us as we said our good-byes. A couple of the other hotel personnel scowled at us, but most of them thanked us for what we had done for the women. The attention was a bit embarrassing, to put it mildly. It was the same at the train depot.

Finally, though, after Annie and Maxwell's long, tearful goodbye and quick hugs from Maxwell for Sullie and me, we three were loaded onto the train and on our way home.

CHAPTER 26

The trip passed quickly. In Glendive we picked up Annie's housekeeper Martha and then made the short trip to Bergen. It was August ninth, and we had been gone for over three months. Nothing had changed. And yet, everything had changed. Bergen was the same, sleepy town, yet it seemed even more tired to me after the bustle of the city. The people were the same. Some of them, mostly women, openly expressed their gratitude to us. Quite a few of the shopkeepers, men and women, stood in their doorways, nodding politely as we passed down the main street toward Annie's house, and I imagined the greeting Valsted, Belzer, and Littman came home to, not just here but in Glendive, too. Quite the opposite of ours I now knew, and my heart gladdened with the thought.

We also received the occasional scowl, mostly from men. One man, who I knew to be a farmer who lived near me, blocked our path, spit on the sidewalk in front of us, and muttered a curse under his breath. When Sullie turned his powerful body to face him and asked him to repeat himself, the man hung his head and slinked away like a scolded dog. We sidestepped the man's spit and continued on.

"Well, isn't that just a fine howdy doody of a welcome?" Annie said. "And here I thought we'd get a damned parade out of the deal! Instead, we get, well-- we get farmer spit!" We all laughed.

Suddenly, I spotted a familiar figure nearly running toward us, a swirl of lavender skirts attempting to slow her. It was Mrs. Carlson, the chatty banker's wife. I sighed and said a quick silent prayer for patience as she waved. "Yoo hoo!" Her loud, high-pitched voice drew the attention of the others on the street. She panted as she drew up in front of us. "Why, it is you three! I just had to come out and welcome you home. I just knew that you were up to something that day you left on the train. Why, I said to my sister, 'Those three are up to something,' but I couldn't for the life of me come up with what it was. But then I read in the *Billings Review* all about the hearings and the court stuff and all of it. Why, who knew what evil lurked among us right here in our tiny little town! I surely didn't! Why, I respected those men. And there might be other towns involved, too! Can you believe it?" She never waited for our reply before turning to me. "And I must express my condolences to you for the loss of Bob, if it's appropriate under the circumstances. Why, when I heard about his passing my heart broke for you. I know he was a no-good son-of-a-gun, but he was still your husband, and I'm sorry about what came to pass with him."

"Thank you, Mrs. Carlson, but now we must be –," I said.

Mrs. Carlson never missed a beat, "But now you are back, and, well, I just want to tell you all how proud I am of you for doing what you did. That took real courage." At long last, she was spent. Her hands stilled and her mouth formed a smile.

"Well, Mrs. Carlson, thank you very much for that welcome," Annie replied right before Mrs. Carlson hurled herself at her, hugging her. Annie's arms tentatively went around the woman as Martha, Sullie, and I gaped. Mrs. Carlson was generous with her affection as she hugged each of us in turn, clapping me on the back before she excused herself to return to her business, which I assumed was to tell the entire town the news.

Finally, we arrived at Annie's house, and Martha, bless her heart, went to the market with all three of our grocery lists. Once she returned, we enjoyed a quiet lunch before Sullie loaded my things into his carriage to take me home. The valise I brought with me when I left home looked small, and I blushed with gratitude and a little bit of shame as he loaded trunks of the beautiful things that Annie had purchased for me in Helena.

Annie's soft vanilla scented arms engulfed me as we said our goodbyes. "Now, don't be sad, Clara. I'll see you in about three weeks for the wedding. You know?" Annie assured me, her one arm around my waist leading me to the buggy. Sullie's warm, strong hands practically lifted me into the seat before he climbed up beside me.

"Thank you for everything, Annie," I managed. "I'll never be able to repay you for your support and kindness and all of the beautiful things you bought me."

"Don't mention it again. You deserve every good thing that comes your way, and don't you even doubt that for a minute. Now, Sullie, I'll see you later, but you'd best get this little lady home." Home. That sounded glorious. And a little worrisome.

"Aye, lass. That I will," Sullie said with a tip of his head and with a quick snap of the reins, we were off.

During the trip to my house in the country, I had such mixed feelings. It was my farm now, and mine alone. But, how would I manage it all? Bob had been the one in charge of finances and much of the outside work of the farm, and although I had experience managing money after my father passed away, I felt overwhelmed with it all. My mind swirled. It was too late in the year now to plant a garden, so I would not have vegetables to eat this fall and to can for the winter. What was I to do without them? Time to figure that out later. Right away, I needed to take care of the animals and clean the shack, of course. Patrick had supposedly come out and taken care of things for me, but I had my doubts. After all, this was not his farm and his animals, so he probably did not bother himself too much with it.

Sullie's low voice quieted my thoughts. "Lassie, what're you thinkin' so intently on?" His gaze was soft and concerned.

"I was just thinking about all that I have to do when I get to the farm. I was feeling a little overwhelmed and apprehensive about it all. There's so much that I don't know how to do...." My voice trailed off and I sniffed at self-pity that threatened to invade me.

"Let me assure you, everythin' is just fine at the farm. But, Clara," Sullie's voice got a little harder, so I looked over at him. He looked into my eyes briefly, and they had darkened to almost black. Something was not right. "There's one important thing that I've not mentioned to you before. I didn't want to cause you pain, lass, but now I must." My hand flew to my throat and my pulse pounded in my temples.

"What is it? I can handle it. Just come out with it, please."

"Well, here it is then. As I told you before, I had Bob's body brought back here after he…after he passed." I nodded as I already knew this. "There's more. The boys, well, your boys came home an' buried him next to your wee babe up on the hill behind the house. Oh, Clara, I'm sorry."

"No, no. That's fine with me. I expected that. It's just that, well--are the boys still here? Did they stay and wait to see me?" My heart pounded hard, anticipating his reply.

He shook his head and my stomach clenched. "No, lass. They didn't stay. Patrick told me that they needed to get back to their own lives, their own ranches and so couldn't or wouldn't stay the extra time to see you or to take care of anythin' here. They pretty much just buried their Pa and left. I'm sorry, Clara. I really am."

"Did - did they leave a letter or some word for me?"

"No."

Even though I had prepared myself for it, the punch of that one little word held so much strength that I bent over, my hands covering my face. Sullie rubbed my back. A few minutes later I straightened, patted my face with my handkerchief, and tried to assemble my thoughts.

"Okay, I can handle this, Sullie." My voice had more strength than it should have, but I felt a conviction that, in time, I could make this all right with my boys. This, I had to believe in order to go on living.

"I know it. Now, look at that." Sullie pointed in the direction we were turning, up the lane to the homestead. "It looks just fine, doesn't it? And, it's all yours, lass." Sullie touched my hand and I soaked in the warmth, both of this wonderful man and of the farm with its little shack that stood black against the tan and gray of the hillsides and the green of the field surrounding it.

"Home." I could breathe again.

A white speck on the porch slowly took the shape of Champ who bounded out to meet us. He was a blur of happiness as he wiggled and yelped. Sullie stopped the carriage and hoisted the little guy up to ride with us. My arms reached out for him, and he nearly toppled me out of the seat as he launched himself into my lap, licking my face and hands and crying with delight. Joy filled my chest and hot tears threatened to fall, but I just held on to the little ball of fur with all my might.

"Patrick told me that this wee guy here would not leave the homestead for the life of him. He tried and tried to get him to come home with him, but the furry one couldn't be coaxed or bribed to go. I guess he was waitin' for you." Sullie reached over and gave the dog a pat on his back.

"Yes, all this time. What a faithful, precious baby he is." Champ pushed himself into my chest as though to soak me up, and I stroked his head as his eyes shut in glee, tongue lolling out the side of his mouth. "If only people were as faithful." I shook my head at the self-pity rising in me and chastised myself for it.

"Oh, Sullie! Look!" I exclaimed and pointed to the large garden plot that I was not here to plant. Long, straight rows of bright green plants reached for the sun, and my heart swelled. "Patrick even planted my garden!"

"That was to be a surprise for you. Patrick enjoyed puttin' it in so much. Made him feel like a real farmer, he said."

"It sure is a nice surprise! I wasn't sure what I was going to do for vegetables this year without it. He's an angel. Please, express my appreciation to him as soon as you can. I might not be able to do it myself very soon as I won't be coming to town until Annie and Max's wedding, I imagine." My spirits lifted further when I noticed the field was green, too. Bob must have managed to plant it before he came to Helena, and the plants that would give me income after harvest were priceless.

The house, once we got to it, was spotless, and although it felt extremely tiny after being at the hotel for so long, it was home. And I reveled in being there. With the promise to come and get me for the wedding, Sullie left after unloading the buggy and bringing in clean water, so then it was just Champ and me. I decided that he no longer had to stay outside since Bob was not here to reprimand me for having him in the house, so I put down some blankets for him by the door and gave him a water dish next to it.

Over the next few days, I settled into my new yet old life. I wrote to my boys, pouring out my heart to them and asking them to forgive me and to contact me. The homestead that was now all mine was, well, lonely. In the past months, I had become accustomed to having my friends around all of the time, and now there was a void in me that I could not fill. I occasionally expected to hear Bob's horse coming up the lane and would stop mid-action and listen for it, shaking my old head at my stupidity whenever I did.

On the third day home, I gathered the courage to go up the hill to the cottonwood tree that shaded my beloved Julia and her dad. Champ came, too, flopping down only an inch or two from the mound of black dirt that covered Bob. I knelt next to him, trying to find the right words. Finally, my heart poured out my mouth.

"Bob, you tell Julia 'hi' for me and give her big hugs and kisses from her mommy. Will you, please?" Champ rested his head on my lap as I continued. "Now, I want you to know a few things if you don't already. One is that I don't hate you for what you did, or what you planned to do to me. That's been already dealt with, I imagine, between you and the Judge that matters. I can't say that I forgive you because I don't yet, but I'm working on it. Not for you, but for me. Another thing is that I thank you for all the good things you gave me. The boys, Julia, a home. All of those are priceless to me, and I wouldn't have them if not for you, so thank you." Champ whined and looked up at me. "And one more thing, Bob, you son-of-a-bitch, to use Annie's language...." I smiled through my tears. "I will not allow you to take my boys from me!" Champ sat up and cocked his head, eyebrows furrowed at the hostility in my voice. "I will do everything in my power to get them back again, and well--" I gestured across Bob's mound with my hands, "there's not one thing you can do about it!" At that I wiped my face, stood with creaks from my knees, and marched down to the house.

A change came over me. A lightness that I had not felt in years. The sun was warmer, the sky was bluer. What a wonderful feeling. Freedom. Independence.

CHAPTER 27

Sullie arrived the day of the wedding. My heart fluttered at the sight of him, and my stomach trembled. Immediately, I noticed that he appeared thinner and paler than I had ever seen him. His lips formed a tense line and barely moved because he was so quiet. Much quieter than normal.

"Sullie, what's wrong?" I asked on the drive to town. He had greeted me at the house, told me how nice I looked in the pale gray suit and pink blouse, helped me into the buggy, and then drove, silently staring at the road. His brows were furrowed and his eyes were dull and dark.

"It's nothing," he said unconvincingly, giving me only a second's glance.

"You can tell me anything. You know that, don't you? I'm your friend, remember? Friends help each other, just like you've done for me since the day, or night, I met you. Now, what is it?" I touched his sleeve and his arm quivered. He stared straight ahead.

"Like I said, it's nothin'. I'm fine. Just leave me be and I'll work it out for myself. Okay?" His voice held a knife's edge, so I did not press the issue. Instead, I filled the air with light, chatty talk about the farm, Champ's antics, and the upcoming nuptials. At mention of the wedding, the lines on Sullie's face deepened, and his lips turned even farther downward.

"Has something happened with Annie and Maxwell? Is that it?" My voice was shrill.

"No. Nothin's happened. I'm just a bit off today is all. Forget about it." Still, he did not look my way, nor did he touch me.

I could not forget about it. Something had happened and I needed to know what.

The wedding was a perfect affair. Annie and Martha had outdone themselves with the decorations and the food. The heady scent of roses filled the house as the yellow flowers were everywhere, some tied with ribbons and others in vases. There were sweet treats of all kinds, punch, tea, coffee, and a gorgeous cake that could have fed a hundred people instead of the twenty of us that were there.

Sullie barely said two words to anyone. He remained sullen all day and kept as much to himself as he could at such an occasion, and I could not help but be concerned for him; however, I knew not to press him. I prayed silently for peace in his heart.

Annie was the happiest I had ever seen her as she and Maxwell said their vows and exchanged rings in front of us. Her gown was a soft ivory silk that flowed around her legs, and the bodice was covered with beautiful pearls and embroidery. I could not imagine where she had acquired such a dress until she told me that it had been her mother's. She had always wondered why she toted the thing all over the country as she moved, and now she had her answer. It was stunning on her, and she carried herself with such confidence and grace. She and Maxwell both oozed happiness.

Patrick attended the wedding, too, and when I thanked the young man for all he had done for me while I was gone, his pale freckly cheeks reddened to match his curly hair. He managed a big grin, though, and told me that it was no bother. He had enjoyed it immensely and that if I needed any help at all to just give him a shout, and he would be there in no time. What a kind young man.

It was a glorious afternoon, filled with laughter and a few tears as Annie and I said our good-byes privately. We promised to write each other every week and to keep each other in our prayers. Seeing her so thrilled about her new life, I could not possibly harbor negative feelings about her leaving. Besides, she would be back once they returned from their honeymoon, a trip to Europe via a ship, of all things. So soon after the Titanic disaster. I would never be so brave. She would return to Bergen to clean out her house, sell what needed to be sold, and take the rest back to Helena with her. And then, she would have to return again once her house sold. Also, she and Maxwell both insisted that Sullie and I come and visit them as often as we could; however, I did not see that happening any time soon as I had almost zero income and a farm to run.

With final hugs for the new Mr. and Mrs. Heinz, Sullie and I left to go home. The ride to my homestead was a silent one, both of us lost in our own thoughts, it seemed. He handed me down from the carriage, gave the wiggly Champ a quick pat, and with a soft, "Good-bye, Clara," he drove away. I was completely perplexed.

My concern over Sullie grew with each new and

more complex scenario that played in my head over the next few days. I knew not what to do, though, as he had asked me to just let it go. I could not do that, but at the same time, I would respect his wishes and stay out of it.

The day after the wedding, I saddled my mare and rode over to the Miller's place. As the sun heated my shoulders and back, I thought about what I wanted to say to Joshua. Mainly, that I was thankful to him for his support and that I was sorry about what happened to Rebecca. As I rode up to his ranch house, a once-white but now peeling two story home with deep porches on three sides, I could not help but notice the disrepair. One of the side windows was covered with a piece of faded wood, the yard was weed-filled with large bare patches, and the fence was standing about as well as a drunkard after a hard night in town. My heart thumped at the sight of Joshua rocking on the front porch, his brown hat creating concealing shadows on his face.

He rose as I approached and dismounted, tying the mare to a sagging hitching post. "Hello, Joshua," I said. "Looks like it's going to be a hot one today."

"Yep."

"I hope it's okay that I came over. I'd like to visit with you for a bit if that's all right."

"Sure," he responded sullenly, his chin against his chest. "Come on up and sit."

"Thank you," I said and sat in the rocker next to his.

"That used to be Reb-- my wife's seat. Right there next to me. That's where she always was and that's where she should be now, Clara." His voice hitched and as he turned his face to me, his eyes were pink and welled with sadness.

"If you'd rather, I can sit on the step," I said and half stood.

"No. You sit there. It's okay." His face was hidden again, and I could barely make out his soft words.

"Joshua, where are the children?" He and Rebecca had a boy who was ten and a girl who was twelve, and I suddenly worried for their welfare. Their father was in no condition to care for them.

"They're with my sister, Catherine, in town today. She came out from Nebraska when, well when I--- you know, when I went out to help you."

"Good. How are the children doing anyway?"

"Okay, I guess. I try not to pain 'em any with too much of all this." He gestured over himself with one hand and looked up at me. A lone tear escaped and fell onto his sleeve. I reached out and patted his forearm.

"How long does your sister get to stay?" I said as lightly as I could, not wanting him to discover how alarmed I was by his condition and how concerned I was for his children. What they must be going through, losing their mother and now this, having to watch their father and their home deteriorate before their eyes.

"She said she'll stay at least until the children are back in school in a week or two. She's been comin' off and on for the past three years. You know since Rebecca—"

"I know. You don't have to say it, Joshua. In fact, I came over today because I want to tell you how thankful I am for your help. That was a brave and selfless thing you did, and the other women, I'm sure, will be eternally grateful to you as well." I leaned my head down and to the side so I could see the man's face, but he turned away.

"It still didn't bring her back, though, now did it?" Joshua's ravaged face turned to me, and I sucked my breath in at his despair. A blue vein bulged and pulsed on his flushed neck, his skin was pale and taut, and his eyes were swollen slits that poured tears down the sharp bones of his cheeks.

"No, it didn't, and nothing will. I'm so sorry for you and for your children. You miss her terribly, I'm sure...," my voice broke, "but I knew her well enough to know that she would want you to continue raising your children the best that you can. You and the children were the most important things in the world to her, and you need to pull yourself together for the sake of your children. For the sake of Rebecca."

"I know that, but I'm just strugglin' with it all again. I was doin' a little better, but then when I went out there and testified, it brought it all back again. I wasn't proper healed, I guess and now it's back. I thought it'd help, you know, goin' out there and telling my story, but it didn't."

"I admire you, though, for your efforts to save the others, and I know that you are a strong man, a man of integrity, one who can get through this again, just as you did before. For the sake of your kids, if for nothing else."

"I just don't know," Joshua said, swiping his face with his sleeve and taking off his sweat-stained hat to run bony fingers through oily hair that hung over his collar. A pungent odor came to me with his movement, and I held my breath a moment until it dissipated.

Just then, the creaks of a buggy coming up the rutted lane caught our attention. Both our heads swung toward it.

"Oh, I bet that's the children and Catherine," I said, standing and smoothing my skirt.

Joshua stood beside me and looked a little less dim. "Yep, I reckon so, and glad I am to see them back." He put his hat on, and we went to meet the buggy laden with bags of groceries and two chattering children who jumped down and with a quick, "Hi, Mrs. Terrell," in unison, ran to their dad. Finally, Joshua stood a little straighter and a small smile played on his face as he listened to their stories of town, their words tumbling over each other.

I introduced myself to Catherine, who gave me a shy smile before inviting me in for a cup of coffee, but I explained I must get back home and walked toward my mare. I turned as Joshua softly said, "Thanks for coming over. I appreciate it and I'm sorry for your loss, too."

I flushed before I thanked him and wished them all well, mounted, and rode off with a wave of my arm. Concern for Joshua and the children's condition filled my chest, but there was little I could do for them except check on them from time to time.

CHAPTER 28

I was kneeling in my garden, weeding and talking to the plants two days later when Champ suddenly came to attention, growling deep in his chest, the hair on his back standing up. Before I could force my old bones to stand, though, he transformed into an ecstatic puppy. He barked in high-pitched glee and ran toward the lane where a lone man was riding up on a horse. I flushed as I saw it was Sullie. My hands were brown and green from the dirt weeds, so I rubbed them together before I wiped my brow and smoothed my hair.

Sullie gave a small wave and said, "Stay where you are. I'll be right over there." He dismounted and tethered his horse. That was when I noticed how incredibly thin he had become. Alarm filled me and I hoped it did not register on my face. He was even more wan and pale than he was the day of Annie's wedding, and smoky half-moons sat below his blue eyes. Something had happened. My heart thudded. As he approached me unsteadily, his clothes now loose on his frame, I decided I must not remain true to his wish that I just let it go. I had to say something.

"Sullie! It's so good to see you," I said as I took a few steps toward him, attempting to brush some of the dirt from the front of my skirt and blouse, which did no good whatsoever. My heart hammered. "Let's go inside where it's cooler and have some lemonade. How about that?"

Sullie stood only a foot or so from me and said, "Thank you, but no. That's not what I came for." And with surprising quickness, he pulled me tightly to his chest. A shudder went through him and his hot breath in my ear was ragged. Stunned and with my arms held against my sides by his, my mind whirled. "I came here for this, Clara. Sweetheart. This."

His arms relaxed their hold on me, yet they trembled as he lowered his mouth to mine, claiming my lips with gentle, moist pulls. My arms, of their own volition, rose to his shoulders and into his soft hair, pulling his mouth tighter to mine and pushing my breasts into his chest. He deepened the kiss with my willingness, and my body responded with hot tingles that spread like the rising sun through it. My chest and neck flushed with a desire I had never felt before. A low moan escaped as he pulled back. My lips felt raw and swollen, but remarkably alive. I bit the lower one, tasting him on it, and could not help but smile as I reluctantly lowered my arms.

Champ wiggled against my leg, whining, and I bent to touch his back. "Not now, Champ. You sit." And he did, but was unable to still himself as he lifted one foot and then the other, feeling our nervousness.

"I need to start at the beginnin', I suppose," Sullie's voice was oddly husky, and I looked up into his handsome face, nodding to encourage him. "Back there in Helena, Clara, I fell flat out in love with you! How about that? I guess I sinned the big one because you were still married to Bob at the time. I tried not to, but I couldn't stop it. I just couldn't get you out of my head. And then Bob was killed. I'm sorry, lass. Really,

301

I am--." I tried to say that he need not be sorry, but he shushed me with a tiny precious kiss. "Don't say anything. Suddenly, you weren't married any more, and I grew hopeful that you might grow to love me, too. But I saw no indication that you did—"

"But, Sullie, I—"

"Shh. Let me finish, lass. So since we returned home, I've tried, I really have tried, to get over it. To stop this crazy lovin' of you. But, I can't. I just can't. I don't think that I can live without you."

Just as my mind began to focus on what was happening, he slid down onto one knee right in my garden. And in one graceful motion, he took both of my hands in one of his, reached the other into his pocket, and pulled out a ring, almost dropping it in the dirt he was shaking so hard. My knees let loose, and I was down in front of him, staring at the ring glistening in the sun. Champ could contain himself no longer and leapt between us, licking first my face and then Sullie's. Our laughter rang in the air, and we both pushed Champ away. He gave us a sharp bark but managed to stay a foot or two from us.

I gasped, "Oh, Sullie! What's happening?"

"Clara, I want you to be my wife, if you'll have me. If you don't want to or if you need more time, I'll understand and try to go on, but my life will only be complete with you in it, I'm sure of it."

My hands shot up to my mouth as my gaze flew from the ring to this dear, solid man kneeling with me in the dirt, his blue eyes glittering expectantly.

"So, what do you say? Will you marry me and be by my side for the rest of our lives?" He steadied me with one hand on my elbow. The other held the ring up to me. Tears slid down my cheeks. "Are those tears of happiness, I hope?" he said and wiped one side of my face.

"Oh, yes. Sullie, yes! I'd be honored to be your wife, and yes, these are tears of pure joy!" I put my left hand out and Sullie slid the gorgeous diamond ring on my finger. It fit perfectly and I gasped at its beauty and significance.

He reached out and softly kissed me and I lost myself in him. Champ's quick high-pitched bark brought us back, and we laughed again at ourselves, kneeling there crushing the green plants.

Each of us put out one hand and Champ jumped into the circle we made, whining and licking us with excitement, mirroring my feelings.

Sullie's eyes were damp as he said, "You've made me the happiest chap in the world, and I thank you for that. I want you to know, though, that I respect your independence and don't want to change you in any way, so whatever it is that you want to do in this life, I just want to be right beside you, supportin' you and lovin' you with all my heart."

I could only nod and look blurrily up at him, my soul filled to bursting with love for this man.

I married the great love of my life just two weeks later in a simple, private ceremony. We would have married sooner, but I wanted to wait and see if my sons and their families would come. They did not and were clear about their disapproval of my marrying so soon after their father's death, even hinting that I had been unfaithful in my marriage to Bob. A deep need to talk this over with Annie rose in me, but she was still on her honeymoon in Europe, and I would not be able to talk to her until she returned. I had just come to accept that when Sullie surprised me by taking me to his office and putting the telephone receiver up to my ear. Annie's voice came through so loudly that I held it about three inches from me. After exchanging pleasantries and congratulations, she listened as I talked about my concerns and how I wanted to make my boys happy, but just did not know how to do it.

Her reply still echoes in my head when the circumstances are right. "Clara, you need to stop trying to please other people, especially those boys. Are they doing any one thing in this world for you? I think not! You need to do something that makes *you* happy, and this is it! Just forget about them and concentrate on you and Sullie. They'll come around and if they don't, then to hell with 'em!" Which is exactly what I did.

After our marriage, we sold the homestead and livestock to Patrick for a small amount that he could afford, and he was able to continue to work for Sullie and run the farm. His energy never ceased to amaze me. Champ and I moved into Sullie's house in town, and we hired Martha to be our housekeeper. She and I became close lifelong friends.

Annie and Maxwell eventually returned to Bergen and straightened out her affairs as best they could. She glowed with the same happiness I felt, and we had a fine time together again, the four of us reminiscing and catching up on all the news. And speaking of news, one day about a week after Annie and Maxwell left for Helena, Sullie rushed into the house waving a newspaper.

"Sweetheart! Come quick!" I rushed from the kitchen drying my hands on a tea towel.

"What in the world? What are you doing home at this hour?" I said, giving him a quick kiss.

"Don't you distract me with those lips, lass. Look here," he said, pointing to an article. "This is the *Dakota Herald* from over in Bismarck. Here, I'll read it to you. 'Officials in North Dakota have begun investigating allegations of sixteen women being unlawfully condemned to life sentences in the state insane asylum. These investigations came about due to recent court cases in Montana, during which it was found that fourteen men had their wives arrested, found guilty of being a danger to society, and then sentenced to spend the remainder of their lives in Montana's state insane asylum. An investigation is underway to determine any wrongdoing in the cases of twenty-two other women incarcerated there as well.'" Sullie's long finger paused as he looked up at me.

"My throat tightened with emotion. "What else, what else?"

I grabbed ahold of his bicep as he continued, "It goes on to say, 'When word came out about the cases in Montana, family members of the women here in North Dakota began to question what was told to them about these women's whereabouts and found out that these women had been sent away to the state insane asylum in Jamestown. Similarities to the Montana women have been discovered, and it appears that proceedings to free them will begin shortly." Sullie ran a hand through his hair and began to pace in front of me, tapping the newspaper against his thigh. "Did you hear that? You didn't know that you'd be savin' even more than just the Montana women, did you?"

"No, I had no idea. This is absolutely wonderful. Just wonderful!" I exclaimed, wringing my hands and dancing from one foot to the other. "But I just wish...." Sullie stopped pacing and quieted my hands with his.

"What do you wish?" He urged me.

"I wish that none of them had to suffer at all. Why did any of this have to happen to them? It's a horrible, frightening thought that this was such a widespread problem."

"You're right, but look at it this way. You can't do one thing about the fact that their husbands had them sent away, but at least you've helped them all get their lives back. You shed light on the darkness, made the wrong right again. Without you, they'd all still be in those horrid places." Suddenly, his strong arms were around me, filling my head with his scent and my heart with his goodness.

"You're right, Sullie. Thank you for always having the right thing to say." I sank into his chest and barely heard his coos as he caressed circles in my back.

For the first time in my life, comfortable serenity filled my every day and passion filled my nights. We followed the cases in North Dakota closely, and eventually, fifteen of the women were found to be merely menopausal and released to their families, which thrilled us to no end. Montana and North Dakota were followed by Wyoming and South Dakota. This was certainly not just a local problem, and I was relieved and grateful that these states were willing to correct the injustices against their women. Occasionally over the next few months, reporters came asking for a statement. I gave none and eventually they stopped contacting me, of which I was relieved.

It came to me one day while I was reflecting on all of this that Sullie and I were like snowflakes, each of us floating through life, fragile individuals, but once we married, we became pressed together forming a snowball. We took on a little of each other's forms, losing part of ourselves but gaining strength through the change. Society is like that, too, made up of individuals who are a little more fragile and uncertain alone than they are when pressed together working toward a common goal, and one small snowball can collect other snowflakes along its course and slowly become larger and stronger, eventually having the ability to make big changes.

AFTERWARD

August 21, 1956
Bergen

I am eighty-six years old now, and thoughts of those days still fill my soul with a tight gladness. Just recently, I lost the love of my life, my Sullie. He was blessed and lucky to the end, drawing his last breath as he slept beside me. I grieve him every single minute of the day, but know that soon I will see him and my Julia again.

Annie and I remain the closest of friends, even though we have lived far apart all these years. She lost Maxwell two years ago to a heart attack and grieves him deeply. Since we both are alone now, she is talking about moving back to Bergen to live with me. How I hope we can make that happen!

If you are wondering, I did manage to renew a relationship of sorts with my sons. My persistence paid off. I wrote them letters every week, and about six months after Sullie and I married, I began to hear back from them occasionally. I was overjoyed and so was Sullie. We started to mend the rift by getting together now and again, and we have built a relationship that is different than before, more distant, but there nonetheless.

Somehow, I managed to forgive Bob for what he did. At least I think I did. I never went back up the hill to visit him; I went to visit Julia, but never him. Is that forgiveness? I don't know, but it works for me.

Ever since those life-changing months in 1920, I have felt somehow invested in the lives of the fourteen women who Judge Valsted, Charles Littman, Doctor Belzer, and those blasted husbands sent to Whispering Pines, and so in the years following this story, I kept in as close of contact as possible with them. Following are short glimpses of the women's lives and of the lives of the men who were involved, if you are curious about them. I apologize for the brevity. I was the lucky one to get to work with Annie, Maxwell, Sullie, and the others to save those women that we could. Unfortunately, we could not save them all.

The Women

Lucretia Valsted - Committed on January 7, 1916 by Judge Edward Valsted, her husband, at age fifty-three. Physically released August 30, 1920. Lived with her daughter, who originally knew nothing of her mother's incarceration, until she died of natural causes in 1939.

Mary Belzer - Committed on January 21, 1916 by Doctor Henry Belzer, her husband, at age fifty-one. A nurse at Whispering Pines accidentally gave Mary too much medication in 1918, which rendered Mary incapacitated and unable to care for herself; therefore, she remained at Whispering Pines until her death in 1933. Doctor Belzer came to see his wife only once.

Sarah Larson - Committed on March 11, 1917 by Frank Larson, her husband, at age fifty-four. Released August 23, 1920. Divorced from Frank, who was remarried to Laura, Sarah moved to Bismarck, North Dakota, where she worked as a seamstress until her death of natural causes in 1934.

Rebecca Miller - Committed on April 9, 1917 by Joshua Miller, her husband, at age fifty. Rebecca committed suicide at Whispering Pines, hanging herself with a bed sheet on June 20, 1917.

Caroline Clement - Committed on April 25, 1917 by Richard Clement, her husband, at age forty-nine. Released August 27, 1920. Caroline moved back to Bergen, where she and Richard lived out the remainder of their lives together. The two passed away within three months of each other in 1940.

Olive Marshall - Committed on May 16, 1917 at age forty-six.
Hilda Marshall - Committed on October 21, 1919 at age forty-seven.
Released September 5, 1920.
Both Olive and Hilda were committed by David Marshall, their husband. David married Hilda within two months of having Olive committed. When Hilda began having "symptoms" similar to Olive's, he quickly had her committed, too. The two women became friends in Whispering Pines, their hatred of David drawing them closer than sisters.

Upon their release, Hilda's son-in-law, a wealthy lawyer living in Baltimore who originally knew nothing of the incarceration, gave Hilda enough money to live out her life comfortably. She decided to move back to Bergen with Olive, and they used the money to buy the theater there, which the two women successfully ran until their deaths. Olive gave up a long fight with cancer and passed away in 1934, and Hilda passed away in 1941 of natural causes.

Johanna Lucki - Committed on June 14, 1917 by William, her husband, at age forty-nine. Released August 29, 1920. Johanna moved to Denver where she lives with her sister.

Hattie Clark - Committed on December 27, 1917 by Samuel, her husband, at age fifty-three. Released September 15, 1920. Hattie moved back to Bergen where Beatrice and Samuel Mulhaney gave her room and board in exchange for working as a cook in their hotel until Hattie retired in 1939. She passed away in 1942 of natural causes.

Hannah Foley - Committed on March 21, 1918 by Jacob, her husband, at age fifty. Released August 28, 1920. Hannah moved to Billings where she attended a Normal School and became a teacher. She taught in a small town south of Billings until she died in a tragic fire at the school in 1929.

Valena Thorpe - Committed on April 29, 1918 by Clarence, her husband, at age fifty-four. Released September 9, 1920. Valena moved to New York City to live with her daughter, who knew nothing of her mother's incarceration, until her death by natural causes in 1948.

Grace Sheffield - Committed on September 16, 1918 by Peter, her husband, at age forty-five. Grace was diagnosed by Doctor Mitchell as mentally insane. He presumed she was a bit unstable when Peter committed her and that the dire living conditions at Whispering Pines caused her to completely break down. She was never released and spent the remainder of her life incarcerated in Whispering Pines, passing away at the age of sixty.

Dorothy Barton - Committed on March 17, 1919 by James, her husband, at age forty-seven. Released August 20, 1920. Dorothy moved back to Bergen to live with James who passed away in a suspicious accident in 1921 when he fell down a flight of stairs into their cellar. The couple was quite wealthy, and Dorothy inherited it all. When Dorothy passed away in 1950, she willed nothing to their only child, Jimmy, who had testified with his father at her "trial." Apparently, she was not a very forgiving woman.

Louisa Fielding - Committed on August 12, 1919 by Jacob Fielding, her husband, at age 56. Released August 28, 1920. Louisa moved back to Beaver County and lived with Jacob until her death of natural causes in 1940.

The Men

Doctor Edward Mitchell - Doctor Mitchell has dedicated a great part of his life since 1920 advocating for the rights of the mentally ill, calling it his purpose in life. He still practices in Helena, and I see his name in the newspapers occasionally when he attempts to get the state to allocate more funds to Whispering Pines or to pay more attention to the needs of the patients there. Most of the time, his pleas fall on deaf ears, but occasionally he succeeds and when he does, I thump my cane on the floor and send praises to Heaven for this dear man.

Joshua Miller - Rebecca and Joshua married late in life. She was thirty-eight and he was thirty-five. Despite my efforts to make him feel that he had done the best he could and that he had helped our cause immensely by testifying, Joshua never recovered from his guilt over sending Rebecca to Whispering Pines and her subsequent suicide. Although he tried his best to be a father to his children, he just could not manage to pull himself from the depths of his depression. He lost his fight on a bitterly cold January morning in 1921 when he rode his oldest horse to the top of a bluff behind their house, sat down under a naked cottonwood tree, took off his right boot and sock, put the barrel of his shotgun under his chin, and used his big toe to pull the trigger. The children were ten and twelve and were taken in by their Aunt Catherine in Nebraska.

Judge Edward Valsted – Shortly after his return from Helena, Valsted was run out of town by the good people of Glendive, and since he could no longer be a judge or a lawyer in this state, he moved on to begin a new life in Portland, Oregon. I heard that he married a widow there and that he was a practicing lawyer until his death. I guess you really can reinvent yourself if your crimes do not follow you. Unfortunately.

Charles Littman - Once he lost his license to practice law and was revealed to the people of Bergen as a morally compromised man, Littman had no other choice than to move away. I think he chose the mountains of West Virginia as his new home. He never married that I know of, and I am unsure if he is alive or dead.

Doctor Henry Belzer – Shortly after his return home from Helena, the good people of Bergen forced Belzer to leave town. Shortly after this, he lost his license to practice medicine in the state of Montana, so he sold his home and moved to California where he lived out the remainder of his life. I heard he married a thirty-four year old woman from there in 1933, right after Mary passed away in Whispering Pines. What she would want with a seventy-three year old man, I will never understand. Probably his money.

Frank Larson - Remained on his farm in Beaver County with his second wife, Laura, until his passing in 1930. He was seventy-two. Laura, who was only seventeen years old when the fifty-eight-year-old Frank married her, lived the life of an abused woman and had no way to support herself and their six young children after Frank died. She was forced to send the children to live with various relatives scattered around the area, and she had no choice but to work as a "lady of the evening" in Bergen until she was able to put enough money away to leave, which she did about five years later. I have no idea where she went or how she is doing.

ACKNOWLEDGMENTS

There are so many people to thank for giving their time, energy, support, and patience to this project; however, I must first give my humble appreciation to God, for it is only because of His guidance, His forming the characters, and His giving them life, that this book is possible. So, thank you, God, for allowing me to be your instrument.

To my ever-patient husband Larry, who gave me the space and time to finish this project and who edited, proofread, and advised along the way – thank you. Your smile lightens my heart when I am down, and your unending support amazes me. Thank you, Larry, for giving me a blank check – literal and figurative – to get this done. I love you beyond words.

For my mom, Diane Nelson, I am eternally grateful. You not only gave me the idea for this story, but supported my efforts in every way. Mom, you graciously shared your wisdom of the time period, the laws, women's rights, and women's health; and were my steady sounding board. You took so much time tirelessly editing the manuscripts, giving me advice and encouragement all throughout this process. And for my dad, Darvin Nelson, your steadfast strength and quiet support mean more to me than you will ever know. Thank you both, for without you, this would not be possible.

I also am indebted to my other unpaid editors, supporters, and cheerleaders. Darla, Randy, and Rose

Torgerson, I thank you for reading the drafts and advising and supporting me all these years.

To author Russell Rowland, I send a huge thank you for giving me so much advice, for answering all of my questions about the writing and publishing process, and for encouraging me at the finish line.

I am also grateful to Kendra for the work she did formatting the cover for me. Thanks, Kendra.

In my quest for knowledge, I encountered so many helpful people who willingly gave me their time and expertise. First, I thank Brian Shovers at the Montana Historical Society for sharing his knowledge of the time period, and in particular of the state hospital in the 1920s. Warren McGee was the go-to man for information about railroads during that time, and I thank him for his help also. Susan Lupton at the State Law Library of Montana researched 1920 state law and sent copies of numerous laws and cases for me to study. Thank you, Susan. Melvin Drake helped a great deal by putting me in contact with a doctor/friend of his who gave me insight into how menopause was viewed and treated in the 1920s and who answered my questions about treatments that were possibly given to the women in the state hospital back then. Thank you to all of you for your wisdom and help.

God bless you all.

ABOUT THE AUTHOR

Deanne Smith was a high school English teacher for twenty years. Recently retired, she can dedicate time to her passions other than teaching: writing, drawing, painting, and traveling. *The Change* is her debut novel. She lives in Montana with her husband Larry and their dog Sheba.

Made in the USA
Charleston, SC
17 December 2014